Swann Song

Swann Song

Kim Pritekel

SAPPHIRE BOOKS

SALINAS, CALIFORNIA

Dedication

For all who have had to start over.

The three songs in this novel were written by me and all three have been recorded, given their voice and music by Jennifer Mitchell, and can be found under her name and the titles: Safe Harbor, Quiet Beauty and Dirty Lullaby on iTunes, Apple Music, Amazon Music or your favorite streaming service.

Acknowledgment

Special thank you to Jennifer Mitchell, who gave Swann her voice.

Chapter One

The world was one big swirl, mixing with the cool breezy night. Christine stepped out of the rental car she had parked right in the middle of the rickety old bridge. She had no idea that bridges like that even existed anymore. They certainly didn't in LA.

The boards creaked under her booted feet, her unsteady body reeling as the chemicals raced through her bloodstream, slamming every nerve ending alive as they passed. Her vision blurred, and the rail she was heading for seemed to recede. She reached out a hand, trying to catch it and bring it back.

Christine, known professionally by her last name, Swann, nearly fell as the rail hit her midsection, knocking her off balance. She giggled to herself, thinking of those warning signs on rearview mirrors: *Warning: Objects may be closer than they appear.*

Grabbing onto the rail, she steadied herself, looking over it and down into the murky depths of the river. Which river? Hell, she couldn't remember. All she knew was it was some river in the podunk town she had found herself in.

Raising a leather-clad leg, she rested her boot against a rung of the railing, grunting slightly as she pushed with her thigh, her other boot finding the top of the railing. She cursed at the splinter that lodged in her hand as she grabbed the nearest support pole, the dangling light attached to it swinging back and forth as she disturbed it with her head.

"Fucker!" she slurred, bringing a hand to her head, then grabbing the pole with both hands as she began to lose her balance again.

Steadying herself, she once again looked down into the water, midnight black despite the bright moonlight. The swinging lantern cast eerie shadows on everything, shadows dancing across the wood planks of the bridge, shadows dancing across Christine's body.

She felt a sting behind her eyes and shook her head to try to get rid of it. She was also trying to shake the memories that were beginning to flood back, her high wearing off, the numbness wearing off. She was starting to be able to think, and she didn't want to think, feel, or remember.

The crowd in front of her, huge and loud, demanding, wanting every part of her that they could get or could take. The band behind her, playing, she knew exchanging glances with each other as Christine stood there, microphone between her hands, forehead resting against the silver head.

She had missed her cue twice already, and she didn't care. She couldn't remember the words; her mind and focus had been stolen by the good hit she'd taken in her dressing room.

"What the fuck is the problem?" the lead guitarist, Joey, had asked after he'd made a stroll up to her, playing the entire time.

The question snapped Christine out of her stupor for a moment. She grinned at him, telling him it was all good, and then turned back to her audience, not seeing any of them, not one single face.

A disaster. A total, fucking disaster. Christine felt the sting in her eyes worsen and then wetness on her cheek, chilled by the breeze. Her eyes refocused on the water below, so inviting, so calming in its chaos. She felt the weightlessness as one boot left the security of the railing. She leaned over even more, seeing her leg dangling above the churning river. She leaned farther, farther, dangerously farther. She got another splinter in her palm as she let go, she realized. It was her last thought.

⁕ ⁕ ⁕ ⁕

Frizzy synthetic red hair brushed across the ceiling of the Dodge Ram. A pale hand slammed against the steering wheel in time with the music on the radio, and a ridiculously pale face, streaked with color, bobbed to the beat of the gloved hand, flopping that frizzy red hair around like a huge bush.

"Yeah, sing it, Sharon!" Willow sang out, her painted eyes closing for just a moment before opening to squint with raucous laughter.

She adored the Dutch band Within Temptation and found their lead singer, Sharon den Adel, particularly wonderful. She admired her style and natural sensuality, something she lacked. Her voice was wonderful, too, and for the mood she was currently in, their up-tempo song "Faster" was exactly what she needed.

Willow loved the buzz she got after doing her gigs on the side, be it personal appearances at a house or Patch Adams-style visits to the pediatric unit at the hospital where she worked. All the energy from the little rascals at the birthday party seemed to flow into her, giving her a natural high like nothing else. Even her main job as a nurse on the children's ward didn't affect her the way dressing up for the kids did, be it Wonder Woman, a rabbit for Easter, an elf on Christmas, or, like tonight, a clown.

She reached down to the volume knob and cranked the sucker, laughing at herself as she sang along, quite horribly, with the next song that came on. The loudness made it worse, because she had absolutely no idea what the words were.

Life was good for Willow Bowman as she drove out of the small town of Woodland, Colorado, an hour or so from Denver, and headed toward her modest ranch just outside of the mountain town.

Her voice gave out finally, probably God's way of telling Willow to shut it, but she continued to bob her head and beat the steering wheel along with the music.

Heading around Dittman's Curve, she approached the bridge, named after some old guy who had done something or other for the town a hundred years ago. What Dittman really needed to do was fix his bridge, she thought.

As she neared the bridge, she noticed a car parked smack-dab in the middle of it, lights off, looking abandoned.

"Shoot," she muttered.

The one-lane bridge was the only way to get to the ranch. Eyes still on the bridge, Willow blindly reached across the console until she felt the passenger seat, then her phone. Movement caught Willow's eye, and she looked to the rail of the bridge.

"Oh, my god!"

Pulling the truck to a stop, she dropped the phone, leaving the engine running and door swinging, and ran to the rail. There was a huge splash in the dark depths. Without another thought, Willow climbed up where she had seen the dark figure before it had jumped and followed suit.

The water was freezing, chilling every part of her, stabbing at her like thousands of tiny knives. It took her a moment to get her bearings, then she began to thrash around in the near complete darkness, using her hands to feel around frantically.

≈.≈≈.≈

It was cold, but Christine had figured it would be. She allowed the cold to embrace her, swallow her. She was angry for a moment as her body's natural survival instincts made her hold her breath, her body far more interested in surviving than her heart.

As she sank deeper into the dark water, her brain became hazed enough to feel it as a comforting cocoon, engulfing her body and vanquishing the demons that lurked above the surface of the water. She felt the numbness begin to overcome her again, that lack of feeling or even ability to feel, inside or out. She welcomed it, prayed for it, *wanted* it.

Something grabbed her wrist, bringing her out of her reverie. She began to thrash, horrid images swarming her mind, scenes from a child's nightmare. She tried to escape the demon that had followed her into the depths, but it refused to let go.

She took in a lungful of water as she tried to scream, then began to thrash anew as she tried to expel it, only to take in more water.

Floating, floating, blackness, sinking, sinking…

※※※※※

Willow broke the surface, synthetic hair now covering one eye, and dragged her find out of the water and onto the banks of the river. It was heavy, but Willow was determined. The body was that of a woman, she saw, one whose own face was half covered by long, dark bangs, the rest of her hair short.

Not bothering to move it away, Willow jutted the woman's jaw back, plugging her nose, and leaned down to blow hot, life-giving air into the open, chilled lips. Sitting back up, she pressed on the tank-top-clad torso, feeling the woman's chances of survival speeding away with each second.

"Come on." She panted with effort before giving another breath.

After several more tries, Willow threw herself back, startled at the feel of water hitting her lips. She looked down, relief filling her as the woman coughed, the movement racking her entire body and throwing her halfway to her side as she spewed a stream of water to the rocky sand beneath her. More coughing and spasms followed.

Willow sat back on her heels, waiting, watching, in deep concern. The woman calmed after a few moments, still coughing, but alive. She slowly rolled onto her back, head turning, then she jumped violently.

※※※※※

"Fuck!" Christine exclaimed as she saw a monster sitting next to her. A mass of smashed red hair covered part of the face, which was streaked with white, black, and blue. A slash of red extended from the lips down the chin and splotched the neck, reminding her of a deranged clown.

"Shh, it's okay," the monster/clown said, her voice soft and kind. She yanked off the bright red mop to reveal wet, shoulder-length light brown hair, which had largely fallen out of the skull cap worn beneath the wig. "Are you okay?" she asked as she put a hand to Christine's arm.

Christine calmed again, finding it funny that she'd been dragged out of the river by a clown. She hated clowns. As a kid they used to creep her out. She nodded, trying to sit up, but the hand that had been on her arm moved to her shoulder.

"Just lie there. Can you breathe?" the woman asked, and Christine nodded, taking several deep breaths just to make sure. "Okay. Stay here." The clown jumped up and ran, though Christine couldn't work out how she was able to do so given the massive shoes she had on.

They must have made great flippers to swim in. This thought sent a giggle through Christine's still fuzzy brain. Within moments she heard rocks crunching underfoot and the low, soft voice of her savior coming back toward her, having a one-sided conversation.

"Okay. Thanks, John. We'll be here." The woman ended the call and lowered her phone, then knelt next to Christine, who lay there, staring up at the sky. Sighing, Christine closed her eyes, resting an arm across them.

Willow couldn't stop the questions from parading across her mind. Why had the woman done this? Was it suicide or an accident? Who was she? From the woman's dress—a black tank top with black leather pants and heavy boots—she doubted she was from the area. Also, the car had a Hertz sticker on the back window.

She sat next to the woman, waiting for the cavalry to arrive. With a suicide attempt, it would be the police as well as an ambulance. Once they arrived and had the woman loaded, it would be about a twenty-five-minute drive back into Woodland to the very hospital where Willow worked.

She began to shiver, the chilly night breeze seeping into the completely saturated material of her once baggy clown suit, which now clung to her like a second skin. She hugged herself and looked down at the woman. "Do you have a name, honey?" she asked quietly, reaching out to brush some of the hair from the woman's face, which was deathly pale.

"It doesn't matter." The arm came down, and blue eyes looked into Willow's briefly before turning away. Finally, the woman sighed. "Christine," she said quietly.

"Nice to meet you, Christine, though I'm sorry it has to be under these kinds of circumstances." Willow gave her a small smile, though no doubt it looked garish and ghoulish with the smeared makeup from her unexpected dip.

Christine gave her a quick look before looking away again. "Yeah," she responded, voice flat. "And you?" she asked, looking Willow up and down. "Bozo?"

Willow stared at her for a moment, confused

and about to protest when she considered her current getup. She chuckled lightly. "Yeah," she muttered, glancing down at herself. "Willow Bowman."

Christine nodded in acknowledgment, then turned to look back up into the heavens as the sound of a siren not far away broke the quiet of the night.

Chapter Two

The lights of Mercy Medical's ER nearly blinded Willow as she parked her truck and hurried in after Toby and Allen, the two EMTs who had shown up at the scene. The sound of chaotic activity surrounded her as she pushed through the ER doors, hurrying alongside the gurney on which Christine had been strapped down.

"Why am I here?" Christine muttered, her head lolling to the side, her face pale with heavy, dark shadows beneath her closed eyes.

To Willow's experienced eye, it seemed that the woman, who now in the light of the well-lit hallways looked to be in her late twenties or early thirties, was coming down off her high. "Just to make sure everything checks out okay," Willow said, holding Christine's hand.

"I don't need to be here," she muttered, then began to cough violently, bringing up more water. She'd had similar fits the entire way in the ambulance, Willow had been told. As doctors and ER nurses emerged onto the scene, Willow knew it was her cue to back off. Christine was no longer her patient.

She grabbed a cup of coffee from the nurse's station and headed out into the waiting room, wanting to get out of the way. She told one of the nurses to notify her the moment they were done with Christine. With such a small hospital, she'd worked in nearly every department, including the ER, more than once.

"Hey, girl, what are you doing here?" Rachel Smith asked, lightly touching Willow's arm where she stood. "And, what the hell happened? You look like you walked through the car wash in your creepy clown stuff."

Willow smirked. "Hey," she said, then sighed. "Guess I decided to go fishing at…" She looked at her watch, noting that the hands weren't moving and a very menacing bubble was floating around the face. "Shoot." She turned to her friend. "Some late hour." She leaned against the wall behind her, exhaustion finally taking root.

"What? What happened?" Rachel leaned her shoulder against the same wall a couple feet away from her colleague.

"Oh, you wouldn't believe it." Willow was about to tell her fellow nurse what had happened when she noticed two men walking through the automatic doors of the lobby.

The two men were definitely not from the area and stuck out like a couple of sore thumbs. One wore a smart black suit and had a large, black leather satchel in his hand. The other was also dressed in finery, though more understated: a white button-up shirt, its sleeves rolled to the mid-forearm, tucked into expensive-looking gray slacks. He wore more rings on one hand than Willow even owned. His slicked-back salt-and-pepper hair gleamed under the lights as brightly as the rings did.

The men immediately began to look around, but when the one with the satchel spotted Rachel in her scrubs he immediately changed course, the other man following. Walking over to her, the man with graying hair yet young skin smiled.

"Excuse me, Nurse," he said, charm oozing from him. "I need to find someone." He eyed both of them, frowning slightly as he looked from Willow's face down to her water-logged clown suit. His expression made her extremely self-conscious. In all the hubbub and the familiarity with her workplace, she hadn't put much concern into her current appearance.

"Who?" Rachel asked, pushing away from the wall.

"Uh…" The man turned to the suit behind him, who handed him a piece of paper. "Willow Bowman? We were told by one of your fine physicians she was here. I understand she's a nurse at this hospital?"

"I'm Willow Bowman," Willow said, also pushing away from the wall. The man looked at her, doubt evident in his dark, piercing eyes. "It's a long story," she said softly. "What can I do for you, mister?"

"Robert Knowles." He extended a hand, which she took after removing her ruined white glove. "I need to speak with you concerning tonight's events. I assume it's why you look like a drowned rat?"

His smile was tight-lipped, and Willow wasn't so sure she liked this guy. "Ah, yeah." She looked down at herself, then back up at him.

He handed a white handkerchief to her before turning back to Rachel. "Is there somewhere we can speak with Ms. Bowman?"

"Sure. Follow me to the conference room." Rachel looked at her friend, who only shrugged as she looked at the handkerchief, made of a finer silk than anything she had ever touched.

"Ms. Bowman can join us once she's cleaned up a bit," Knowles said.

Yeah, Willow didn't like him.

⁂

She splashed water all along the white sink, rinsing off the last vestiges of makeup, then looked at herself in the mirror. Her hair was a tangled mess, and finger-combing could do only so much. She needed a brush, which was in her truck. For the time being, she pulled it up into an incredibly messy bun, which would have to do. Her eyes, light green like her grandmother's, reflected how tired she was and were irritated and red from the filthy water of the river.

Her face clean, there wasn't much she could do about her attire. She had unbuttoned the coverall-type clown suit, letting the top hang down, arms flapping around her legs. She was glad she'd worn a tank top underneath it, and even more glad that it was dark blue and not white.

Pushing open the doors of the conference room, Willow saw the two men, the suit standing over a laptop, a tiny printer buzzing away next to it, spitting out a sheet of paper. Robert Knowles was sitting at the head of the table, his fingers steepled under his chin. An expensive gold watch glittered against a tanned wrist. She also noticed a large, gold pinky ring on his right hand in addition to the others that adorned his fingers.

"Ah, Ms. Bowman." He greeted her with a smile, looking a bit more approving as he looked her over again, this time his gaze settling on her breasts for a moment before moving back to her face. "Please, have a seat." He indicated the chair to his left.

Willow took it, glancing at the suit across the

table from her, who had yet to speak. She knew she was safe but felt very uncomfortable with those two. "What's this about?" she asked, looking back to Knowles, who sighed and sat forward in his chair.

"Have you spoken with anyone about what happened tonight? Other than emergency personnel, of course," he asked.

"No. Listen, Mr. Knowles—"

"*Ms.* Bowman," he interrupted, not unkindly, but certainly firm.

Stunned into silence, Willow started as something was put before her by the suit. Looking at it, she realized it was a check. Her eyes flew up to meet his hard gaze. "This is a check for thirty-five thousand dollars," she said, her voice breathless and even more confused.

"And all yours," Knowles said. "If"—he held up a well-manicured finger—"you do one simple thing for us."

"Us? What, you and the suit?" she asked, nodding toward the other man who was already back typing on the laptop. Robert Knowles chuckled, making Willow's skin crawl.

"No. Jack is simply Swann's attorney," Knowles said, a tight smile on his lips. "What you'll be doing will be for her, me, and Swann's reputation."

Willow stared at him, utterly baffled for a moment, his words flowing through her head, trying to make sense of what he was telling her. Swann. She had said her name was Christine. Why did he refer to her as Swann? She thought back to the woman she'd fished out of the water, the face, pale, dark hair, blue eyes, leather pants, black tank top…

"Holy shit!" Her eyes widened, and her hand

flew to her mouth. The men exchanged a glance, then Robert looked at her again. "I pulled…I pulled *Swann* out of Chandler River?" she squeaked out. He nodded. "Swann, as in won six Grammys last year?" He nodded once more.

"Perhaps now you see just how important it is that we get your full cooperation with this," he said.

The paper from the printer was slid in front of her. It looked like a contract of sorts. "What is this?" she asked, hands shaking now as she was beginning to understand the gravity of the situation.

"It's your promise that you'll keep what happened tonight to yourself," Robert said simply.

She picked it up and began to read it over, trying several times before she was able to focus. "So," Willow drawled, her eyes still sweeping over the document. "You're saying I get the money if I keep my trap shut?"

"Ms. Bowman, Swann has a great many fans who are young girls, girls in their teens, early twenties. These fans look up to her, emulate her. In her music they find inspiration for their own lives, as well as words they can relate to. These girls would be devastated to find out their heroine, their role model, has fallen from grace."

Willow looked up at the man, the corner of her mouth quirking at his spew of crap. "You play a good game, Mr. Knowles." She chuckled lightly.

His brows drew together in irritation. "Then let me put it to you this way, *Ms.* Bowman. If this got out, Swann would be finished. Better?" He sighed, flopping back in the chair, his hand going to his forehead. "Cleaning up this mess is going to cost her enough as it is."

Willow's ire and amusement died down as what he was saying really sunk in. She wondered if the singer had told her that her name was Christine to try to mask her identity. She had no idea.

Clearing her throat, she instead asked, "How did you know where to find her?" It was more than obvious those "citified" boys had no clue which end was up out there in the sticks.

Knowles glanced up at her. "Swann's tour manager knew the circumstances under which she left tonight," he explained curtly. "He was concerned." The man wiped at a smudge on the polished table with a fingertip. "Luckily, there aren't all that many hospitals in this area."

Willow turned back to the contract under her hand, then glanced over at the check. Instantly, as if the lawyer were reading her thoughts, a gold pen appeared before her. She took it, tapping it against her chin as she read over the document once more. She met his expectant gaze.

"I'll sign your contract here, Mr. Knowles, but I don't want your money. Your daughter, or whatever, needs help, not to hand out bribes."

"I'm her manager," he clarified. "And, the check stays here, Ms. Bowman. Whether you chose to cash it or not is entirely up to you."

She nodded, scribbling her signature across the dotted line.

"This is a legal document, Ms. Bowman," Lawyer Jack said, taking the pen and contract from her before the ink had a chance to dry. "If you were to breach it, Swann can and will take legal action against you. Do you understand this?"

Willow nodded, sighing warily. "Yes."

"Thank you," Robert Knowles said, standing. "Good evening to you."

With amazing efficiency, the attorney packed up the laptop and printer, and both men were on their way.

Willow glanced at the check, taking it in her fingers. "Holy crap," she whispered. "I just saved the life of the woman who won the Grammy for best female vocalist last year."

❧ ❧ ❧ ❧

The check secured in the glove compartment of her truck for safekeeping, Willow headed to the female employees' changing room. Glad to find a pair of scrubs in her locker that were not too smelly, she hurried into the shower, stripping out of her pasted-on clothing and stepping under the warm, calming spray.

She felt her skin thawing, but her heart was still like ice. She kept seeing Christine—er, Swann—lying there on the riverbank, so vulnerable, death hovering in the air.

Willow could not reconcile in her own mind the face of the woman she had rescued that night with the woman she had seen on television and on CDs and magazine covers. What had caused someone like that, who had the world at her feet and money and fame in abundance, to do something so drastic?

She wondered if the toxicology reports would tell them anything. The look in the woman's eyes had been dazed and fuzzy and her pupils were very dilated, which the near drowning could only partially explain. Willow had a hunch there was more to it, and Robert Knowles's reaction to the situation—almost nonchalantly irritated, as though this wasn't the first time something like this had happened—deepened that hunch.

She stepped out of the small stall, pushing the curtain aside. Grabbing a towel, she quickly dried herself and slipped into the scrubs. She had no shoes and eyed the big red ones.

Opting to not look like Patch Adams yet again for the night, she stuck some surgical booties over her shower flip-flops and headed out to get some information.

The air in the ER was cool and sterilized. She went in search of Swann's chart, hoping she hadn't been moved yet. She knew by Colorado law she'd be taken in for an M1 Hold, which was a seventy-two-hour period of observation in the mental wing of the hospital. It was reserved for patients deemed to be in danger of harming themselves or others, and with her suicide attempt, drug-fueled or not, it was the singer's fate.

Willow found her in cubical three, the curtain closed around the small space. She'd been transferred from the gurney she'd been brought in on to the bed in the cube. She was still dressed in her damp clothing, though much of her body was swaddled in emergency blankets.

She looked down at the closed eyes, long, dark lashes that any woman would envy, and a face at peace in slumber. She knew when those eyes were open that they were a penetrating, dark blue, often elevated with smoky eye makeup, long washed away.

She studied the face, with its high, prominent cheekbones and strong jaw. The skin was very pale, and blue veins were visible beneath the surface. Her hair looked dark black against the paleness of her skin and the white bedding beneath her. It was short around the back and sides, but the bangs were long, often covering an eye in pictures. Now, a few wisps rested against her face. Gently, Willow pushed those strands away.

She took one of Swann's hands in her own. The skin was warm, and she was relieved beyond belief not to find it as cold and stiff as it had been at the river. She didn't know this woman, other than her music. Her voice was beautiful, soulful, and strong, her songs often wondering about life and the part everyone played in it.

It was strange, standing next to her unmoving, sleeping form, Willow swore she could feel a sadness coming from the singer. It was unsettling, but it made her want to somehow make it better—no doubt the nurse in her responding to a person in need. But, the need was strong.

❧ ❧ ❧ ❧

The drive home was long. As Willow drove across the Dittman Bridge, a shiver passed through her and her eyes were drawn to the spot where Swann had jumped. A wave of nausea washed over her. Taking several deep breaths, she forced her eyes straight ahead as she drove the last ten miles to her ranch.

"Mmm, must have been some party," Kevin mumbled, still half-asleep as he rolled over, awakened by Willow climbing into bed.

"Had an emergency at the hospital," Willow whispered, settling her tired body against the soft mattress.

"Everything okay?" her husband asked, sounding a bit more awake, though his eyes were still closed.

"Mm-hmm," she murmured with a heavy, tired sigh. "Talk tomorrow," she slurred, already asleep. It had been a long day.

Chapter Three

The day outside was gray, the rain having stopped falling only an hour earlier. Christine gazed out, noting that the sky didn't look quite as pregnant as it had earlier. She brought her knees up in the chair, pressing them against her chest and wrapping her arms around them.

As she rested her chin on her knees, she sighed deeply. She felt strange, somehow changed beyond recognition from the person she had been this time two days earlier.

A soul-altering choice, the counselor lady had called it after she'd administered a mental health evaluation that morning. Christine guessed they wanted to see if she was crazy or just really fucked up. She voted for both. She craved a cigarette like nothing else, cursing herself for quitting.

So. She'd finally tried it, finally gone over the edge that she had always been able to step back from before. Christine shivered, realizing how close she'd come to succeeding in ending it all. She also realized how close she was to not caring.

She flinched slightly at the sound of the key in the door to her room, but she didn't turn around. Her gaze was still fixed on the gray world outside her window, glass with little metal crisscross mesh embedded into it. There was quiet murmuring just outside the room, then footfalls, followed by the heavy sound of her door being closed and locked.

"Hello, Christine."

"Bob."

Her manager was silent as he took a seat on the bed behind her chair. She could hear the squeak of the bedsprings and smell his cologne. The room was sparsely furnished. Simple bed—no rails, no bars, but bolted down—and the chair she sat in. A bathroom off to the side with a pedestal sink and toilet. Everything nice and snug, nothing she could harm herself with.

"Quite a mess you've gotten yourself into here," he said, his voice quiet, tired.

"So it would seem," she muttered, not bothering to look at him, in truth not wanting to see the disappointment she knew she'd find there.

"Everything's been taken care of—hospital staff, doctors, ambulance drivers, the police, and the crazy little clown who fished you out." He snickered. "Apparently she's a nurse of some sort here. You gave her your real name. Why?"

The silence grew heavy. Christine changed position slightly, letting one foot slip to the floor, still holding the other leg tightly. She kept her posture, staring out the window, though she no longer saw the day beyond. Finally, she responded to his question, her voice flat. "What would you rather I had done? 'Hey there, I'm Swann, yeah, *that* Swann. Want me to autograph your tits while we're down here?'"

"Why'd you do it?" he finally asked, breaking the silence with the effect of a sledgehammer through glass.

"I don't want to talk about it with you, Bob." Christine's voice was low, tacitly suggesting a change of topic. He didn't bite.

"You could have drowned, Christine," he said, insistence in his voice.

She smirked. "I've been drowning for years, Bob," she whispered. "What finally made you notice?"

"That's a little dramatic, isn't it?" he asked with mild amusement in his voice. Christine said nothing. *Precisely why I don't go to you for anything, bud.* "Christine," he said, clearly unaware of just how much ire she felt for him. "I'm your friend."

"Friend?" She turned on him then, popping up from the chair with blue eyes blazing brilliantly, expensive white teeth bared. "No, I don't think so. I'm no friend to you. I'm your meal ticket. Always have been."

"Christine…"

"No!" she snapped. "If I meant anything to you, you never would have scheduled this tour. I told you I needed a break, that I was struggling. You knew." She turned back to the window, hugging herself as she paced, jaw muscles clenching.

"But the album—"

"Fuck the album," she yelled before flopping back down into the chair, a hand running through her long bangs. "What about me?" she almost whispered. "Not like what I thought or wanted has ever mattered." She glared back at him. "Should have fired your ass years ago."

"You'd be nothing without me, and you know it."

"Maybe not. But I'd still have me." Turning back to the window, her shoulders falling, she said sourly, "Do something useful, Bob. Get me the fuck out of here."

She wasn't surprised to see a whole host of media as she stepped out of her apartment building in Brooklyn, headed to the car that would take her to the airport.

Swann! Swann! Over here! How do you feel? Is it true you're going into rehab? What do you have to say to your fans?

All the questions were being shouted at her, the huge crowd standing back with their phones in the air to catch every second. She knew she'd be all over social media in about five minutes, so decided to make it count.

Handing her bag to her best friend Adam, she nodded toward the black SUV waiting at the curb. Getting the idea, he continued on as she turned and faced the mob, raising her hands.

"Hey!" she called out to get everyone to quiet down.

A new flurry of questions were hollered at her by many different voices. "Okay, okay, okay! Calm down now."

She waited until the questions stopped and, though she had phones, cameras, and microphones shoved in her face, she kept her cool.

"Sometimes we all just need a little extra help to get over a bump in life. Something not talked about enough, in my opinion." She made sure to look as many reporters in the eye as she could, including a few bystanders. "So, I'm fine, I'll be fine, and I say, be good to yourself."

She scanned the multitude of cameras, searching for one that had a big network logo. She chose the closest one to her that she hoped would reach all the way to Colorado.

"And," she added, looking directly into the lens. "Hey, Bozo. Thanks." She knew nobody would get what she was talking about, but the message wasn't for them. "Peace out!" she called to the group, flashing two fingers as she headed into the waiting SUV.

❧ ❧ ❧ ❧

Eyes closed and her body swaying with the music she was creating, Christine ran knowing fingers across the piano keys. She had written more music in the past two months than she had in two years. As the emotion passed through her, it filled her with a peace that only music could give her, the creation and execution of it giving her a sense of control that she didn't have anywhere else in her life.

During her stay at Promises, she'd started having the dreams again and remembering things she had thought long dead. Demons of her past, events—some self-invoked, others thrust upon her—that haunted her and dogged her nocturnal steps.

Her therapist at the exclusive rehab center told her that now that her body and mind were free of the poisons she had been feeding them, the gates were wide open for her to face whatever had caused her to run in the first place.

And therein lay the problem: she didn't want to face the ghosts.

She stroked the ivories with a lover's caress. Music was the only thing that hadn't betrayed her or demanded something from her. Music gave itself to her, allowing her to bring it forth into the world freely and willingly, never asking questions or wanting answers.

It just *was*.

Through music Christine could tell a story, share a part of herself without the accessibility and direct vulnerability that talking about it would have. No one knew the real her, and that was how she wanted it. It was why she used her last name professionally— only a handful of people knew her first name at all, let alone used it without fear of being gutted.

She had always been so grateful that when Bob had found her in that shithole bar in Queens, she'd been doing her own stuff. She'd been ballsy enough at fourteen to tell him she would only ever do her own stuff and that if he wanted anything different, he knew where he could shove it.

He'd laughed, and that was basically where her creative freedom had stopped. If she were to play for Bob the piece she was playing now, he would laugh, then tell her to burn it; it had no place in *his* show.

She didn't want to think about all of that. Those thoughts dogged her days as it was. Right now, all she wanted to do was lose herself in her music and forget about all the things that were wrong in her life. That was part of the problem. She'd seamlessly, intentionally ignored everything problematic, the anxiety building and building but not dealing with any of it, until the weight of it all had started to overwhelm and then finally control her.

Her counselor said that was why she had turned to drugs. She wanted to numb the internal turmoil and pain. Self-medicating, she'd said. That was a term Christine had heard before but had never fully understood it until she'd been shown the irrefutable proof that she'd been doing it her entire life, even if through her self-imposed isolation.

Christine snorted softly at the irony. As she'd detoxed, gone through the process of learning new coping skills and opening to the idea that perhaps legitimate anti-anxiety medication may help more than cocaine, the original addiction had arisen anew: music. One addiction for another. Her creative juices had started to churn within her soul, demanding to be let out. She was happy to oblige.

Her fingers came to a halt as a knock sounded on the door to her suite. "Come in," she called, pushing the bench back and standing, carefully closing the lid of the baby grand as the door opened, then swiftly closed. "Good afternoon, Margaret."

"Hello, Swann. Were you practicing?" Margaret asked, arranging her bulk on the couch that faced its twin, where Christine seated herself.

"Composing, actually." Christine ran her arm along the length of the back of the couch, her head slightly tilted as she studied the woman sitting across from her.

Margaret Olson looked at the white Baldwin, then to her patient. "I see no music." Christine tapped her temple. "All up here," she said with a grin.

"Ah." The older woman shook her head as she got settled. "If only I had one-tenth of your talent," Margaret said with a sigh, making the singer chuckle. She tapped on a tablet that she set on her lap, sliding her finger this way and that as she got to what she needed. "All right. Last time you talked about dreams that were coming back." She glanced up at Christine, then gazed back down at her notes from their previous session. "Have you had any more since last week?"

Christine blew out a breath, glancing out the French doors that overlooked the beautifully manicured grounds of the exclusive rehab center. "Yes."

"When was this?" Margaret asked, plucking the stylus from its nook on the little computer, ready to scribe.

"Sunday night," Christine said, her voice quiet, almost fearful. As Christine began to speak, her voice remained quiet, almost haunted. "The alley again."

"Tell me about that alley, Swann."

It was dark, the best time to be up and about. That's when it was easiest to score a little extra money. She hated to do it, but if she had learned anything from those bastards who fucked and gave birth to her, it was that everyone did what they had to do.

With a sigh, Christine headed down the dark streets of Queens, New York. It amazed her what a shit place it was considering the irony of its name. Whatever. Royal pain in the ass, maybe. Speaking of which, hers sure hurt. Guy from the night before... What the fuck had she been thinking, letting him do that? She couldn't believe people got off on that shit. Oh well. He'd given her dinner for the next week from that. Backdoor men, that's what Adam called those guys. What-the-fuck-ever.

She turned into an alley, a faster way to get to the street she wanted to work. She really needed to get a gig, and soon. This street shit was for the birds. Damn, it was cold. She wrapped her arms around herself, then quickly dropped them. Dude needed to see what he was buying. She rolled her eyes.

The streets were slow, a few cars passing now and

then, and she was beginning to get impatient. The boots she wore, fake leather and extremely shiny, reached to just below her knees and were crazy uncomfortable. Her thighs were bare to just below her ass, where the mini she wore ended. God, she hated skirts. Her legs felt like they were about to get frostbite. Luckily, this piece-of-shit outfit came with a little jacket. Her tits may have been cold, nipples like rocks and about to file a restraining order against her, but by golly her arms were relatively warm.

Ohhhh, a car! Dark in color, its headlights nearly blinded Christine as it pulled to the curb, squeaking to a stop next to her. The window rolled down with a mechanized buzz.

Walking over to the small sedan, she leaned down, making sure plenty of her size Ds could be seen in the low-cut shirt. "Hey, sugar," she said sweetly. Looking in, she saw a man—big surprise. His hair was short, kind of choppy, like his barber had gone a little nuts with the scissors, or perhaps pruning shears.

"How much, sweetheart?" he asked, his voice surprisingly high pitched.

"Well, that's all up to you. What's on your mind?" Christine asked, grinning and cocking an eyebrow. God, he made her skin crawl.

"Stand back a little, honey, so I can get a look at you." He leaned slightly over the passenger seat.

Standing upright, she held her arms out, turning in a small circle. She turned back to face the car, hand on her hip. His face was buried in shadow, but she thought she could hear a small moan coming from the car. It took everything in her to not vomit on his front tire.

"Get in," he said, his voice taking on an unmis-

takably aroused tone. Suddenly his less-than-attractive mug was alive and well as the dome light lit the cab of the car when he pushed open the passenger-side door.

Stepping to the car again, Christine noted the tenting action going on in his trousers. Hiding her disgust, she climbed into the front passenger seat. But, when she did, something quickly caught her eye on the empty back seat. She noticed a tear in the material of the bench seat, a neat little cut that looked to be about an inch or so long with stains all around it.

"Great, let's go," he said, looking at her right leg, which was still out of the car. "Can't drive unless you close the door, honey."

She gripped the handle along the inside of the door, about to pull it closed, but something told her not to. Something was screaming at her to not pull her leg in or close that door. Confused, she turned to look at the man behind the wheel. He stared back at her. As she watched, his face began to change. His unattractive features began to turn downright frightening as, she swore, his eyes darkened.

"Close the door," he demanded.

She cried out when her right hand was grabbed and she was damn near tugged out of her boots as she landed on the sidewalk, the cold, rough cement skinning her hands and chin. She looked up to see Adam standing over her, his stance wide and threatening as he yelled at the man in the car.

Stunned from hitting her head, she couldn't understand him for a moment, but she knew she'd never seen her friend, her protector, like that before. As time went from slow and thick to speedy and loud, she brought her arms up instinctually as the car screeched away from the curb, the still-open door edge slicing her thigh as it whipped by.

Crying out, Christine looked down at it, watching as blood began to bubble up from the cut. She looked up at Adam, stunned, confused, and afraid.

Christine hugged herself, rocking slightly. There was silence in the room for a long moment before her therapist broke it.

"These dreams are pretty vivid," Margaret said, her voice quiet.

Christine nodded. "Yes, they are." She sighed, running a hand through her hair, leaving it in disarray. The counselor was silent for a moment, and Christine could feel her eyes on her. She hadn't looked at Margaret once during the entire telling of her story.

"How did you feel about that?" Margaret asked gently. "The fact that Adam saved you from potentially being his next victim?"

Christine looked at the woman for a moment, not sure what to say to the kind, knowing smile she saw. She turned away again. The kindness was too much, and she didn't deserve it. "I don't know that I would have cared. There wasn't much to save, you know?" Christine leaned back into the soft cushions, her hands tucked behind her head and her eyes on the older woman.

"Adam had seen the missing girl get into that same car, with that same man, right?" Christin nodded. "Did they catch him?"

"Yeah." She snorted. "But not before the bastard nabbed three more girls."

"Did you know them?"

Christine was quiet for a moment, her mind reeling back, then slowly she nodded. "Yes," she whispered.

After a long silence, Margaret said, "You're to be released from here in a few weeks." A statement, not a question.

Christine smirked, grateful for the change in topic. "So they say."

"What will you do? Do you feel you're ready?"

"Well, if you're asking if I'll take another dive off a bridge, the answer is hell no."

"Why not?" Margaret asked, crossing one leg over the other. "What's different now?"

Christine took a long, deep breath and blew it out. "I almost hurt somebody else," she finally said. "That's not okay."

"The nurse."

"The nurse," Christine said with a nod.

"And, what of your fans? Are you afraid of losing them? Or, that you lost them after this?" Margaret asked kindly.

"They'll come back," she said, her voice so low it was almost a whisper. "They always do. Bob will make sure of that."

Chapter Four

You about done with my air compressor, there, Kevin?"

Willow's head shot up from the fence she was working on. Her husband, wiping his forehead with the handkerchief he always kept in his back pocket, headed over to greet Richard Dean, their closest neighbor at three miles away.

"Hey there, Dick. Yeah, sorry about that. Come on into the garage. I'll get it for you," he said, patting the old man's back.

Willow smiled as she turned back to her work. She had been telling Kevin for months to get the thing back to Dick, but he hadn't listened. Stubborn male. She had no idea what he'd been using the thing for in the first place.

"Ouch, dang it!" She snatched her finger away from the wire cutters that had pinched the skin on her index finger, making it bleed.

She stuck the wound into her mouth, a mumbled curse around the finger aimed at the fence. Examining her hand, she saw that it was just a small cut.

Once her work had been interrupted, Willow realized just how hot it was. She looked up into the May sky, blue as a robin's egg and unseasonably warm for the time of year and their altitude. Snatching the tied kerchief from her hair that held it back out of her face, she wiped her face down with it, then beat the cloth against her thigh and decided to go in for some iced tea to cool down.

The walk back to the house was a long one, but beautiful and peaceful. The soft whinnies and snorts of the neighbor's horses could be heard, as well as the squawk of their chickens in their pen. Their dogs were out running, making those chickens squawk, but it was okay. Life over the past six days had been good.

Willow wanted to get animals of their own, and they certainly had the land for them, but Kevin was against it. His argument was they didn't have the time, nor necessarily the money, to keep up a full ranch. She didn't fully agree, and would love to have a house full of life, be it from furry babies or, dare she say, a human one. But, early on, she'd agreed. They needed to focus on their careers and the two of them and, a bit later on, the house.

Willow and Kevin had taken some well-deserved vacation time, using it to get to repairs and improvements on the ranch they'd been wanting to do for a couple years but had never seemed to find the time for.

She knew her best friends, Remmy and Julie, were confused as to why they didn't take the opportunity to go somewhere romantic, just the two of them away from the daily grind, but she also knew they'd never understand if she tried to explain it to them. So, she never did—to anyone.

It was Saturday, and she'd be going back to work Monday night. She had been thinking about having a barbecue the following day. Something she'd have to bring up to Kevin.

"Hey, honey?" Kevin called, pulling Willow from her thoughts.

She smiled. "Speaking of the devil," she muttered. "Yeah?" she called back, stopping just shy of the square plot of grass that was the "backyard" on the two hundred and sixty-five acres of land they owned.

Kevin came out from the shade of the garage, his hand shielding his eyes from the sun.

"Have you seen the attachments to the air compressor?"

She shook her head. "Nope. Did you look in your work bench?"

"Why would they be in there?" he called back, sounding less than accepting of her suggestion, and headed back into the garage.

Willow walked toward the house again. She held up her hand and all five fingers, ticking them down. "Five, four, three, two…"

"Here they are!"

"You don't say," she muttered, pushing the slider open and entering the house. She knew damn well that he'd never admit to finding the attachments in the Bermuda Triangle of Colorado known as his work bench.

The back sliding glass door opened into the space that was once used as a dining room by her grandparents, whom she'd inherited the house and property from. Now, it was used as a makeshift office for Kevin until they got the two-story farmhouse renovated and updated to what they wanted it to be.

Heading into the kitchen and over to the fridge, she pulled it open and surveyed the contents, looking for the jug of iced tea she had brewed the night before. Moving aside Kevin's gallon of Gatorade, she spotted the green top of the pitcher.

Sighing with contentment, she pulled the jug free

and poured the dark gold liquid into a glass, drinking half of it down before she could even get to the freezer for ice. Breathing heavily as she wiped her mouth with the back of her hand, she refilled the glass, adding a few cubes of ice.

Carrying her tea into the living room, Willow set it down on the end table before sitting on the recliner. She removed her boots, then kicked up the footrest and got settled as she grabbed her tablet to browse social media.

She was terrible about looking at it regularly, probably the only thirty-five-year-old out there who forgot to check it more than a couple times a week at best. She put in a lot of hours at the hospital and then more with the animals. By the time her day was done, she wanted to sleep, not scroll through political posts or one group slamming another group for the gripe of the day.

As she scrolled through her newsfeed, the headline of an article caught her eye.

Swann Ready To Spread Her Wings Again!

The article included a picture of the singer, which immediately grabbed Willow's attention. Swann was looking straight into the camera, clearly a professional shot. She was gorgeous. Her dark blue eyes were staring into the camera, almost seeming to stare into the very soul of the observer.

Willow met that gaze for a long moment before having to avert her eyes. She was bemused that a static picture on Facebook had won a staring contest. Swann's hair was as it so often was, messy and dripping into her face. One could take it as either "freshly fucked" or "fuck you," depending on one's perception of the singer.

She wore her ever-present tank top, though the one in the picture was white. A leather choker was around her throat, a pair of silver wings dangling from it. True to her signed word, Willow hadn't said anything to anyone, not even Kevin, about what had happened that very cold night. She'd thought of the singer every time she'd driven over Dittman Bridge. Now, maybe she'd get some closure. She clicked on the article.

Singer/songwriter, Swann, who mysteriously dropped from public view earlier this year, has announced that the concert tour for her latest album, Swan Song, *which was canceled in February after she was rumored to go into rehab—a rumor denied by her manager, Robert Knowles—has been rescheduled.*

"All tickets to the canceled performances, including an encore appearance in Denver, Colorado, will be honored for Swann's rescheduled concerts in those cities," said the singer's agent, Mark Hutchins, who added that Swann was feeling great and in good spirits and was looking forward to seeing her fans. The video below was taken the night the singer was flown to California to reportedly enter rehab.

Willow was so relieved to read that Swann had either chosen—or been forced—to get help. She was glad she'd made it out okay and, apparently, felt well enough to go back out on the road. She chewed on her bottom lip before tapping the video to play it. The scene was at night outside of a tall, brick tenement building in Brooklyn, NY, according to the caption.

The woman who had introduced herself as Christine stood near a shiny black luxury SUV.

The singer looked thin, dressed in baggy jeans and an oversized hoodie against what was clearly a cold night, as her breaths were nothing more than puffs of steam. She was inundated by people shouting questions and comments to her. It would have driven Willow nuts, but the singer handled it with calm.

Handing her bag to a handsome young man, Swann nodded toward the black SUV waiting at the curb. The man continued on as she turned and faced the mob, raising her hands. It took her several tries to quell the flurry of questions and get the crowd to quiet down.

"Sometimes we all just need a little extra help to get over a bump in life. Something not talked about enough, in my opinion. So, I'm fine, I'll be fine, and I say, be good to yourself."

Willow watched as Swann gathered herself and then looked directly into one of the cameras. "Hey, Bozo. Thanks," she said softly, then yelled to the crowd, "Peace out!" before flashing two fingers as the video ended.

Willow sat there for a long moment, stunned, with her mouth hanging open. She watched the short video again, then one more time. There was no way Swann could be talking to her. But, looking at the date of the video, she saw that it was just a few short days after the bridge incident and when Christine had called her Bozo.

Sitting back, she studied the picture at the top of the article, making herself look into those dark blue eyes, hearing those words again in her head. *Hey, Bozo. Thanks.* She smiled, touched that someone of such high esteem in the music world and in pop culture would actually even think of a simple nurse from the outskirts of Woodland, Colorado.

"What's got you smiling like that?" Kevin asked, bending down and looking at the screen of her tablet. He placed a chaste kiss on her cheek before plopping down on the couch, letting out a long, tired groan as he put his feet up on the coffee table. "Who's that?"

Willow met his interested gaze and instantly felt a twinge of irritation at the question and him looking at her screen. What was that about? She'd never kept anything from him, never even gave it a thought. Yes, she'd signed a nondisclosure agreement—she now understood that's what the document was—with Guido and the Suit, but she certainly could trust her own husband, especially after thirteen years together, eleven of them married. But her annoyance and hesitation weren't so much about knowing she *could* trust him as it was that she inexplicably wanted to keep this all for herself.

Mentally rolling her eyes at her own nonsense, she smiled. "Swann. She's a singer," she explained, knowing her old-school, George Jones, Johnny-Cash-and-friends-loving husband would have no clue who that was.

"Ah," he said, grabbing the remote for the TV. "Cool."

Setting her tablet aside, she raised her iced tea to her lips. "So, I was thinking," she began.

He didn't even spare her a glance as he flipped through channels. "Okay."

"Tomorrow is our last day before we both head back to work," she said, shrugging a shoulder nonchalantly. "Why not have a barbecue? I can ask Julie and

Remmy…"

He scrunched his face a bit. "You know I don't like spending time with them."

"…and Matt and Monica." She'd never understood why he seemed to dislike her best friends one minute and embrace them the next. "I know you and Matt love to talk baseball."

"Yeah, but their kid, Leia, is kind of a brat."

She rolled her eyes. "I know you have little to no patience for kids, Kevin, but Leia is only four. What do you expect?" She lightly nudged his thigh with her sock-covered foot. "Come on. It'll be fun. We can keep Leia busy with Richard's horses at the fence line."

He let out a heavy sigh and ran a hand through his sandy blond hair. Giving her the side-eye, finally he nodded. "Okay."

❧ ❧ ❧ ❧

Willow stepped out onto the wraparound porch of the smoky-blue two-story house. The newly painted white trim was something else she and Kevin had accomplished during their working vacation. It had taken thirty years off the old farmhouse.

She smiled, closing her eyes as she inhaled the early Sunday morning air, hands wrapped firmly around her mug of coffee. She loved the way two worlds were merging as the sun peeked over the flat plains and Rocky Mountains of her beloved Centennial State. She heard the songs of male crickets frantically rubbing their back legs together, desperate for a mate and saluting the ebbing night, melding with the songs of the birds in the dozens of trees around the house, helping to birth a new day.

This was her time, a time of peace and tranquility where she could regroup and gather strength from the dawning of new life. She was usually just arriving home around this time, drinking her coffee and watching the day reborn as Kevin got up and prepared for work.

He worked for the school district, taking care of all their IT needs. That's how they'd met, at Woodland Middle School. Fresh out of nursing school, Willow had gotten in with the district as a school nurse. It was also where she'd met Julie Wilson, her best friend, who taught at the school. Within a year she'd gotten in at the hospital, where she'd been ever since.

She looked out over the pastures, hearing the horses start to wake, snorting, their hooves stomping lightly on the ground. In the distance she saw the headlights of Macy Allen's car as she delivered the morning paper to the outlying farms and ranches. Willow usually passed the small blue car on her way in from the hospital.

Sipping from her mug, she made her way slowly down the stairs of the porch to the flagstone path that led to the edge of the landscaped part of their yard and ended in the dirt road to the gates of their property. She noted the colors that spread across the sky, pinks and oranges stretching fingers through the clouds, with rays falling through the cracks to spotlight scenes on the plains.

Memories of an earlier time began to flood Willow's mind. Her grandfather had been born in the farmhouse in 1918, his parents building expansions and even adding another story to the tiny, one-room house as their family began to grow. Seven children later, everyone began to disperse and find their own place in life.

Willow's grandfather, Earnest, had stayed on, loving the land far too much to leave it. His brothers had gone off to fight in World War II while he remained at the homestead, the sole son left to oversee the ranch. His father, aged and weathered by that time, was far too weak to run things.

Earnest Paxton lost three of his four brothers in the war, as well as one sister, Rose, who had gone over as a WASP. The other sister, Lucille, had married and moved off to New Jersey. Earnest's remaining brother, Carl, had no interest in the life of a farmer/rancher; he made his way west to explore the world of real estate, making his fortune in San Francisco.

Deep in these memories, Willow walked to the fence, which she needed to finish fixing. She pushed the gate open and headed across the road to the mailbox, standing tall before a ditch filled with water for irrigation. Grabbing the newspaper from its designated box mounted on the pole, she tucked it under her arm and headed back across the road.

Willow had spent hours and hours and hours with her grandmother on this land. Myra Paxton… now she was an interesting woman. Born in Rifle, Colorado at the height of the Great Depression, she was the third of six children, born to poor farmhands. Having no interest in farm life, she ran away from home at the age of sixteen, going off with the strongman of a carnival that was passing through town.

By that time, World War II was over and the population was desperate to have its spirits raised, so many of their young men having not come home. The carnival was a great success, and Myra traveled all around the United States and Canada with Dale, working as a weight guesser on the midway and as a dancer in one of the many shows.

Eventually tiring of the carnival life, Myra decided to find her own way. She began hitching rides along Route 66, where a lonely driver named Earnest Paxton picked her up in 1951. They were together until the day Earnest had died. Myra and Earnest had only one child, a bouncing baby boy, who eventually became Willow's father and inherited his mother's youthful wandering spirit.

Throughout Willow's youth, he moved them from this house to the next, one town to the next, and even spreading across state lines. She had no real childhood home to speak of, never living anywhere longer than a few years.

The ranch became her sanctuary, something that she knew she always could return to, something that would be in the same place, look the same, feel the same, *be* the same. Willow spent nearly all of her summers there and, when her parents lived close enough, her weekends too.

Her grandmother once even called Willow's mother, Helen, to see if there was a problem at home because the girl wanted to spend so much time at the ranch. Helen had been hurt by the question, but Willow hadn't the heart to tell her mother that it was because she felt she had no stability with her own parents, and so she sought what she craved with her grandparents.

It had been even worse when Willow's parents divorced during her sophomore year of high school. She felt lost and adrift. Once again, the ranch had provided the emotional nourishment she needed. She had even gone so far as to consider moving in with her grandparents indefinitely.

But by that time, Earnest was getting sick and Myra had enough to deal with, so Willow had stayed with her mother and Helen's new boyfriend, Shawn, who eventually became Willow's stepfather, and somebody she'd endured.

When Earnest died, Myra decided the ranch was too much to take care of. Since her son had his own life and home and absolutely no interest in taking on another residence, and her granddaughter had always loved the place so much, Myra had left the ranch in its entirety, repairs and all, to Willow.

During the instability of her childhood, Willow had closed a lot of doors that led to the deeper parts of herself. Gaining friends only to lose them a year or two later had made her turn inward for comfort—when she wasn't at the ranch, anyway. She'd locked away so much of herself during those years that in some ways, she still didn't entirely know who she was.

That's where her marriage came in very handy. Nobody knew the truth. On the outside, she and Kevin were the perfect fit. One of her friends once told her they were Barbie and Ken. She looked nothing like Barbie, but she had to admit, Kevin did look something like a Ken doll. A very handsome man, fit, great personality. The best part for her? He was predictably safe.

Chapter Five

Christine set the silver tray of empty dishes in the hall outside the door to her suite.

Belching loudly, she put her hand to her stomach, feeling full and content, muttering, "Excuse me" to the empty room.

She walked over to the French doors and looked out. She'd miss the view when she left. It was amazing how vibrant and beautiful things were to her again. Through the haze of the past ten years, the world around her had started to lose its color, flavor, and beauty. How had she allowed herself to become numb to the sounds of life? Weren't they music of a sort?

Wrapping her arms around herself, she leaned against the open doors, not quite stepping out onto the balcony. She had done that one night and nearly fainted. Looking down had reminded her entirely too much of that lost night in Colorado three months earlier.

She was heading home that day, and Christine was glad of it. She wanted her own house, her own bed. Plus, she missed Milly. That surprised her. The housekeeper had been with her for just over two years and had quickly become a cherished friend, as well as one hell of an employee.

Milly had no family in California to speak of, and her son was clear across the country in Nashville trying to become the next big country star. Christine wondered who on earth listened to that country babble. The stuff gave her ulcers. How could anyone have that many problems in one song?

Glancing over her shoulder at the unexpected sound of a knock, she headed back across the room and pulled the door open, noting her packed and piled luggage nearby. Her eyes widened at the smiling face that waited on the other side.

"Adam!" Finding herself almost picked up in his thin arms, Christine hugged her old friend for all she was worth, thrilled beyond words to see him there, even if she did feel embarrassed. Even though she'd just seen him three months before, it felt like forever. He was the little kernel of normality that she'd always leaned on since she'd been a kid.

"Hey, gorgeous," he said, his deep voice resonating through her.

"What are you doing here?" she asked, her embarrassment coming out as anger in that moment. "I don't want you to see me here."

She tried to push him away, but he had none of it, instead pulling her into a hug. She finally stopped fighting and fell into it. He held her, chin resting on top of her dark head.

"I heard you might need a friend. So here I am, friend. Or bellhop."

"How'd you know where I was?" she asked. "And, how the hell did you get in here?"

"Bob," he said, which she knew answered both questions. "You must be pretty damn angry at him for him to resort to calling me." He pulled out of the hug, heavy dark eyebrows drawn. "Did he force you to go here?"

Christine shook her head, amused. "No. For

once I made the correct decision for my life. Come on, let's sit."

"Jesus, this place is posh. Isn't this where Robert Downey, Jr. stayed?" Adam asked, looking around with wide, dark eyes, clearly impressed, as they both sat down. "Like, I mean, if Iron Man stayed in this room, I'm going to shit myself. I'm not all that impressed by the glitz and glamour of your life, Chris, but—"

"I almost did it, Adam," she blurted, looking down at her hands in her lap.

"What?" He stopped mid-stream as he geeked out over his favorite actor. He seemed to catch up to what she'd said and the meaning behind the simple words. He swallowed, sitting up straighter. "How?" he asked, his voice almost choking over the single word.

Christine chuckled ruefully, unable to look at him. "I jumped off this old, rickety bridge into a river."

Adam was quiet for a long moment, and she didn't feel the need to fill the silence. She gave him space to absorb what she'd said, though still didn't look at him.

"Why didn't you call me?" he whispered. "I would have been there in a heartbeat."

She turned to her friend now, seeing the pain on his face. She hated knowing that she'd put it there. "I know." She reached across the space between where they sat on separate couches and squeezed his knee to try and soothe his hurt before sitting back down. "I lost control." She shook her head to emphasize her point. "I lost it."

"What were you on?" His voice was low and serious. He'd had his own bout back in the day, so she knew he knew all too well.

"Everything. Anything." She sighed, glancing at the hand that grabbed hers, holding it tight. "I was taking anything I could get my hands on, Adam. I totally fucked up, bud. I may have ruined my career."

"I heard about the concert in Denver," he said quietly.

She met his gaze then quickly looked away, ashamed.

"It was all over the news, in the papers. They said it was because you had worn yourself to exhaustion, but I knew something was wrong." He squeezed her hand until she looked at him. "You were with us in New York after. Why didn't you tell me?"

"I was embarrassed," she said quietly. "Didn't know how to say it."

He nodded, the two sitting in silence for a long moment before he said, "And don't worry, Chris. There's no way you could ruin your career. They love you. Don't you know that?"

"I don't know, Adam," she said, blowing out a long, slow breath. "I just don't know anymore."

"I do have one question," he said, meeting her gaze. "How did you get out of the river?"

Christine grinned, feeling foolish. "A clown saved me."

"What?" Her friend looked at her as though she were crazy. "Jesus, you really were on some bad shit."

She laughed, letting it roll out of her throat with abandon. It felt good. He grinned, confused. "No, really. It was this woman, a nurse or something, who was dressed as a clown. Scared the shit out of me, too. I hate clowns."

"Oh, man," Adam said, joining her in her laughter. "Why was she dressed as a clown?"

Christine shrugged, wiping her eyes, crying from laughing so hard. "I have no idea."

⁂

Eyes closed, Christine inhaled deeply, just the barest touch of a smile curling the corner of her lips. Opening her eyes, she looked around. Everything was just as she'd left it before starting her tour—scattered sheets of blank sheet music feathered out over the wood floor in the shadow of her beloved grand piano. Finished work was still resting on top, the lid down.

Walking over to the instrument, she fingered some of the pages, her mind automatically conjuring up the music, following the notes with her eyes for a brief moment before memory finished the song.

Striding past the piano, she walked over to the bar at the far end of the spacious, sparsely furnished room. The late morning sunlight filtered in through the massive windows that overlooked the Pacific, coloring everything bright and clean.

She opened one of the cabinets next to the small bar fridge and was surprised to see it empty. "Milly," she murmured, a pleased smile quickly spreading over her face.

She could easily imagine her little firebrand of a housekeeper rummaging through every cabinet, closet, and drawer to find all the contraband, having herself a little party at the sink, dumping it all down the drain.

Walking back across the room, her bare feet padding over the cool, oak boards, she seated herself at the Baldwin and lovingly lifted the lid. Reaching out a finger, she tapped middle C, listening to that one beautiful note resonating in the room that stood two stories tall, an outer wall of glass providing a view into the Japanese gardens with the ocean beyond.

Closing her eyes, she sat straight and began to play, her fingers racing over the keys, the music flowing like water, her ears drinking it in. She needed to feel the music. Her body swayed with her emotions, rising and falling, cresting only to slam down again upon the rocky shores of melancholy.

Though the music was sad, composed upon a bed of bad memories, Christine could not have been happier.

ᔕᔕᔕᔕ

Reading what her Communications Coordinator had sent her via email and social media, Christine took a slow, careful sip of her coffee. It was amazing how good it tasted when sober. She relished the chocolate and hazelnut notes of the flavored coffee and creamer.

Marci had the unfortunate job of going through all of Christine's communications, be them from Robert, studios, venues, or fans. No doubt the last category was her least favorite part of the job. She clicked on an email from Marci that had the subject line: *Is this your clown?*

Curious, Christine set her coffee mug aside and clicked the video that was in the body of the email, which Marci explained had been sent to the Facebook page for Swann and her band. In the video was a woman dressed in dark green medical scrubs, her hospital ID badge clicked on the vee of her collar. She looked like she was standing in a hospital hallway, as they all looked fairly similar.

Christine noticed that the woman was absolutely beautiful. She looked to be in her late twenties or maybe early thirties. Her wavy light brown hair was pulled back into a ponytail, framing a lovely face. The word that came to mind was *angelic*. Her eyes were a beautiful light green and so open and friendly.

"Um," the woman said, looking uncomfortable standing there. "Hi, Christine or Swann. I suppose that's what's appropriate. Um, my name is Willow Bowman. Um, I saw what you said when the press was talking to you before you went into rehab. Well, that's what I heard, so no idea if that's true or not," she quickly amended, making Christine smile. "But, um, anyway, when you said, 'Hey, Bozo. Thank you.' No idea if you were referring to this Bozo," she said, placing her hand on her chest. This elicited an outright laugh from Christine, totally charmed. "But, just in case you did." She smiled a smile so filled with genuine kindness that it stopped Christine in her tracks. All she could do was stare. "You're welcome," Willow said softly, a small tilt to her head. Then, with a little wave, the video ended.

Christine watched it several more times, unable to believe it was the same woman who had pulled her out of the water that night. She was such a small woman, but when she looked into her eyes, she saw it, saw her. Also her voice. It was such a soothing voice, quiet and very pleasant.

Sitting back in the desk chair of her Malibu home office, she considered what to do next. Grabbing her mug to sip, she stared at the screen on her computer.

🙠 🙠 🙠 🙠

"Okay, here's the plan." Bob clicked a button on

the small remote that rested unseen in his hand. "We follow basically the same route as last time." A list of cities in various states all around the country popped up on the large, white screen he'd pulled down from the ceiling in his darkened office. Another click and bullets appeared next to certain cities. "In these places you'll be meeting with camera crews for pre-arranged conferences, in which," he said, looking sharply at Christine. "You will continue with the story of fatigue and overdoing it. Got it?"

She nodded dumbly, her eyes on the screen but her mind in outer space. She tugged at her bottom lip with her fingers as she slowly propelled the chair back and forth, using her feet for leverage. "But, you know, the rumors are flying," she said.

"Rumors aren't facts," he said absently, returning to his presentation. "Good deal."

He clicked again and went through a quick slide show of the various venues she'd be playing at, including Empower Field at Mile High in Denver.

"The good thing about doing this now instead of February is that in Colorado you'll be in the stadium this time as opposed to the Pepsi Center, where we were before. More seats, more people, more zeros in the paycheck."

"For who?" she muttered, gaze reaching the ceiling before falling back to him.

Bob looked at her, clicker at the ready. He ignored the comment and moved on to the next slide. It showed Christine at an earlier show, hair wild around her face, makeup dark and smoky. She recognized the pants she wore—black leather, slung low on her hips, and black boots. Very similar to what she wore at every show. The top, however, was new and clearly computer generated.

"What is this? I don't own a top like that. Hell, it's not a top, Bob, it's a friggin' bra!"

"I know," he said with a grin, obviously proud of himself. "I had Wayne play a bit with a picture of you during the Toronto tour, cut and paste with his computer, and voilà!" He indicated the picture. "This is our new look."

"No way." Christine sat forward in her chair, her hands clutching the edge of the conference table, ready to rise and strike. "I am thirty-one years old, Bob, and the skanky fifteen-year-old look is out. You have me looking like a goddamn prostitute!"

"Old habits die hard, eh, Christine?" he murmured with a raised eyebrow.

Before she could even think, she reached over and grabbed him by the front of his two-thousand-dollar suit and swung, his head bouncing back from smacking against the chair he sat in. Immediately blood began to trickle from his nose. He touched it with the tip of a well-manicured finger.

She looked at him, deeply wounded and stunned, both at what he'd said and what she'd done. "Son of a bitch," she muttered, angry at herself. She walked over to the bar at the corner of his office and snagged a towel, wetting part of it before throwing it at him.

He used it to dab at his nose. "Damn it, Christine. You need to do something to get back on the map. You've been out of the game for six whole months. *And* you fucked up during a goddamn tour!" He winced as he wiped the blood from his nose, looking at the towel before throwing it to the large glass conference table. "We've got to get you back in the spotlight."

"And dressing me like a whore is the way to go?"

she yelled, hands on hips from where she stood by the bar.

"If it keeps the dykes' tongues hard and the guys' cocks hard and hands on their wallets, yes."

She looked at him with her face like stone, hatred running through her veins. Biting her tongue, she decided to change the subject. She wasn't going to win this fight right now, so opted to stop before she ended up in jail for murder. Shifting gears, she said, "By the way, I'm doing much better. Thanks for asking."

"I know you are." He tossed the clicker across the table. "I've spoken with your doctors."

"Figured. And?"

"And what?" He rested his temple against his fist, studying his client with hooded eyes.

"Forget it." She headed toward the door. The meeting was over.

"Christine."

She stopped, her hand on the door. She glared at him over her shoulder.

"Why should I give you my pity or congratulations?" he asked, now on his feet. "You did it to yourself."

She stared him down, neither of their gazes wavering. He was pushing her more and more, and she wasn't sure how much longer she could take it. His condescension and insults, once veiled, were beginning to see the light of day in all their hateful splendor.

Without another word, Christine walked out, leaving the door open behind her. Bob called out after her, "Fittings are set up for Wednesday."

Chapter Six

Willow was tired after a long night. She'd be glad when her round of nights were over and she could move back to days. She'd been doing it for nearly a year now, and it was kicking her behind. The human body wasn't meant to be up all night and sleep during the day, unless it was a vampire, which she was not. She was a morning person, not a go-to-bed-in-the-morning person.

Folded newspaper tucked under her arm, she climbed the stairs to the porch and used her key to unlock the front door and let herself into the house. She heard the news on the TV in the kitchen and heard movement in there.

"Hey," she said.

Kevin, still dressed in his boxers and the T-shirt he slept in, glanced at her from the coffeepot, then turned back to his task. "Hey."

Able to feel the temperature in the kitchen fall about twenty degrees, Willow studied her husband, whom she knew very well. It was late summer and right on time—the time of year he began to get moody and distant. She wouldn't be surprised if he'd slept in the guest bedroom the night before, even though she wasn't there.

"Damn it," he muttered, trying to pull the foil off the top of a new bottle of creamer, his large fingers not able to get a good hold on the little flap provided.

"Can you get this?" he asked, voice gruff as he held out the bottle to her.

"Of course." She used a steak knife to make a slice in the top of the foil and use the opening to tear the foil away. He sighed and rolled his eyes, seeming irritated at himself for not doing the same.

"Honey," she said, setting the foil-free bottle on the counter next to where he stood. "Everything okay?" After so many years she felt she knew, but wanted to cover all bases first.

He looked at her, eyebrows drawn. "Yes, why?"

She walked over to him, placing a hand on his chest. He flinched a bit, but she stayed put. "Honey," she said gently. "I think you need a shower."

He looked at her as though she'd lost her mind. "Do you seriously think I'd leave for work without one?" he snapped.

"Kevin," she said a bit more firmly. "You need a shower."

He met her gaze for a long moment before it hit him. Nodding, he glanced away, looking sheepish. "Right," he muttered. He seemed to calm but almost looked sad for a moment. "Okay." He leaned over and gave her a peck on the forehead before leaving the room.

Willow grabbed two mugs from the cabinet and set them on the counter next to the coffee maker. She stood there as it sputtered to a finish, the fragrant nectar wonderful as it filled the room.

When she'd first met Kevin, she in her early twenties and him pushing later twenties, they'd hit it off immediately. Yes, he wasn't handsome and all that, but he was such a nice guy. He was intelligent, very funny, and just a joy to be around.

The thing she'd liked about him the most was he hadn't been pushy with her in any way. He'd ask before he hugged her or touched her for any real reason other than to get her attention. She'd never been around a man who was such a gentleman. She'd agreed to have coffee with him, which had stretched into dinner. Soon enough, they were a couple.

She'd been thrilled to just be able to get to know him without pressures of sex, something she'd struggled with since her teen years. Her grandfather, being of that strange generation, would always ask her, "Got a boyfriend, yet?" It was easy at eleven years old to giggle and say, "Grandpa! I'm only eleven!"

But, as she got older, it got harder and harder to find a response, let alone a reason other than, "No, focusing on my schoolwork for a good scholarship." When she'd met Kevin, she finally felt like she could perhaps have what others had: a companion, somebody to do things with; laughter and even some affection, without the pressure of sex.

There had been many, many men she'd found herself attracted to—or, more accurately, found attractive—but she never seemed to feel the same draw or sexual pull that her friends did. She looked at guys and found them attractive: kind smile, strong back, great jawline. She looked at women and also found them attractive: beautiful eyes, alluring silhouette, soft-looking skin.

Thoughts, like everyone had.

Kevin and Willow had been together nearly ten months before they had sex for the first time. Willow knew it was unusual, as most of her girlfriends either had sex right away, had one-night stands, or at least slept with their boyfriend within the first couple months of dating. Kevin hadn't pushed the issue, so Willow felt like she had time.

When it happened, they'd both been surprised; it hadn't been planned, nor did either of them even exhibit behavior that might hint at that direction. But, after it did, they'd decided to move in together. It had been nice, like moving in with her best friend. They'd had sex about a month after, then again a few months later, then at perhaps six months, then every now and then.

She had to think about it to remember when the last time had been. She thought perhaps a year, maybe? No—it had been after the party for his co-worker's son who had graduated from college.

"Three years ago," she whispered, pouring two mugs of coffee. "Wow."

One day, several years ago, she'd come home from work for lunch, which she rarely did, and had found Kevin masturbating in the shower. She'd been shocked at first, then hurt. He hadn't touched her in many months at that point, yet clearly had a need. He'd been deeply embarrassed and, almost like a little boy busted by his mother, ashamed. A long, in-depth conversation had ensued.

Before that day, Willow had never even heard the term "asexual" before. Kevin admitted he didn't know a lot about it, but knew it seemed to fit him, his lack of need for sexual fulfillment as he was fulfilled with her in other ways.

Initially Willow had been hurt and upset, but upon reflection she realized that their lack of a consistent sex life was what had kept her there, kept her feeling safe. She knew she had some inner demons but wasn't in a place to delve into them. She had sexual needs, but she took care of them on her own. Like Kevin, she got the other things from him that she needed—affection, companionship, safety.

Over time, however, she'd come to understand that, in Kevin's case, he would build up life pressures and frustrations, perhaps even with himself, and would begin to lash out. And, like that day she'd walked in on him masturbating, she realized there were times he needed to listen to his body and seek release, though he didn't always realize it himself.

She prepared a cup the way he liked it when she heard him moving around upstairs and knew his shower was finished. Sure enough, a freshly showered and shaved Kevin made his way downstairs moments later. He wore his pressed slacks and dress shirt, his tie hanging loose around his neck.

"Thank you," he said softly, leaving a kiss on her cheek as he took the cup of coffee she handed him. He seemed lighter, the furrow between his eyes gone, but she could see something else was bothering him.

She prepared her own cup, waiting as she knew he'd talk when he was ready.

"I'm sorry, Willow," he finally said, leaning back against the counter.

"For what?" she asked, taking an experimental sip of the coffee to determine if she'd added enough flavored creamer.

"I saw the other day that you ordered a little… something for your private time." There was no accusation, no bitterness, just a touch of sadness in his tone. "I'm sorry I can't be what you need—"

"Stop." She set her mug aside and walked over to him, moving his hands out of the way as she began to work on his tie. "We've been together a long time now, Kevin," she began, sparing a glance up into his troubled blue eyes. "You're an amazing man. A good husband and wonderful friend." She smiled at him. "We've made it work. As we've always said, if and when it no longer works, then we'll make changes." She left a gentle kiss on his lips, patting his chest after soothing the newly knotted tie. "Have a good day at work."

❧❧❧❧

Willow hummed along to the music, actually singing when she knew the words, as she got ready to meet Julie for coffee in Woodland. Before the events at Dittman Bridge she'd been a fan of Swann and had a lot of her music on her playlists, but since that night—and certainly since the "Bozo" video and seeing the article that the singer was taking the steps necessary to help herself past what seemed to be a very rough patch in her life—she'd been listening with a more appreciative ear.

Swann's music was different from the average group or singer. It was dark, yet not somber or depressing. It tended to have a more serious message or observation of life. She absolutely loved Swann's voice. Her music could be danced to or, she supposed, had sex to, and with the smoky, sultry quality of her voice, the latter was definitely not hard to imagine.

She stopped, her hand mid-stroke as she brushed her hair. That last thought had hit her in the stomach like a sledgehammer. She suddenly felt very uncomfortable about where her mind had just gone.

She looked at her reflection in the bathroom mirror and, for just a moment, she saw somebody she didn't recognize. She saw a woman whose face was slightly flushed, who had a fire in her eyes that turned the usual light green dark. She quickly looked away and took a deep, steadying breath.

She quickly swept her hair up into a ponytail, as it was a hot late summer day, even in the mountains, and headed into the bedroom to turn off the music and finish up to leave the house. She felt a strange sense of guilt, but she wasn't entirely sure why.

Trying to push her unease away, she grabbed her phone to shoot off a quick text to Kevin to let him know she was heading out for her coffee date and would be home for dinner. Text sent, she was about to put her phone down when she saw a social media message come in. Tapping on it, she saw it was a message from Swann's public page, and a video made by Swann herself.

Slowly lowering herself to sit on the bed, Willow tapped the arrow to play the video message. In it, the woman that she'd pulled from the river looked relaxed, reclining on a couch, from what could be seen. She wore none of her usual dark eye makeup, her complexion looking much better than that of the thin, pale woman Willow had seen before. She looked young and healthy and, frankly, beautiful.

"Good morning," she said with a lopsided grin that Willow found utterly charming. "I hope you'll forgive me for responding so late, but I did get your video, and *yes* you were the Bozo in question." Willow couldn't help but smile sheepishly at that, even as she sat there alone. "I'm glad you got the message. So, I was kinda wondering what you're doing a month from today?"

Willow felt her heart flutter and a wave of nausea

flow through her, and had no idea why. "Um," she muttered, mind racing down the calendar. "Why?"

As if hearing her, Swann continued. "I ask because we're ramping up our tour, you know, the one I kinda messed up last winter?" Again, that lopsided grin. Willow had to imagine the singer had gotten away with a lot of mischief in her life using that grin. "So, we'll be in Denver at Empower Field at Mile High that night, and I personally want to invite you and a guest to be *my* special guest at the concert," she said, placing her hand on her T-shirt-clad chest.

"Oh, my god," Willow whispered, a hand going to her mouth.

"So, if you're interested, message me back here with a 'Hell, yeah!' and your email address so I can be sure to get digital tickets sent to you."

"Hell, yeah," Willow muttered, quickly. Without thinking, she responded as she was asked to do, giving the pertinent information. She hit send and was about to set her phone down when she gasped, as her message was instantly responded to.

Swann: Hey, there! So glad you want to go. I think you'll have a good time.

Willow read the message, her heart racing in her chest. She'd just been personally messaged by a ridiculously famous person! She was nobody special, just a random individual who had been in the right place at the right time. Anybody would have done what she'd done that night.

Taking a deep breath, Willow responded.

Willow: Good morning. ☒ Yes, I think it will be a

wonderful show, but you certainly don't need to send tickets. I'm happy to pay for them.

     Swann: Absolutely not, so get that craziness out of your mind. I want you there, and I want you there as my guest. Copy?

Willow grinned, thoroughly amused and touched. She nodded. "Copy," she whispered.

     Willow: Roger that.
     Swann: Good girl. What are you up to today?
     Willow: I'm actually about to meet my best friend for coffee. You?

She let out a long, slow breath, hoping it was okay that she asked. How was this woman just so nice? Friendly. How was she so…normal?

     Swann: I'm heading out myself in just a few minutes to the studio, get a few things laid down on the new album before we head out to begin the tour.

"This is just crazy. 'You know,'" she muttered. "'Just gonna go record an album, no bigs.'" She shook her head.

     Willow: I'm guessing you're going to be far more productive than I am today.
     I'm feeling a bit like a slacker.
     Swann: LMAO! Hardly! You save lives, I make noise. You win in the productivity category. But, I digress. You have a wonderful time and tell your friend some random chick in California that she doesn't know said hello. Have a mocha breve for me. Sadly, I can't

have caffeine while recording.

Willow: Oh, sad day! Can't imagine no caffeine. I pass my award for productivity to you, and I'll even slip some caffeine into it.

Swann: Ohhh, sneaky, sneaky! I love it. ⊠ Have a great day, Willow.

Willow: Thank you. You do the same, Swann.

Swann: Call me Christine. That's my actual first name.

Willow gasped, remembering when the singer had told her that at the river. "Christine," she said softly, tasting the name on her tongue. She liked it, a slow smile spreading on her lips.

Willow: Christine it is. Have a wonderful day and best of luck at the studio, Christine.

The conversation ended and Willow felt her body fill with almost uncontainable energy. She jumped up from the bed and waved balled fists around like a baby excited about a new moment in its young life. She blew out several deep breaths, trying to calm down.

"Holy cow," she whispered. "Okay. Relax, calm down, Willow. She's just a person." One more breath and she grabbed her phone and headed out of the bedroom.

❧ ❧ ❧ ❧

The Coffee Shop was a main hangout in Woodland, and they made incredible muffins. Willow sat across from Julie, a woman who was adorable with her short, sporty blond hair and eyes that were so kind and always had a little twinkle in them. She was five or six years older than Willow. Her wife, Remmy, was just as amazing, a true goof at heart.

"So, let me get this straight," Julie said slowly, eyeing her friend who sat across the table. "You're telling me that you fished Swann out of the river?"

Willow nodded, sipping her mocha breve, something she'd never had before but would certainly order again. "Yes."

"Why didn't you tell me?" the teacher asked, sounding a little hurt. "Not only is it huge that it's a famous person, but mostly, how unbelievably traumatic for you."

"I didn't tell anyone," Willow said quietly.

"Not even Kevin?" Julie pushed. When Willow shook her head, Julie looked at her strangely. "My god, NDA or not, the first thing I would have done was tell Remmy."

Willow hadn't exactly dug deep into that fact. She had no answers, so simply pushed it away. "Yes, well, somehow your wife can read you like an open book and would've known in an instant that something was wrong." She grinned. "Probably could tell *you* what had happened."

Julie laughed, nodding. "You are not wrong." She grew serious and eyed her friend. "So, why are you telling me now?"

"Um." Willow hedged, feeling a little shy and definitely excited. "Turns out Swann is finishing the tour that was interrupted earlier in the year, and she's giving me two tickets to go see the concert at the stadium next month, for me and a friend. You are my best friend, so I want you to go with me."

"Seriously?" Julie exclaimed, slamming her

hands on the table as she shot forward in her seat. She looked around and gave a sheepish grin to a few other customers who stared at her at her outburst. Turning back to an amused Willow, she said, softer, "Seriously?"

"Seriously. Buckle up, 'cause I think it's going to be a good show."

Chapter Seven

They both flinched at the sound of breaking glass. Adam looked around frantically for the source. His frightened eyes finally met Christine's in the darkness of the alley.

"Are you sure you wanna go in there?" he whispered.

Looking up and down the trash-filled alley, she sighed, nodding as she met his gaze. "I have to, man."

"No, you don't. Chris, we'll find another way. You can stay with us again for a few days. You know Mom won't mind—"

"It's not about finding a place to stay, Adam," she exclaimed, glaring at him. "Or having money for a place. Man, this is my chance!" Her voice was filled with passion, as were her eyes. "I can't chicken out, so don't you fuck this up for me, neither."

"But this place is a dive, Chris. You're not even old enough to get in this place, let alone sing here." He grabbed her by the shirt, dragging her into the shadows as two men started to fight in the mouth of the alley, one thrown out into the street, the other following.

The truth of the matter was, Christine was scared to death. The Diamond Back was not exactly top-of-the-line entertainment in Manhattan, but it was the only gig she could get, so she was taking it.

She wanted to explain that to her friend, but she knew he wouldn't understand. He didn't get how *much she wanted to sing and play her guitar. Adam didn't have a passion of his own, other than finding trouble and trying to keep her out of it, so he could never understand.*

"Listen," she said, gently pulling her arm out of his grasp. "I'm gonna do this, so either you can sneak in with me to listen or you can grab the next train home. Your choice." She turned and headed toward the back door to the bar, showing far more confidence and bravado than she actually felt.

"Wait." Adam snagged her arm, nearly pulling her off her feet. She glared at him. "I just worry, okay?"

"Yeah, I know." Christine grinned at him, tapping him playfully on the cheek. "I love you too, bud. Now I have to go."

This time he didn't stop her, and she made her way into the dark, smoky bar. The stage was tiny and behind a screen of chain-link fencing. The Diamond Back was known for its fights and rowdy patrons, so she was glad it was there. It was her first appearance there, though she'd played at any number of other cheesy joints. It was quick money, usually in the neighborhood of about seventy-five to a hundred bucks. It meant she didn't have to swing a trick for a couple of weeks. She was thrilled.

Grabbing her guitar, which had been slung at her back, Christine stepped on stage. There was no house band that night, and she certainly didn't have a band of her own, so it was just her. Oh, and Pluck, her guitar. She had on the best pair of jeans she owned, only a couple holes instead of connect-the-dots holes, topped by a black T-shirt. She was stylin'.

Adjusting the microphone, she looked out at the crowd, which was mostly men in very dangerous-looking chains and leather, looking at her rather expectantly, some a little hungrily. So, she was supposed to entertain the gorillas, eh? Standing on that five-by-five-foot stage, just her, a microphone, a stool, and a shitload of courage.

"Hi," Christine said, the microphone screeching shrilly and earning her boos from the crowd.

"Hey, honey, ain't I seen you somewhere?" someone yelled out.

She felt the hair on the back of her neck stiffen. Fuck, all she needed was to run into a customer. Thinking fast, unable to see the guy's face as the lights were in hers, Christine quirked a grin. "I don't know, you been to Hef's mansion lately?"

To her surprise and relief that got a round of laughter. Before any more questions or comments could be shot her way, Christine lowered the guitar strap over her shoulder and placed her fingers on the instrument's neck.

"Here we go, boys."

Looking down at her fingers as they strummed the strings, she got herself in the right frame of mind, head beginning to bob with the acoustic beat she was creating. She decided to ease this crowd into her own stuff, first warming up with a few classics. Bob Seger, Bonnie Raitt, then really get them excited with "Holding Out For A Hero" by Bonnie Tyler. Her voice wasn't as gruff as the original, but she could hold her own.

Those boys were whooping and cheering. She had their full attention, so she decided to do a song she'd written recently. "Okay, this next song is called 'Clutch,' and it was written by yours truly."

They cheered her on, surprisingly supportive. Damn, she was having fun! She couldn't remember ever *having such a responsive audience before. She would definitely be coming back to this dive.*

With more drinks shoved in front of her than she could remember, she watched as the bartender popped the top off another Corona and slid it over to her. She took a swig of the golden liquid, a very satisfied smile spreading across her face. She'd only been slated to do one set, but she'd been asked to stay for three.

"Hey, you were awesome."

Christine turned on her barstool to see one of the less scary guys standing there, a young woman standing next to him. He had his arm draped across her shoulders. "Thanks."

"What's your name, so when you make it huge I can say, 'Fuck, yeah! I saw her when!'"

She grinned, but panicked. She didn't want to give him her first name, and she hadn't been introduced, just tossed out to feed the lions. "Um, Swann," she said, knowing nobody knew her last name but Adam.

"All right," he said, nodding. "Well, great show."

She watched the couple walk away when she felt a presence on her other side. She turned right as he spoke.

"Are you even old enough to drink that?"

She raised an eyebrow. "Excuse me?"

She turned to see a man lowering himself down to sit on the stool next to hers, one manicured hand casually dangling off the edge of the scarred bar. He was dressed in a gray suit, dark gray tie perfectly knotted. His hair was dark and immaculately slicked back from a tanned face.

"Who the fuck are you?" she demanded.

"My name is Robert Knowles, and I'm wondering if you're old enough to drink that." He indicated the cold one dangling by the neck from her calloused fingers.

"Fuck off, Bob." Christine muttered, turning her stool and her back to him.

"How old are you, kid?" he asked in the same low, smooth tone.

"Old enough to know where the sun don't shine and to stick my bottle there." She glared at him over her shoulder, and he laughed.

"Look," he said, leaning toward her. "I'm not here to cause problems for you or bust you. I was walking by this...bar," he said grudgingly, looking around with distaste. "When I heard you singing."

Christine turned her stool again, glancing over at him. She looked him up and down, nose wrinkled. "Great. So I got me an old guy for a fan. Lucky me."

"No, but perhaps you'll have an 'old guy' as a manager."

"I know I know you," a man slurred, walking up behind Christine, his hot, beer-scented breath on the back of her neck.

She started, whirling around and nearly swallowing her tongue. Her eyes were wide as she took in the drunk but very familiar-looking man. "I-I don't know you," she managed.

"Bullshit," he said with a sloppy grin. "You sucked my—"

"She's never met you before in her life," Robert Knowles said, having magically appeared behind the man.

He grabbed him by his shirt and pulled him away from a shocked and terrified Christine. Somehow his action hadn't been aggressive as much as seeming "helpful" as he held the man up who was about to fall over. He just seemed to be so drunk that he didn't realize it was Knowles's move that made him unsteady *in the first place.*

The man looked at Robert, blinking several times. "But, I do. She was in my car last week."

Robert gave him a charming smile, slapping the man on the shoulder. "Couldn't be," he said. "She was with me in Los Angeles last week."

"Really?" The man studied Robert with squinting eyes, clearly the wheels of his pickled brain trying to work out the details of what he'd just been told compared to what he thought he knew. It would have been amusing if Christine hadn't been so mortified. "Oh," the man finally said, grinning. He looked at the singer. "I'm sorry, miss."

She waved it off. "Happens." She watched the man stumble off into the crowd before turning back to the man who'd just saved her behind. "How'd you know?"

He met her gaze. "Girls like you are a dime a dozen," he said. "But your kind of raw talent isn't."

She looked at him, trying to read his eyes. This dude was serious! Turning to fully face him, she tilted her head, eyeing him as she sipped her beer.

"Here's my card. I'll be in town for another few days." He reached into the inside breast pocket of his suit jacket, bringing out a very thick wallet. Opening it up, he dug for a moment, then withdrew a black business card, handing it to her tucked between two of those manicured fingers. "If I don't hear from you before I leave New York, I'll never take your call again." He tossed some money onto the bar, clearly ready to leave. "I hope I do, Swann. You've got quite a talent."

In her private room at the back of the bus, Christine lay on her bed, hands tucked behind her head as her mind wandered. She'd already taken a nap, lulled by the gentle sway of the Prevost making its way across the country.

She hadn't thought about that night in a very long time, the night she'd met Bob. She had called him. She remembered it so clearly. She'd been standing out in the pouring rain as she'd used the pay phone to call the number on the card. She'd honestly expected it to be a bunch of BS, and there'd either be no Robert Knowles at the end of the line, or he was a pimp, using the line of music manager to get her to work for him.

She smirked, thinking that wasn't entirely off the mark of what he really was. She'd sung, all right, sung her heart out for basically pennies in the early years, before she knew she had any rights. Even then, there was still a heavy price to pay, a price that had weighed her down for nearly twenty years with Bob.

It didn't take long before he'd come through on his promise, getting her out of the shithole she called a home in New York and had given her a room in his house all the way across the country in LA. He was already established in the industry, so it wasn't hard to get her in front of the right people.

Over time, he'd proven he could be trusted, never laying a finger on her nor letting anyone else—and people had certainly tried. Fresh meat was delivered all the way from the Big Apple for the sampling. In his protectiveness of her and his guidance, he'd become her friend and her confessor. Once he had all her secrets, which took time to get, the true nature of their relationship was revealed.

She was to be his cash cow, a living, breathing,

singing ATM. He made it clear she'd better be careful how much she complained, because the tabloids were always looking for something new and juicy, and the common folk just loved to see the rich and privileged fall. She'd been rewarded handsomely for her talent and her obedience. But, she thought as she lay in that bus headed to their next city, every dog has its day.

⁂

"Check, check, check. Check one, check one, check one."

As the sound engineers and set builders did their thing, Christine met up with the boys in the band to discuss how the show was to go that night.

"Why only here?" Jed asked, looking over the folding chairs and music stands that were leaned against the wall in the tunnel that was being used to store props until they were needed. The drummer looked at her, hands on hips. "We've already been in, like, thirty cities. Why didn't we do this song then?"

"Because I want to do it here in Denver first," Christine explained, though she knew it wasn't much of an explanation. When Jed blinked at her, she shook her head. "Forget it. You'll understand."

"So, are we doing this song and all this?" Bug, their lead guitarist, indicated the chairs and music stands. "From here on out?"

"Yeah," Christine said, nodding as she looked over everything, counting the chairs. There were twenty, just as she requested, as well as twenty musicians to fill them in every city on the tour.

The four members of her band eyed each other but said nothing more, simply shook their heads and walked away. She knew there had been some damage done by her behavior over the last couple years, fully coming to a head that night in February. After rehab, she'd invited them over to her house for dinner and explanations and apologies for dessert.

She knew they cared and understood, but she also knew she was how they fed their families and paid their bills. Bug, a.k.a. Davey Rickles, was the only one who'd been with her since the beginning. The other three positions had come and gone, tried on and discarded for lack of fit. Her current band had been together for six years, and she loved those guys.

Walking from the tunnel up the stairs to the stage, she looked out over the massive venue. During a regular Broncos football game the stadium held about seventy-six thousand people. During the show that night, it would be upward of a hundred thousand, as the field was also utilized for more people.

They were the more expensive seats by far, though there was a small roped-off area for special guests, one of which stayed in Christine's mind. She was nervous and hoped Willow would like it.

Chapter Eight

Keys in hand, Willow stood looking at Kevin. She knew he was upset with her, and frankly, she didn't blame him. She had been wrong. She should have told him about that night on the bridge months ago. Now that she'd been forced to because the concert was tonight, he was hurt.

"I hope you guys have fun," he said, his tone quiet and flat. He spared a glance over the rim of his coffee cup as he took a sip.

"Do you want me to bring you anything?" she asked. "We don't get to Denver all that often, so I can get you those cookies you love."

He shrugged, noncommittal.

She knew she wasn't going to get anywhere when he was like this, so she walked over to him and cupped his face between her hands, leaving a kiss on his lips. "I love you. Be good."

He smirked. "Love you too. Be safe."

She felt bad leaving him there, knowing she should be taking him with her, but somehow—and again she couldn't figure out why—it was something she needed for herself. She could also tell herself that he didn't like that kind of music and couldn't pick out a song by Swann if a giant S was stamped on the front of the choice on iTunes. But, there was more to it and she knew it, she just couldn't quite put her finger on it.

She hurried out into the warm afternoon to her

truck. She still had to drive to Woodland and pick up Julie before heading on to Denver. She noticed the inside of her truck was a little dusty, which was impossible to avoid living out in the country. Not wanting to be embarrassed for Julie to get in, she leaned over and opened her glove box to grab the wet wipes she kept in there.

Something caught her eye, and they widened as a hand went to her mouth with a gasp. "Oh, shit," she muttered behind her hand as she grabbed the check, long forgotten in the aftermath of everything and life in general.

She brought it out and looked at it, again noting the amount. She looked back to the house, only able to imagine how angry Kevin would be that she hadn't told him about the check either. Truth was, she'd totally forgotten about it.

With a heavy sigh, she swapped wet wipes for the check, closing the glove box once more.

⁂

"I have never seen so many women in all my life," Willow muttered.

"I guess that's what happens when you're a lesbian icon," Julie said back, eyeing all the excited women around them.

"What do you mean?" Willow asked, just barely avoiding being hit in the head by two very excited women who met up in wide-armed hugs and squeals as they were led through the maze of the stadium to their seats. "What, is she like Melissa Etheridge or something?"

"Of the alternative music world, yes."

Willow felt like a fish out of water. They'd arrived in Denver, had a nice dinner, gotten Kevin his cookies, then drove to the stadium. Even though they'd gotten there early, the place was packed, inside and out. Once they'd gotten up the stairs, the usher had scanned her phone with the digital ticket Christine had sent. She'd been surprised, and a bit concerned, when whatever information had come up on the woman's scanner had her grabbing her walkie-talkie and calling for a guy named Stanley, who they were currently trying to keep up with.

She had no idea where they were going, but when they burst out of a tunnel and onto the ground level—in other words, *on the field*—Willow was all eyes and open mouth. She glanced over at Julie, who was just as stunned.

"Ladies," Stanley said, unclasping a red velvet rope for them to enter. Inside the roped-off area, they continued on to a few stairs that led to a small "island," as it were. It was a raised platform, almost like a tiny little stage by itself, connected to the main stage by a long, narrow catwalk. Around them would soon be a sea of people.

Again, the women exchanged a look before they acquiesced. Once they were seated, Stanley hurried back to the rope, opening it for himself and closing it before disappearing into the throngs of people.

"This is crazy," Willow whispered to Julie, who nodded.

"Nothing like a front-row seat to a concert with a hundred thousand of your closest screaming friends."

Willow chuckled, feeling strange and very vulnerable as they sat there. The main stage was at one end of the field, a metal box of sorts hanging overhead with one on either side, no doubt for rigging purposes and perhaps safety. The huge stadium screens were active and lit, obviously to broadcast a better view to those in the stands.

It was growing later, the sun going down as people were packing into the stands and on the field in the seats provided there. The buzzing of voices and laughter was nearly deafening. Willow was nervous and she was anxious. She wondered in that moment, as the show was about to start, how Christine was feeling.

"Would you be horrified if I get the chance to ask Swann to sign this for Remmy?" Julie said loud enough to be heard. She tugged on the Swann shirt she wore.

Willow burst into laughter and shook her head. "No. I very much doubt we'll meet her, but hey, why not?" she added with a shrug.

The huge, bright-as-the-sun stadium lights began to flash, alerting everyone it was getting close. Suddenly, a loud, booming voice sounded through the public address system. "Ladies and gentlemen, please find your seats. The show will begin shortly."

A wave of excited energy crashed through Willow, sending chills down her spine. She looked at the main stage and saw a white grand piano, which surprised her as there wasn't much piano music in Swann's songs. She saw the drum kit up on its dais and the fort of keyboards waiting to be played.

The lights around the stage went dark, leaving the area in blackness. One by one, the lights all around the stadium began to click off, Willow's heart lurching with each one. She felt Julie grab her hand. She met her gaze.

"Here we go," Julie said quietly as silence spread over the massive stadium like a blanket.

Willow nodded, blowing out a heavy breath, which caught her hair and puffed it out for a moment. She'd worn her hair down, all one length, so her long bangs fell slightly over her face. She reached up and tucked them behind her ears as she waited on her little island of two.

The lights were nearly completely dimmed now, only enough light to show that the area on and in front of the darkened stage was filling with gray smoke. A pulsing drumbeat began, low, almost too quiet to be heard, but it could certainly be felt. It was almost tribal. Willow's bones pulsed with it.

"Mmm, you feel that?" a smoky, deep voice riding on velvet said, sensuous as it spread throughout the stadium. The audience started to get anxious. Willow and Julie looked at each other, matching grins spreading across their faces. The excitement was palpable.

The beat was getting louder, and blue lights were slowly rising, pushing their way through the smoke. All around the stage were sparkling lights, creating the effect of a night filled with fog. The coolness from the dry ice creating the smoke could be felt by those closest to the stage, including Willow and Julie.

"You feel it? Like a heartbeat," the voice said, followed by a long sigh.

"She's got a really sexy voice," Julie whispered. Willow nodded in agreement, her eyes searching the stage. "I wish I sounded like that when I talked dirty."

Dark figures began to appear as more lights rose—members of the band. A low guitar joined in with the beat.

"Feel it. Want it. Taste it," the voice whispered, as if in the throes of passion.

The audience was going nuts now, screaming, whistling. Willow could hardly breathe. She gasped as a small burst of light illuminated the drummer from below, casting his features in freakish shadows, his sticks in continuous motion.

"That's right. Let's get a little light on the subject." The voice breathed over the audience.

Willow was surprised to feel a little shiver down her spine, her excitement building with everyone else's.

Another burst of light and the guitarist was revealed, followed by the bass and keyboard players in swift succession. There was now a ring of smoky figures around the outer edges of the stage, at or with their instruments. The center was still in impenetrable darkness.

The drumbeat was at a feverish pitch now, resonating in the bones of the excited, anxious fans, nearly out of their minds with anticipation. Suddenly all music stopped, and a heavy silence filled the large space and everyone in it. Willow was almost holding her breath, hearing her own heartbeat fill her ears.

A sensuous sigh, then a blinding light. Thousands of pairs of eyes squinted at the burst. Mad cheering erupted once vision had cleared and they saw Swann standing center stage, head arched back and eyes closed, the silver light above her shining down like the very touch of God.

She wore her signature leather pants, which Willow had never seen look so good on another human being. She wore a fitted white button-up shirt, though it was only closed by a single button, leaving plenty of cleavage cupped in an exposed black leather bra. Her flat, muscular stomach showed off a diamond stud glinting from her belly button.

Her dark hair was wild, partially covering one eye. She was the picture of sensuous strength and danger.

A heartbeat passed with the cheers at a deafening pitch, then the music began in earnest. There was a blast of fire and smoke, and Swann was visible in all her glory, the light full-on, blue eyes gazing out upon her sea of fans. She held the microphone in her right hand as she began to sing.

Willow, caught up in the rush of excitement with everyone else, was on her feet singing, cheering, and yes, even screaming. She almost swooned like a schoolgirl when Christine, in the middle of a fast, beat-heavy song, looked right over at her and gave her a quick wink before turning back to the rest of the tens of thousands.

About an hour into the concert, Swann walked up to the front of the stage, the band not launching into another song. "We're gonna do something a little special next," she said into the microphone, her speaking voice like a warm blanket comforting all present after sixty minutes of nonstop thrills. "So, if you'll give me a second to change into something a little more…comfortable." She grinned as everyone lost their heads all over again.

"God *damn* she's sexy!" Julie exclaimed, fanning her shirt.

Willow burst into laughter. She knew how deeply in love with her wife Julie was, so for her to say that, Julie was feeling some kind of way. They all were. She couldn't deny that her body was absolutely pulsing, and she had no idea what to do about it.

The stage went completely dark, and Willow had to admit that she was grateful for a moment to breathe. She sat down in her chair, as did Julie, both reaching down to the bottles of water that had been waiting at their seats, taking a long sip to cool down even as the night air was cooling off.

After a handful of minutes, a slow, lonely cello began to play while the stage was still dark. The deep, somber tone stopped all the chatter that had begun. A rise in applause caught Willow's attention and she looked back to the stage. Silvery light began to gently illuminate the stage and a lone figure was visible near the end of the grand piano, a woman sitting in a chair with the cello cradled tenderly between her legs, her bow stroking the strings lovingly.

Christine stepped out of the darkness and into the light that rained down on the piano, the rest of the stage in darkness. Willow couldn't help but smile as she clapped with everyone else. She was amused, as it looked like the singer literally had changed into something more comfortable.

She was wearing a pair of fitted jeans that no woman should look that good in, somehow tight while also looking insanely soft and comfortable, like a favorite pair turned velvet from years of wear. The tailored women's button-up she wore was similar to the one earlier but more casual, and certainly more buttoned, though still revealing a bit of cleavage to tease the eye.

As she strolled to the front of the stage, she ran her hand through her hair, pushing it away from her face, which garnered her more applause and whistles. She surprised Willow by walking right past the microphone on its stand and to the catwalk, headed right to them.

"Oh my god," Julie whispered. "She's coming over here."

Willow swallowed hard as the singer walked right up to her. She was absolutely stunning in her casual, nonchalant manner. She oozed confidence and raw sexuality that seemed to be inherent. She gave her the same lopsided grin she had in the video as she held out her hand to the nurse. She noticed that Christine was wearing a couple silver rings, though she could only see their undersides. She was also wearing a black leather band around her wrist.

She reached up and took Christine's hand, so soft, and was gently pulled to her feet. They stood looking at each other for a moment, and Willow realized that the singer was a few inches taller than her right before she was pulled into a tight, full-body hug.

Willow's eyes closed at the softness of the other woman. Her warmth and the scent of her perfume, musky yet with its own brand of femininity, was so different than the cold, wet flesh of their first encounter. She reveled in it, knowing that Christine was okay and, from all appearances, was thriving.

"Thank you," Christine whispered into her ear, holding her tight.

Willow nodded, so moved by the moment she was unable to speak.

After a long moment, the crowd around them going wild at what was happening, Christine pulled out of the hug but took her hand again, leading the way back along the catwalk toward the stage.

Willow looked around, feeling nauseous as she

saw an endless sea of faces. She wondered how on earth Christine did this every night.

The singer led them to the piano where she sat down, urging Willow to sit with her. There was a microphone mounted to the top of the instrument.

"I'd like to introduce you all to a very special woman," she said, her voice booming out over the stadium. A few cat whistles reached their ears, making Willow blush deeply. "Stop it," Christine admonished the audience playfully. When it quieted down, she spoke again. "Her name is Willow, and she has the absolute kindest heart of anyone I've ever met."

Christine looked over at Willow for a long beat, something passing between them. Willow felt it to the bottom of her soul. For a moment she was taken back to that night, the cold, the shock, the fear, the adrenaline, the relief. Christine seemed to have felt it too, because she gave her a small smile, as though saying, *I understand.*

"You see," Christine continued to the audience. "One night last winter, I found myself very, very lost, falling into darkness so deep and so thick that all I wanted was for it to end." She looked away from Willow and out to her fans. "I jumped off a bridge," she said, her voice clear and matter-of-fact. Willow was shocked by her candor. "Willow literally jumped in and pulled my sorry ass out." She met Willow's gaze again. "A complete stranger," she said. "No clue who I was, just knew that somebody was in trouble."

An eerie silence filled the stadium for just a moment before applause slowly began to spread, like a wave of fire over the tens of thousands there. People rose to their feet, clapping. There were no cheers, no whistling, just an understanding of the gravity of what

Christine had just told them.

Christine leaned over and said into Willow's ear, "They're applauding for you."

Willow had no idea what to think or what to say, so simply raised her hand as if to say, *Thank you, I hear you.*

After several minutes of a standing ovation, the crowd began to find their seats again, expectation in the air. "I wrote this song for you," Christine said, raising her hands to the keyboard of the beautiful piano. "It's called 'Safe Harbor.'"

The cello began again, Christine waiting a beat or two before she began to play, the tune simple yet elegant, haunting. She glanced over at Willow, giving her that same calming smile. Willow didn't know what to think, so overwhelmed by everything. She took a deep breath as she waited to see what was next.

Christine closed her eyes as she began to sing, her voice so beautiful.

Lost at sea
Waves crashin' all around me
Don't know where I am

No sound no light
The monster always lies
Just excuses no more plans

I step on over to the ledge
No need no push to the edge
Scars haunt me where I am

A soft light lit the back of the stage, which revealed just the barest bit of an outline of a small orchestra, light glinting off violin bodies and a few other instruments, all of which softly joined the song, along with the cello.

> *Pull me up pull me out*
> *Save my life with your sweet mouth*
> *You're my safe harbor*

Rocky shores nightmare real
Leather wet and heartbeat still
You're my safe harbor
You're my safe harbor

This angel is she real or just a lie
Go and heal or stay and die
Memories come and memories flee
When I look do I start to see me

Skies of blue no clouds of gray
Laughin' sun no cryin' rain
Because you took my hand

Pull me up pull me out
Save my life with your sweet mouth
You're my safe harbor

Rocky shores nightmare real
Leather wet and heartbeat still
You're my safe harbor
You're my safe harbor
You're my safe harbor
My safe harbor

Silent tears were falling down Willow's cheeks

by the end of the song, her emotions swelling to such an overwhelmed state that she could hardly think straight. As the last notes of the song died down, the stadium erupted in applause, again everyone on their feet.

Christine smiled at Willow, reaching up to gently use her thumb to wipe away a tear before she took her in another hug, the two holding each other as they sat on the piano bench.

Chapter Nine

"What the fuck was that?" Eddie, the bass player, demanded once the concert was over and the band was alone in the staging area where all their road cases waited for instruments to be repacked. "Violins?" he screeched. "Flutes? We'll be the fucking laughing stock, Chris!"

"Hey, calm down," Bug said, glaring at the youngest member of the band, both in age and time spent with them.

"Shut it, Bug," he sniped, turning his ire back to the singer. "That orchestra, piano shit isn't who we are."

"Maybe it's who *I* am at times, Eddie," Christine fired back, finger-combing her hair as she knew they had company coming. "Unlike some people in this room, I'm not a one-trick pony. Besides, it gives you a nice ten-minute break in the set, and let's face it, sometimes you need it."

There was a stunned silence for a long moment before Eddie cursed under his breath and went into his dressing room, slamming the door behind him. The other three band members and some of the other tour staff stood there looking at each other. Eddie was usually more quiet, Bug the hothead.

Christine, troubled by the outburst, cleared her throat. "Come on," she said. "We've got media coming back here and those with backstage passes. Everybody get ready."

She went to her dressing room, closing the door behind her. She leaned back against the cool wood, her eyes falling closed. She was tired, as it had been a grueling schedule after so many months off the road. But, mostly, she felt emotionally spent.

It had taken a lot for her to get back to work. For the first time in a long time, she'd done it alone, no chemical help. Margaret had told her it wouldn't be easy, and she wasn't wrong. However, she was supremely proud of herself for waking up every morning with a full memory of the day before, the night before, and her actions regarding both.

For the first time in a long time, she knew that whatever she was feeling—good, bad, or other—were true feelings, not enflamed or doused by whatever poison she'd put in her body that day. For the first time in a long time, she could take pride in what she'd just done—rocked the very world of more than a hundred thousand women and men, all because of her talent, not drug-fueled energy.

Then there was what Eddie had gotten so fired up about. Christine pushed away from the door and walked over to the vanity table set up for her to get ready. A light-bordered mirror reflected a woman who had regained the weight she'd lost due to her recreational choices taking the place of any real consistent food of consequence.

She felt good, was sleeping better, was using the coping skills she'd learned during her time in both Colorado and California, and was truly doing her best, her full heart in it, to be the woman she really wanted to be.

She took a deep, steadying breath, then planted

herself strictly in the moment. Her night wasn't done, nor was the performing. She had fans to meet and they expected to see Swann, the sexy, devil-may-care singer who was as fearless as her lyrics. She smirked as she wiped away sweat and any running makeup from the heat.

She made sure she got it all, as she knew however she looked in about five minutes would be splashed across newspapers and websites around the world. Her sellout tour was getting massive attention simply because her personal life had derailed the last tour and folks loved to watch the train wreck. The addition of the surprise song and guest that night further meant that she was in for it, especially from Bob.

As she reapplied her makeup to get back into character, she thought about the massive blowup that would be coming. She knew that that night's concert was being filmed for a future documentary on Swann, and it certainly wasn't why she chose to debut "Safe Harbor" or the emotional reunion with Willow. But, she knew Bob would see it, and no doubt, somewhere inside, she *wanted* him to see it.

Lowering her hand that held the mascara brush, Christine turned her head this way and that, making sure her handiwork was good. Satisfied, she reached for her eyeshadow. The irony was, she hated wearing makeup in her everyday life and only did it if she was making a public appearance or doing something specific to her music career. It was part of her uniform, part of her armor.

Tucking all of her "warrior paint" back into the travel bag, she took a good look at herself. She fixed her hair, chuckling to herself that people had no idea how much work it actually took to look like she'd just stumbled out of bed and into her day.

Happy with the image, she stood from the chair and unbuttoned her shirt as she walked over to where she had her wardrobe hanging. She flung the white shirt she'd been wearing during her song for Willow and removed her bra, replacing it with the leather bra Bob had such a hard-on for, topping it with a worn denim vest.

Walking back to the vanity, she looked at her body in the mirror. The stupid bra was visible, as was a good amount of cleavage. No matter if she went down to a hundred pounds, she'd still be large-breasted for her frame. But sex sold—she knew that better than most—and she acknowledged that for those who would be coming backstage, image was most important.

She grabbed her perfume and spritzed some fresh on. She squared her shoulders and allowed that little devilish smile to cross her lips. Swann was firmly in place, and just in time. A knock at her door alerted her to the fact that it was time; they'd arrived.

She checked her earrings, making sure they were all still there—five in the left ear, three in the right—then opened the door and met with her audience. It was the typical crowd, the butch lesbian who tries to play it cool then eventually loses her shit. The mousy housewife who oozes the mom vibe but eventually loses her shit. And, her favorite, the tough guy with his girl, trying to prove to her that he can be cool, too.

She smiled, stood for pictures, signed autographs, and obliged in general chitchat, all the while knowing that if she had a dollar for every time somebody ogled her boobs, she could retire. She also could do these meet-and-greets in her sleep, kind of an emotionless autopilot. So she was completely surprised by the butterflies that invaded her stomach when the door to the back area opened and the two women she'd been waiting for entered.

When she'd first seen Willow that night, sitting with her cute blond friend on the smaller stage, Christine's breath had caught. She knew the nurse had a big heart. She knew she was kind and clearly very giving. She knew that she was terrified of clowns. What she hadn't realized was just how beautiful she was.

The night of the bridge incident, it obviously hadn't been a factor. When she'd watched Willow's video to her and finally seen the scrubs-clad woman behind the smeared clown makeup, yes, she'd found her beautiful. But that was nothing like what she was seeing in this moment.

As Willow walked through the door, dressed in simple jeans and a women's V-neck shirt that showed off a trim figure, Christine was momentarily rendered speechless. Her hair was down, reaching past her shoulders. It was wavy and framed an angelic face with delicate features and absolutely stunning green eyes filled with so much life. Her gaze fell to her mouth, the lips full and looking so soft.

Carrying far more impact than Willow's physical appearance, however, was her general presence. She had such a quiet, peaceful energy. Christine found that her calm was what she found so alluring, even more than the gorgeous face or sexy body the nurse possessed.

Pushing her thoughts out of the gutter, Christine finished with the couple she was currently taking a selfie with, then accepted a small hug from the woman before she and the man walked away.

"Welcome," Christine said to Willow and her

guest, who was looking at her with huge eyes, like she'd just realized that Santa Claus was real. "Excellent to see you again, Willow," she said, grinning at the nurse. "And, who's this?"

"Hello," Willow said quietly, almost shy. "Um, this is my best friend, Julie Wilson. She's a teacher in Woodland."

Christine turned her focus on Julie. "Very nice to meet you, best friend Julie Wilson." She took one of Julie's hands and kissed her knuckles. "So, a teacher and a nurse are best friends," she said, eyeing the women. "Do superheroes always hang out together, or are you two special?"

Willow smiled sheepishly, looking away. "Um, yes," she said, finally meeting Christine's gaze. "We hold a convention every year in Woodland. Where we met."

Christine threw her head back as a loud bark of laughter left her lips. "Can I get an invite? You know, maybe I can meet a hottie. I've got a thing for knee boots and capes."

"I see," Willow said, nodding. "I'll certainly make sure we can find an extra chair for you next year."

"I'll hold you to that," Christine murmured.

Willow smiled at her, though it was shy and unsure, making Christine think of a schoolgirl with a crush. Christine could be a terrible flirt, and she'd used it to her advantage with many a beautiful woman. She realized in that moment she was being drawn into her usual tricks, and it shook her out of her sexual reverie. Though she was very attracted to the nurse, this was not a woman she wanted to sweet-talk into her bed. Willow had saved her life, and she owed her deep appreciation and respect.

Resetting, Christine gave Willow a friendly smile. "I really hope you enjoyed the show," she said casually, ditching the tone she knew affected those she intended it to.

"I did," Willow said, her own tone lighter, her body language a bit more relaxed. "Honestly, it's the best concert I've ever been to." She looked down for a moment at her fingers, which played with the plastic backstage pass that hung from a lanyard around her neck. She seemed to be collecting her thoughts. Finally, she looked up again, meeting Christine's gaze. "I really loved that song," she said softly. "Um…" She looked down again. "It was really beautiful. Deeply moving."

Christine smiled, touched by the emotion she saw in those green eyes and heard in her soft voice. "Thank you. You inspired it."

Willow met her gaze again, and something seemed to pass between them in that instant: a mutual understanding of the specialness of their bond from the harrowing circumstances of their meeting—even if they never met again.

Christine felt eyes on her and turned to see Julie watching the two of them, a strange expression on her face. It was almost a knowing smile. "So," Christine said, turning to her. "Thank you so much for coming with Willow. I really hope you gals had a wonderful night together."

"We did," Julie said. "It was truly an amazing night." She and Willow exchanged a quick glance before she looked back to the singer. "I was wondering if I could ask a favor."

"Shoot," Christine said. "What's up?"

Julie raised an eyebrow as she tugged lightly on

her T-shirt. "This belongs to my wife, Remmy, who is a huge fan. If I don't at least ask if you'll autograph her shirt, I'm going to be on the couch for a long, long time."

Christine grinned. "Oh, no no no, we can't have that now, can we?" She held up a finger to tell Julie and Willow to stay put. She walked over to a table where some of the band's merchandise was stowed in boxes.

She found a large poster of the tour's main promotional image. Swann stood front and center, arms crossed over her chest and feet set apart, her look ready to rumble. Her bandmates stood behind her, all of them cast in eerie shadows from a light source above.

Grabbing a silver Sharpie, she walked back to the two women. "How about we do a little video for your wife, hmm?" she suggested with a quirked brow.

Julie looked like she was about to jump out of her skin with excitement as she tapped and swiped on her phone until she got to the video function. "Okay."

"Would you mind doing the honors?" Christine asked Willow, nodding toward the phone.

"Sure." Willow took the phone from Julie and aimed it at the two. "Tell me when to start."

"Go for it." Sure the video was started, Christine grinned into the tiny round lens. "Hey, Remmy. As you can see, I'm here with your wife, and she informed me there would be dire consequences if she didn't cajole me to sign your shirt." She grinned when she saw Julie cover her face with her hands for a moment, her face flushed. "Now, I thought better of this. See, if I sign this," she said, lightly tugging at the sleeve. "A perfectly good shirt goes to waste. Right? So, I'll sign this for you."

Christine held up the poster for the camera before signaling to Julie to turn around, using her back as a writing surface. She removed the cap of the Sharpie with her teeth, then with expert strokes wrote: *To Remmy. Love, Swann.*

Moving away from Julie, who turned back to face her, Christine handed the poster to her. "Here you are, madam."

"Thank you," Julie said, looking at it. "She's going to love this."

Christine placed her arm around Julie's shoulders and looked back into the camera. "Remmy, I'm sorry you weren't able to join us tonight, but know that I'm grateful your wife and Willow were able to come play for a couple hours. Take care."

"Got it," Willow said, lowering the phone and handing it back to her friend.

"I can't believe you did this," Julie said, glancing down at the poster, her phone, then the singer, a look of awe on her face. "Thank you."

Christine gave her a genuine smile. "My pleasure." She accepted a hug from the teacher then turned to the nurse, knowing their time was coming to an end. "It was my absolute pleasure to have you both here tonight. I thank you."

"Swann?" Christine turned toward the unfamiliar voice to see that the woman provided by the stadium to manage the backstage access was waving to get her attention.

Christine met her gaze and nodded. On a lark, she turned to Willow. "Can I see your phone?"

Willow looked at her, confused. "Um, sure." She dug it out of her pocket and held it out to her.

"Do me a favor and get to your contacts,"

Christine instructed. The nurse nodded and did as asked. Christine took the phone from her and created a new contact named *CS* and inputted her number. Somehow, she knew the information was safe with her. She saved it, then held the phone out to its owner. When Willow reached for it, Christine held on for just a moment, their fingers touching. "If you ever need anything," she said softly, for Willow's ears only. "Or, if you just feel like filling me in on the happenings of Woodland."

Willow smiled, looking down at their hands both holding the phone, then said, "I work in Woodland but live about thirty minutes outside of it. On a ranch."

"Really?" Christine asked, intrigued. "With horses and goats?"

Willow's smile grew as she shook her head, looking amused. "No. We don't have any animals at the moment. My husband isn't a fan."

"Tsk tsk," Christine chastised playfully. "Animals are amazing. Thinking of getting a cat."

"Well, then you could give her or him loves from me, too. I love cats," Willow said, tucking her phone back into her pocket.

"Here, kitty, kitty, kitty," Christine teased. "You get home safe. Thank you for coming." She took Willow into a hug, unable to get enough of her warmth. Willow returned it, the two saying nothing for a long moment before the nurse backed away.

"Bye," she said softly.

Christine raised her hand and gave a little wave as she watched the two women walk away, Willow glancing over her shoulder a couple times before she disappeared through the door.

Chapter Ten

She stood at the coffee station slowly stirring her coffee, the plastic stir stick going round and round as she stared off into space. She was jolted back into the small snack room that held vending machines, an industrial-sized coffeemaker and a few tables and chairs. The actual cafeteria was on the main floor of the hospital, but little snack spots like this offered something quick for those visiting loved ones.

"Willow!"

Jerking at the sudden voice just behind her, Willow hissed when hot coffee sloshed out of the paper cup and onto her hand and the counter that her cup sat on. "Shit," she muttered, tugging a napkin free from the holder on the counter. "What?" she asked irritably, glancing to her friend and colleague as she wiped up the mess.

"They've been paging you for almost ten minutes," Rachel explained. "Where have you been?"

"Here," Willow said, indicating the small around they stood in, confused. "There's no way, I haven't even *been* here for ten minutes." She looked at the watch on her wrist, shocked to see that, no, she hadn't been there for ten minutes, she'd been there for sixteen. "Shit," she whispered again, running a hand over her hair, which was pulled back into a tight ponytail.

"Well, they need you," Rachel said, giving her

the stink eye before hurrying out of the snack room.

Angry at herself and genuinely shocked at how much time had just vanished, she looked down at her coffee, which had cooled off substantially. With a disgusted look, more at herself than the cool coffee, she tossed the entire thing into the trash and hurried back to her ward.

Later that day, Rachel caught up with Willow as she was filling meds for her afternoon rounds. She heard somebody enter the room and glanced over. She could tell by the look on her friend's face that it wasn't going to be a fun chat. "Hey."

"Hey, yourself." Rachel watched her for a moment, the rolling cart next to Willow topped with a line of little plastic cups waiting for various pills to be dropped into them. "So, what happened earlier this morning?"

Willow shrugged, turning back to her task. This was certainly not something she could dare afford to mess up. "I think the move back to days just has me a little wacko," she said. "It's been an adjustment."

"Uh-huh," Rachel said, crossing her arms over her chest. "I've worked with you for how many years, how many shift changes?" She shook her head. "I don't buy it."

"You're nothing if not honest," Willow muttered, feeling a bit caged, and it wasn't because Rachel was cutting off the exit.

"Is everything okay with Kevin?" Rachel prodded gently.

"Yeah," Willow said, nodding as she met Rachel's gaze. "Fine."

"Is everything okay with *you*?"

Not sure how to answer that, Willow simply

nodded, giving her friend a brave smile. "Fine."

"I'm not trying to push or piss you off, but you've seemed distracted or a bit in la-la land for the past couple weeks. You're the best damn nurse I've ever known, and I've been doing this for twenty-two years. Nobody is more dedicated."

Willow nodded, feeling completely undeserving of the compliment. She knew her head had been in the clouds, and she wasn't entirely sure what to do about it. It wasn't something she felt she could necessarily talk about. "Thanks," she said softly.

Rachel walked over and gave her a tight one-armed squeeze. "Just a heads-up. I know Kerry plans to talk to you about it this morning." With that, her friend and colleague left the room.

Left alone, she blew out a long, heavy breath. The head nurse and her supervisor, Kerry Norton, was a ballbuster and no one wanted to get on their bad side. "Crap."

❧❧❧❧

The rain had been pouring as Willow had driven home from that rough day. She loved the rain, loved the snow, just not driving in it. Pulling onto the property, she was finally able to breathe a sigh of relief, so grateful that the Dittman Bridge hadn't been washed out from the swell of the river.

Her new hours got her home about an hour before Kevin, so once she got parked at the house, she sent him a text, letting him know that as of now, his path home was clear. Gathering her things, she climbed out of the truck and hurried to the house, squealing as cold rain made its way down the back of her scrubs.

Nearly launching herself up the stairs to the porch, she turned and looked out over the day. It was actually quite beautiful, as a small parting of the clouds was allowing a single ray of sun to shine down onto the rain-soaked land beneath. She felt the need to capture it, so raised her phone and clicked off a few pictures.

Sitting on the porch swing, she looked at her pictures and, for no real reason, decided to send one to Christine. It was a strange need to share such a miracle of nature with her. It had been two weeks exactly since the most amazing night of her life, and though she'd had the surprising new contact in her phone that whole time, she'd yet to use it.

She brought up CS in her text app and attached the best of the pictures she'd just taken.

Willow: A soggy homecoming, but I found this remarkable. Hope you're having a wonderful Tuesday afternoon wherever you are. Oh, this is Willow, btw. In Colorado.

She was nervous as she hit send, and half expected to get a message back from somebody asking who the hell was sending them pictures. A little bemused by her own behavior, she unlocked the house and let herself in. She headed upstairs to use the restroom and brush her hair out before putting it back up into a ponytail to keep it out of the way so she could get dinner started.

As she changed out of her scrubs into dry, comfortable clothes, her phone alerted that she had a text. She picked it up off the dresser to see a message from

CS. She gasped and her heart stopped.

CS: Well, hello Willow from Colorado! It's funny you should send that, because I took this picture not ten minutes ago. Perhaps the rainbow here in Chicago is headed your way, hmm?

The picture was of the Chicago skyline with a beautiful rainbow stretching over the top of it. "Wow," she whispered.

Willow: That's absolutely stunning! I hope it brings you good luck for your show tonight?
CS: Yes, getting ready to head to the venue now.
Willow: Must say, I feel a little envious of those waiting for the show. Such an amazing experience.
CS: I'm so pleased. ⊠ We'll get you to another show, I promise. Was that your ranch?
Willow: Yes. I took the picture from my front porch.
CS: Such a dream, to have so much space and quiet. Bet it's heaven on earth.

Willow smiled at that. She'd always seen it as her little piece of heaven, that's for sure. On a whim, she found a picture of the old farmhouse, taken right after they'd painted it earlier that summer. She attached it to her next text.

Willow: This land has been in my family for a long time. It was left to me. Here's the old Farmhouse. My husband and I painted it recently. Needed it! Perhaps you could come visit sometime. Get away from the crazy life of an adored rock star.

CS: I. Would. Love. That. I want to talk to you more about that, but I have to go. Arrived at Soldier Field. Have a wonderful night!

Willow: Break a leg!! (Not sure if that's said for concerts too.)

CS: LMAO! You're too cute for your own good. Night!

Willow: Goodnight. I'll listen to some of your songs in support.

CS: Give me a few, I'll send you something.

Her heart still racing and adrenaline flowing through her at how incredulous the last few minutes of activity were, Willow shook her head, trying to wrap her mind around the fact that she'd just been texting with Swann.

She finished defragging physically from a long day at the hospital before grabbing her phone and heading downstairs to the kitchen to do something with the frozen chicken she'd put in the fridge the night before.

Willow went about her business for dinner prep. Within a few minutes, she had a text alert. Setting the baking pan she'd pulled out of the cabinet down on the counter, she grabbed her phone and opened the text app to see a message from Christine. When she saw it was a video, her heart skipped a beat and she leaned back against the counter to watch.

Christine was straddling a stool, dressed in a casual T-shirt. She wore no makeup and her hair was out of her face. She had an acoustic guitar in her hands. "Here ya go," she said. "A private little concert for you."

Willow turned up the volume on her phone as

the singer began a simple, yet absolutely incredible rendition of "Safe Harbor" accompanied only by her guitar. Her voice was clear and beautiful. It amazed her just how much talent that woman had. She watched Christine's face as she sang. The singer's eyes closed often, her face so expressive as she seemed to feel every word.

She held the final note until it slowly faded away. Her eyes opened and she gave Willow a smile.

"I hope you enjoyed today's edition of, 'Randomly texted song.' Tomorrow we'll be doing our colors." With a wave, the video ended.

Willow burst into laughter even as she swiped at her tears, moved yet again by the song and what was behind it. She responded.

Willow: Brava!!!!! Now I have a lullaby to go to sleep.

CS: Oh hell, if I'd known that, I'd have gone full-on Swann makeup. Well, may have sent you nightmares. Never mind!

Willow laughed again, then proceeded to watch the video at least ten times before getting around to dinner.

☙ ❧ ☙ ❧

The stage was dark, save for a single light shining down on them from far above, raining down soft, silvery light. A sea of empty seats surrounded the stage. There was no band, no instruments, just them.

Right hand in Christine's left, left hand on the singer's right shoulder, and Christine's hand resting against her back, they danced. She had no idea where the music was coming from, but it was soft and slow, just piano. She felt so comfortable with her, in her arms, and smiled when Christine spun her around before they retook their dancing position.

The music stopped, yet they kept dancing, bodies swaying together. Christine brought their joined hands up behind her neck, lightly stroking Willow's to indicate she should leave it there, her other hand automatically moving up to join it. Christine's arms wrapped around her back, pulling her tighter against her.

Willow looked into her face, so beautiful, her eyes such a deep, dark blue, like the deepest ocean, and just as stormy. Christine leaned forward, Willow's eyes sliding closed just a second before the softest lips touched her own. She responded, one of her hands moving up into the darkness that was Christine's hair, the short strands so soft.

The kiss deepened, Christine's tongue stroking hers like a lover's caress. In that moment, Christine's kiss became the sole focus of her world. So soft, so sensuous, so completely right.

Willow's eyes shot open as she gasped. Her heart was racing and her body was pulsing. It took her several moments to realize where she was, in her bedroom lying next to her sleeping husband. She was confused. It had been so real.

Hand falling across her closed eyes, she tried to calm herself, but she was so terribly aroused. Truth was, she couldn't remember ever being aroused enough that it was painful. She throbbed, and her panties were absolutely soaked.

My god.

She could still feel the softness of her hair on her fingers. She could still feel her tongue, so gentle, yet stoking a passion deep within her. She squeezed her eyes shut, covering her face with both hands as she feared she may scream in confusion.

No, she thought. No, no. It was just a dream. *Then why does your clit feel like it's about to explode?* Willow considered her options. She thought of going to take a cool shower, calm down, quiet her body down. Somehow, she knew that wasn't going to do it. Not this time.

Her next thought was to go to the guest bedroom and take care of it herself. She had a new toy that she hadn't used yet. Feeling a little better, Willow took a deep breath and pulled her hands away from her face. She lay there for a moment, and it was a mistake, because she had the instant image of her and Christine lying on a bed, and Christine was on top of her, kissing her.

"No," she whispered. "No." She was a married woman, damnit, and he was lying right there.

She looked over at Kevin, who was lying on his back, one hand up over his head, the other resting on his T-shirt-clad stomach. She scooted over to him and reached beneath the sheet, which was hiked up to his waist. She found the entrance flap to his boxers and did what she needed to do to get the results she wanted.

Kevin snorted as he awoke, blinking, confused and sleepy. "What are you doing?" he slurred.

"I need this," she whispered, pulling the sheet down. "You don't have to do anything."

She peeled her panties down and straddled his hips. His body responded to her aggressive, quick movements. It didn't take very long before he let out a little gasp and she let out a little sob as nerve endings and biology did their job, completing the act.

Feeling even more confused, and guilty, she gently climbed off him. She grabbed her soiled panties and slid off the bed, heading to the bathroom. She didn't want to cry in front of him, confusing him any more than she already had.

❦ ❦ ❦ ❦

The next morning, Willow went about doing her morning tasks. She'd taken a shower after…well, just after, and had leaned against the tile in the stall as she cried. The orgasm hadn't been with Kevin in mind. It may have been his body, technically, but it wasn't about him. She didn't know what to do with that information. Was it cheating?

Taking a deep breath, she continued to pack her snacks for the day. She didn't often have time to stop for an official lunch, so she mostly packed quick and easy finger foods like baby carrots and trail mix.

Kevin entered the room in his usual dress shirt, ironed slacks, and loose tie around his neck. He poured coffee into the mug she'd left for him after pouring her own.

There was an awkward silence between them, and Willow hated herself for it. She had no idea where his head was at. It wasn't like the times they'd had sex when it hadn't been planned, and she knew last night was very different than her usual behavior. Though she was usually the one who initiated it, she was never aggressive or forceful.

"Supposed to cool down this weekend," he muttered, pouring flavored creamer into his black coffee.

"Oh yeah?" she responded. "Perhaps summer is finally going to give in to fall?"

"Hope so. Over it." He brought the mug to his lips, taking a slow, measured sip of the hot brew.

"Want me to pack you a lunch?" she asked.

"No. Mark invited me to grab a burger with him today."

"Okay. Have a good time. Tell him I said hello," Willow said, giving him a sweet smile.

He leaned over and gave her a peck on the cheek. "Will do." He took his coffee upstairs to continue getting ready.

She watched him go, not sure what to think. She could tell things were a bit off initially, but he could be so hard to read at times. She let out a long, shaky breath as she continued to pack her lunch.

Chapter Eleven

As the car she'd hired drove along the PCH, Christine was getting more and more excited. It had been a very long tour, and she was very ready to get home. Since they'd already done the international part of the tour before her little meltdown in February, they'd only had to do the domestic portion. Cut the time on the road in half.

The black SUV took the turn into her driveway slow, as it was a hairpin turn on an already dangerous stretch of road, no matter how beautiful it was. The driver opened her door for her, and she smiled at him in acknowledgment. As he went to the hatch to remove her luggage, she pulled out some money from her wallet to hand him, which he took with bowed gratitude.

Her home in Malibu was the only really big thing she'd ever splurged on. It made sense for her to live in California as that's where the studio was and all her bandmates were based there. She figured if she had to stay there, she was going to stay in style, so with her first multi-million-dollar payday, she'd begun to make plans for her retreat.

From the long driveway, the house looked like a small, one-story bungalow, but it was deceiving. The bulk of the fifty-eight-hundred-square-foot house trickled down the cliffside to the private beach below. The house sported four bedrooms, five bathrooms, a chef's kitchen, and—the reason she'd bought the house—a massive entertaining room, which she used as her music room.

She peeked into the window of her four-car garage tucked at the back of the driveway and saw that her cars were intact and that Milly's car was also there. Seemed as if everything had gone just fine while she was gone.

She shrugged into her backpack and tugged her massive roller bag behind her. Inside the house, she smelled the fruity cleaning products Milly used and was so glad to come home to a nice, clean house. The housekeeper knew that while Christine was gone she was welcome to do as she pleased, just as long as things were clean when the singer got home.

"Honey, I'm home!" she called out as she headed to her bedroom, which was the second largest room in the house and where she spent her time when she wasn't in the music room. She stopped when she heard the scurrying feet of her trusted housekeeper running up to her.

"He's here," she whispered, nodding past Christine to her bedroom.

"Who?"

"Mr. Knowles. He's been here for about an hour waiting for you."

Christine rolled her eyes. "Lovely." She leaned down and left a daughter-like kiss on the older woman's plump cheek. "Thanks. I brought you some cool stuff."

Christine took a moment to put her armor back on, just as she'd gotten to take it off, walking through LAX with a baseball cap pulled low and track pants and T-shirt. Hadn't been stopped once and it had been swell. Now, here she went again. She knew he wouldn't waste much time once she got back, though hadn't expected him to literally be in her house. She was, however, glad he'd showed at least a small amount of decorum and had left her alone on tour.

"What are you doing in here?" she asked, walking into the bedroom that was really more of a suite of rooms than just a large sleeping area with bathroom or closet.

"We need to talk," he said simply from the sitting nook. It was a small living room-type area with a fireplace, couch, and an armchair. A TV was mounted above the mantel. He downed the rest of his drink, setting the tumbler on the table next to him. It looked like his usual scotch on the rocks, though the rocks looked to be mostly melted. She wondered where the scotch had come from.

"What's to talk about?" Christine called from the bedroom portion, where her huge four-poster waited for her to curl up that night. She heaved her backpack onto the bed then grunted loudly as she did the same with her roller bag.

"Plenty," Knowles said as he strolled into the room. Christine noted his perfectly tailored slacks with a white button-up shirt tucked into them, sleeves rolled up to mid-forearm. That was his "sloppy" look.

"Such as?" she asked, looking away from him to begin unpacking. Tired of their "talks," she worried she'd draw blood as she bit her bottom lip in order to not scream at him to leave.

"Such as, what was that garbage you pulled out of your ass starting in Denver? That was *not* on the roster, Christine." Folding his arms across his chest, he took an aggressive stance.

"I wrote that song, Bob. I wanted to try it out on a live audience, and it worked. They loved it." She turned back to her mission, tossing a thong and pair of socks onto the bed next to the jeans and tank she'd just pulled from the suitcase. She'd chosen those particular articles of clothing to make him uncomfortable. She also wasn't about to share with him just how much that "garbage" meant to her and the reasons she'd written it.

"You sitting at a piano, spotlight on you, singing some bullshit song backed by a goddamn orchestra is *not* you, and it will *never* be you." He took a menacing step toward the bed. "Got me?"

She glared at him. "Are you threatening me?"

"I'm simply telling you how it is. I've not steered you wrong in almost twenty years, and I'm not about to start now," he growled, staring her down.

She met and held his gaze. "I'm a big girl now," she said, her voice low and dangerous. "I'm not that same naïve kid off the streets,"

"You think you can take care of yourself?" he asked, his voice rising, though still under careful control. "Then why the fuck were you in rehab not six months ago?" He smirked when she flinched. "And, why the hell did some backwoods redneck in a clown suit have to fish you out of a fucking river?"

Her jaw muscles frantically spasming, anger building, she slowly walked over to him, standing not six inches from him. "Don't kid yourself, Bob," she growled. "My problems are my own, but know this: you're at the root of many of them. You're only going to push me so far, and then that'll be that." She leaned in close, nearly close enough to kiss him. "Got me?"

Knowles stared back at her but said nothing. She

could tell that she'd rocked his world with that little speech, as she typically backed down from him when he was trying to intimidate her. She could see a tinge of fear in his eyes and she loved it.

"Now, get out of here. I just got done making you a fucktastic amount of money and I'm tired."

She watched with great satisfaction as he backed away, breaking the stare-down first. He said nothing, simply turned and left. She stood there, a bit shaken. Her eyes fell closed as she took several deep breaths, starting when the front door of the house distantly slammed closed.

❧❧❧❧

Night had fallen and Christine had unpacked, taken a shower, eaten, and now strolled through her Japanese garden with a cup of coffee. It was beautiful out, the light breeze coming off the ocean below calming.

The incredible smells of the plants and flowers that had been meticulously chosen, planted, and cared for by her gardener surrounded her. The landscaping team had done an amazing job, creating archways and even a fountain, the gurgling water peaceful. She sipped her coffee and looked out over the ocean, a lone ship way out to sea, its lights reflective on the water.

She was tired, but it was that good kind where you're tired because you gave all you had to give and now it's time to rest. Productive tired. She walked over to one of the benches scattered along the path of the garden and let out a contented sigh. She slung her arms out along the length of the backrest and crossed one leg over the other.

For some strange reason, Willow popped into her mind. She wondered what she'd think of the garden. Being a bit of a country girl, would she like the ocean? Had she ever been? Maybe her husband had taken her.

She took a long, slow sip of her coffee, staring over the rim of the mug. That last thought had left a very bitter taste in her mouth that the chocolate-hazelnut-flavored coffee creamer wasn't able to sweeten. Since that first day she'd gotten the picture of the ranch and the storm clouds, they'd texted often, at least every couple of days, depending on how busy one or the other was.

She had absolutely no explanation why, but she wished Willow were there with her in that moment, sitting in the garden. They didn't even have to be saying anything, just sitting quietly. It was her energy she missed, she craved. The quiet, the calm. Quiet beauty. Yes, that's what Willow was to her—quiet beauty.

She sent her thoughts in a different direction, as thinking about Willow, a married woman, was far too defeating. What had Margaret said? Self-talk can make your day or break your day. So, she turned her thoughts toward something she had a bit more control over.

Music.

She needed to call the guys to the house so they could start tossing around more ideas for the new album. Plus, she needed to work things out with Eddie. He was barely talking to her, but she tried not to read too much into that. By the end of any tour, one, if not all of them, was grouchy as hell and plain tired of all of it and missing their normal lives.

She considered the music she'd written over the years, the style that had won them the fan base they had. It made her think back to the early days when Robert had shoved bubble-gum down her throat until she choked on it. She didn't feel she had a lot of room to complain considering all he'd done for her. But, after a few years, she felt suffocated by cute boys and nail polish.

On her eighteenth birthday, he'd asked her what she wanted. Her response? To record one of her own songs. He'd eyed her for a long, breathless moment, then finally agreed and given her the space to do it. She'd written a song in three days: "Razor Wire."

It was the immature version of the stuff Swann had done now for more than a decade. Bob had loved it. Funny thing was, he had no idea it was about her feeling imprisoned under his tutelage. She sure as hell wasn't going to tell him, because the song was a huge hit and the entire album was her first to go platinum. He never mentioned bubble gum again, not even a stick of Wrigley's.

Here they were once more. She felt like she was outgrowing her own empire. As she took another sip of her coffee, the ship far out there blew its horn. Such a lonely sound, much like the whistle of a midnight train in the darkness somewhere.

She continued to sip her coffee, alone in her garden.

❧ ❧ ❧ ❧

"Eat up, boys," Christine said, indicating the long tables that were set up in the music room and were loaded with platters of food she'd had catered for the annual planning session.

She'd never seen anyone rival the appetite her band members had. Jed alone could put away an entire pan of spaghetti. He was six foot three and weighed about two hundred pounds. Her guys built mini-pyramids on their plates then carried them to the table that was in the corner of the room that she used for serious writing sessions that the piano didn't accompany.

Making a plate for herself, Christine grabbed a Coke from the cooler filled with ice, soda, and beer. She took her place at the table with Bug to her left, Jed to her right, and Eddie and Bernard across the way.

The group chatted about everything and nothing as they ate. Usually after returning from a long tour, the five of them needed a break from each other and didn't hang out much, except for Christine and Bug. She saw him as a close friend, so they at least communicated. But, after returning this time, he'd taken his wife of twenty-three years on a vacation with just the two of them. A good man, good husband, and good father, though his kids were grown now. She respected Bug, and often went to him for life advice, which clearly she hadn't always taken.

"So," Eddie said, wiping his hands on his napkin as he pushed his mostly empty plate away from him. "We need to address the five-hundred-pound gorilla in the room."

"I ain't eaten that much yet," Jed muttered, shoving more nachos into his mouth.

Christine and the rest laughed, all except Eddie. She knew what was coming. "All right, what's on your mind, Ed?"

"I've been thinking more about the piano bullshit and all that on this last tour. Now," he continued, and she could tell he was trying to keep his well-known temper under control. "I know you had some serious shit go down last winter and all that mess. I know that chick helped you and everything. So," he said with a shrug as he sat back in his chair. "Is the violin crap just for that song, like, a thank-you song for her or to get in her pants or whatever, or is this crap staying?"

Now it was Christine's turn to try and control her temper. She took a drink of her Coke before setting the can down on the table. "Yes, Eddie, that song was part of a thank-you to *Willow*." She nearly ground out the name between clenched teeth, as opposed to "some chick." "But mostly for me to work out my feelings on what happened. As are," she added, "Most of my songs."

"Okay, but that doesn't answer all of my question," Eddie said. "That style ain't you at all. Never was."

Christine didn't answer verbally, but instead scooted back from the table and walked over to the piano. She grabbed the three-ring binder she'd bought to finally organize all of her compositions, rather than leaving them scattered in chaotic piles all over the floor. She placed it in front of him, then retook her seat.

"What's this?" He opened the hard plastic cover and flipped through page after page after page. He met her gaze. "What's this?" he asked again, shoving the binder aside, where Bug grabbed it, quietly looking through the works.

"This is a collection of my compositions for the past fifteen years," Christine explained. "Been comping since I was a kid."

"Some of these are pretty amazing," Bug murmured, humming a few bars here and there.

"So." Eddie, laughing nervously, ran a hand over hair that was thinning so was kept cut pretty short. "What you're saying then, you've always been a wannabe crooner?"

She smirked as she, too, sat back in her chair, her head slightly tilted as she went into warrior mode. "I'm not Frank Sinatra, Eddie. But there's a hell of a lot more to life and music than leather, bars, and heavy guitar."

"Cute. I didn't sign up to play for no Andrea Bo-fuckin-celli."

"I'm shocked you know who that is."

"Shut the fuck up, Jed." Eddie turned his full ire on Christine. "So, that's it, then? Do you not see people are laughing their asses off at the shit you did? What the fuck!"

"Clearly you haven't been on our social media, Ed," Bug said, sliding his phone across the table to Eddie, page open to the messages praising the new song.

"Fuck this shit!" Eddie raged, pushing away from the table so hard the chair fell over backward. "I quit! I ain't gonna be some faggot with a fuckin' cello." He slapped Bernard on the shoulder. "Come on, let's go."

Bernard, their keyboardist who rarely spoke, looked up at Eddie and shook his head. "Not going."

"Fucking pussy," Eddie yelled. "All of you guys! Fucking pussies." With that, he stormed out of the room and then the house.

Everyone was left in stunned silence for a

moment before Bug muttered, "Well, we need a new drummer."

His deadpan comment was enough to break the tension, and laughter prevailed. Christine ran her hands through her hair, blowing out a breath. "Well." She chuckled. "That went better than I expected." She looked over to Jed. "You know who Andrea Bocelli is?"

"Absolutely," he said, sitting back in the chair and crossing his arms over his chest. "Sarah Brightman, Renee Fleming, all of it. I love that stuff."

Christine stared at him, shocked. "Damn. Day of revelations."

"Look." Bug reached across the table to snag his phone. "It's true," he said, holding up the phone. "Fans loved it. But I don't think we can get away with totally changing who Swann is," he said, indicating everyone at the table to mean the band, their image. "However," he said, indicating the binder. "There is some seriously good stuff here, lady." He looked at Christine. "I think we should maybe do one song an album or something." He glanced at the remaining two guys. "What do you guys think?"

Bernard smiled and looked down at his hands, fingers lightly tapping out a beat on the table. "I can play the violin."

"Shut up!" Bug said. "No way."

"Yes, way." He gave the bassist a shit-eating grin. "First instrument I ever learned."

"He's been hiding this from us for eight years," Bug muttered conspiratorially to Christine, who grinned in response.

"You know," Jed added, looking at the singer. "If you really want to spread your wings, why not try a musical?" He shrugged. "Seriously. Cyndi did it, Elton did it."

"Did what?"

"Branched out and wrote something for the theater. And I know a really great lady who lives in Denver—Christian Scott. Retired from the stage now, but she's one of the world's best choreographers and is still connected to the business." He shrugged again. "Nothing else, she can get you in touch with the right people."

Christine stared at him as though he was from Mars. "Yeah, I saw her years ago in that amazing show, *Angel*. How the hell do you know her?"

Jed grinned. "My dad was in a few shows with her off-Broadway back in the day. Still friends."

Christine blinked. "How the hell do I not know this stuff about you guys?" she asked, looking from Jed to Bernard then Bug.

"Think that says a lot more about you than us, Boss," Bug said, taking a sip from his beer.

"Assholes," she muttered.

Chapter Twelve

Willow felt like the air had been completely knocked out of her. She sat there feeling almost lightheaded from her shock and dread. "There's no way," she finally managed, shaking her head, finally looking at her expectant doctor. "Absolutely no way."

"Well." Dr. Armijo, who had been her general practitioner for years, leaned back against the wall from the rolling stool she sat on. "Have you had sexual intercourse in the last couple months?"

Her first instinct was to say no, but then her eyes closed and her head dropped into her hands. "Oh no," she whispered. She let out a heavy breath and her hands fell away from her face, slapping down onto her thighs on the examination table.

"Listen," the doctor said, pushing to her feet and walking over to her. "You're a very healthy thirty-five-year-old woman, Willow. I see no reason why this shouldn't be a normal, healthy pregnancy." She paused, looking into her patient's eyes. "That is, should you keep it."

Not sure whether to laugh or cry, Willow nodded. "Of course I'll keep it."

Dr. Armijo gave an understanding smile. "I never assume. Every woman has a right to make her own choices."

Nodding again, even as she felt numbness shroud her since she was overwhelmed, Willow slid off the table. "So, now what?"

"Well," the doc said, placing a kind hand on Willow's shoulder. "Go home and take a deep breath. Then find a good OB/GYN. I can recommend a few for you if you wish. I know one that is in Denver who travels here, to Woodland. She's wonderful."

It was becoming real. Far too real. "Okay. Can I have her information, please?"

Dr. Armijo pulled her into a tight hug. "Anything I can do, hon?"

Willow shook her head. "No." She gave her a brave smile after the doctor pulled out of the hug. "Thank you, Theresa."

She felt like a zombie as she walked to her truck. It was a cold, gray, early November day with fat, pregnant clouds threatening to explode. How appropriate, she thought. She climbed in and closed the door. She didn't even get her seat belt on or key into the ignition before she burst into tears.

She sat there for a long time, crying until the tears dried up and her face felt tight and her eyes burned. She reached over to her glove compartment and grabbed the little package of tissues, using a couple to wipe her eyes, face, and nose. She took a deep breath, trying to decide what to do next. Her phone alerted that she had a text message.

Picking up her phone, she saw that it was Christine, which brought fresh tears as she so badly needed to see a friendly face in that moment. Wiping her eyes with a new tissue, she looked at the text, which was a simple, *Hope you're having an amazing day.* ☒

On impulse, just wanting to connect with someone so she wasn't alone, she typed out a quick response: *Can you talk?*

Within seconds, her phone rang. Her stomach clenched with nerves, and she wiped at her eyes again before answering. "Hey."

"Hi. Is everything okay?" Christine asked, concern in her voice.

"Yes." Willow sighed. "No. I don't know." She squeezed her eyes shut as the tears began again. "Sorry."

"Hey, hey, talk to me," Christine said gently.

"I'm pregnant," Willow blurted through a fresh waterfall. "I'm not supposed to be. Kevin doesn't want kids and we never have sex ever anyway, so it's no big deal. I'm not on birth control, no reason. And then, one night..." She stopped her rambling as she remembered exactly why what had happened that night had happened, and it had everything to do with the woman on the other end of the line—even if she tried desperately to deny that. "It just happened," she finished weakly.

"Sweetheart," Christine said softly. "I don't believe anything in life is accidental or arbitrary. You're an amazing person, and that little soul inside you clearly needed someone special to take care of it. So, it chose you."

Those sweet words of course made her start crying all over again. "God, I'm pathetic today. I'm sorry." She sniffled, wiping her nose. "That is the most beautiful thing anybody has ever said to me."

"It's true, you know," Christine said, her smile apparent in her voice. "Listen, Willow, I know I haven't known you very long, but I feel like, I don't know, somehow I've known you forever. It's like..." She trailed off, sounding as though she were trying to find the words. "Like I know you. I know you're scared, I know this wasn't what was planned for your marriage. But you chose Kevin to marry, which tells me he's got to be a good person. It's gonna be okay."

Willow's tears slowly came to an end, Christine's kind words washing over her like a comforting blanket. "Thank you," she whispered. She smiled. "Truly, thank you for that. I'm sorry to just burst in on your day. I have no doubt you have more important things to do than deal with my drama." A little shiver passed through her at the low chuckle on the other end of the line.

"If making a peanut butter and jelly sandwich qualifies as better things to do than talk to you, not sure what that says about me."

"Peanut butter and jelly?" Willow gasped. "Oh, no, no, no! See, I need to make you some real food."

"Well, it's homemade jelly."

"Did you make it?" Willow asked, amused.

"No." The singer laughed. "But, it's still homemade."

"Come for Thanksgiving," Willow blurted, eyes widening and hand going to her mouth after the words tumbled out. Her eyes squeezed shut as her face scrunched up in a, *you idiot* face.

"Okay."

Her eyes flew open. "Okay? Really?"

"Yes. Usually I don't celebrate, but I think I need to change that non-tradition this year."

Willow's belly flipped in an excited somersault. "I agree." She grew serious for a moment. "Christine? Thank you. I needed to hear a friendly voice."

"Well, then, we're all set," Christine said. "I can be friendly, and I have a voice."

Willow grinned. "You certainly do."

✿✿✿✿

Dinner was a quiet affair for Willow that night. She had no appetite and was grateful as Kevin droned on and on about a problem at work. She was fairly clueless when it came to his IT stuff, and usually asked questions to have some semblance of an idea of what he was talking about, but that night she just let him talk. If he was talking, she didn't have to.

"So," he said at length. "How was your day? How'd your doctor's appointment go?"

Here we go. Willow felt like she was about to throw up but managed to push it down. "Um, I need to talk to you about that, actually."

He eyed her. "Everything okay?" Kevin asked, concern in his voice and eyes.

"Yes. Basically." She looked down at her plate for a moment, food barely touched. "Um, Kevin, I'm pregnant."

Kevin, who had been bringing his glass up to his mouth, froze, his eyes wide as he stared at her. He lowered the glass slowly as he took a deep breath. "I see." He cleared his throat. "Um, Wednesday Kyle will be in, so I can leave around nine or ten if you want to get an appointment. I can be there with you. Get it done."

She stared at him. "Get what done?" she asked slowly.

Kevin looked confused. "Willow," he said. "We're not having kids. We talked about this. You agreed, years ago."

"That may have been the case, Kevin," she said, her voice low and flat. "But I am *not* having an abortion." She threw her napkin down onto her plate and shoved back from the table, heading upstairs.

❧ ❧ ❧ ❧

It was weekly Sunday fall football, and Willow and Kevin were at Remmy and Julie's house to watch the Broncos play and eat homemade pizza. Kevin was in the living room with the other die-hard fans watching the game.

Willow was in the kitchen with Julie and Remmy. Pizzas were in the oven, so the three women were munching on snacks that had been set out in large bowls, and Julie was making margaritas. Willow eyed the drinks, one of her favorite cocktails, but knew it was a no-no.

She'd shared her news with Kevin more than a week ago, and the two had barely spoken since. He'd slept in the guest room, she in the master. She knew he was angry with her, and though she understood, she wasn't going to let his silent treatment change her mind. Now, as she'd had more time to let the news sink in, she was getting happy about it. She had yet, however, to tell anyone else. Other than her husband, only Christine knew.

"Here you are, my sweet," Julie said, handing Remmy a margarita, getting a kiss in return.

Willow watched the two women. They'd been together a long time and still were clearly deeply in love. Their connection was evident to anyone who saw them, whether you knew them or not. They were perfect for each other, Julie serious yet personable while Remmy was quiet and observant, yet a total goof.

She loved being around them, and their energy together was beautiful. She realized as she leaned against the cooking island that she wanted that in a relationship too. She wanted to have fun with the person she was with. She wanted the silly, inside jokes and meaningful looks and touches.

"Thank you, baby," Remmy murmured against Julie's lips, patting her behind playfully.

"And, how tipsy do you want to be before dinner, lady?" Julie asked, looking at Willow with raised eyebrows.

"Oh, uh, I can't," she said, waving off the offer.

"What do you mean, 'you can't'?" Remmy said. "You love these things," she added, holding up her own drink.

"I do, but...I can't."

Julie and Remmy looked at her, then at each other. Remmy shook her, just barely perceptible. Julie looked back to Willow, shock on her face. "You and me, lunch this week," she said quietly.

❧ ❧ ❧ ❧

The football game over, a few long faces sat around the dinner table as the home team had lost. Willow was chewing a bite of the amazing pizza when Matt asked, "You guys coming over for Thanksgiving?"

"Well, I actually have to work on Thanksgiving," Willow said after swallowing her food and taking a drink of water to help it down. "So, we talked about doing ours on Wednesday instead."

"Um." Kevin spared a glance at her before looking back to his plate. "Don wants to do Thanksgiving in his new house this year. So..." He shrugged. "I'll be going over there."

Willow stared at him, willing him to look at her again, which eventually he did. His eyes were guarded. "Don, as in your brother, Don? The one who lives in Maryland?"

"The very one," he said with a nod.

She was incredulous. "So," she said slowly. "You'll be going alone, then, since I have to work?"

He nodded. The look he gave her was one of challenge. Finally, he turned and looked at the rest of the table, turning on the charm to gain sympathy for his plight. "My brother just went through a divorce, and I want to be there to support him, first holidays alone and all. This one," he said with a light laugh, hitching his thumb in Willow's direction. "Works crazy hours this time of year, so…"

Willow was hurt, but she had a little poison dart of her own. "I invited a friend to join us, Kevin," she said.

He looked at her, heavy eyebrows drawn. "Who?"

"Her name is Christine," Willow said nonchalantly. Across the table, Remmy choked on her drink. "I guess we'll just enjoy dinner on our own."

"We are definitely having lunch this week," Julie muttered.

❧❧❧❧

Willow stood at the kitchen counter sorting through mail that had come in over the past week. She'd been working extra shifts and Kevin hadn't been around much either, so it had piled up. He walked over to the freezer and dug out a carton of ice cream.

Neither talked as he set up on the counter opposite from her.

"So, is this Christine another lesbian?" he asked, digging the ice cream scoop out of the gadget drawer.

She glanced over at him. "What?"

"This friend of yours you invited—without asking or telling me, by the way—is she a lesbian too?"

Though Willow knew what the rumor was, truth was, she'd never asked. "I wouldn't know," she quipped. "Being a lesbian isn't exactly a qualification to be a friend of mine." She tossed the junk mail into the trash, slapping the other mail back onto the counter. "And…'ask you or tell you,' you mean like you did regarding Maryland?"

"It just came up," he said with a shrug, back to her as he messed with the ice cream.

"So did the invitation to my friend. And, what is it with you and Julie and Remmy lately? They are nothing but nice to you and you talk crap about them."

"Because they make me uncomfortable," he said, half turning to look at her. "What is it with those two? Always touching, kissing. Are they in heat?"

"No, Kevin, that's what married people do." Willow slammed her hand on the counter, frustration hitting a boiling point. "They touch, they kiss, they have fun together, they *fuck*!" The word seemed to echo around them, slowly fading away. A long, heavy silence filled the space between them.

He nodded, turning back to his bowl and ice cream for a moment. His head fell a bit, shoulders blades bunching like a tiger getting ready to pounce. He blew out a breath before facing her, arms crossed over his chest. "Is that what happened?" he asked. "That night. You wanted to 'fuck'?"

She rolled her eyes and looked away, running a hand through her hair. She didn't know what to say.

"You've never given me an explanation for that, Willow."

She looked back over at him, confused. "An explanation? For what? You're my husband, Kevin!" She waved her fists like a two-year-old with her declaration, so filled with frustration that had absolutely no outlet. "I understand our situation is different. Believe me, I understand. But why should I have to be interrogated about the fact that I have needs?"

"We've talked about this—"

"Yes, we've talked about this!" She spun around in a circle. "Whoopty-fucking-do." She looked at him, so desperately wanting him to understand. "Do you ever hear yourself? You treat me like I'm five years old." She deepened her voice to imitate his. "'We've talked about this.' Yes, Daddy, we have." She brought up her hand, ticking off items on the fingers of one with the other. "You don't want sex. Check. You don't want animals. Check. You don't want kids. Check."

"Yet, you're pregnant," he said snidely. "How convenient."

She stared at him, hurt, angry, frustrated. Shaking her head, she grabbed the small stack of bills and pushed away from the counter. "I can't," she said, waving off anything he might try to say. "I just can't." With that, she headed upstairs, slamming the master bedroom door behind her with finality.

Chapter Thirteen

T hank you," Christine said, accepting her change and the wrapped bouquet of flowers from the merchant.

She headed back out into the cold, late November day. Walking over to the waiting driver and his car, she inhaled the air, so fresh, so clean. Unfortunately, a moment that may have looked cool and casual was destroyed as her lungs revolted against the cold air and sent her into a coughing fit.

Finally recovering, she climbed back into the car and closed the door behind her and buckled up. "Okay," she said to the man whose reflected gaze watched her, waiting for instructions. He nodded and got them going again.

After landing at DIA, Christine had hired the Uber and headed to the address she'd been given. Thus far she hadn't been recognized in baseball cap and comfy travel clothes, but she didn't want to take the chance of exposing Willow to the possibility, so she arranged for her own transport. She knew every aspect of Willow's life would be picked apart, and that wasn't fair to her.

As the car had sped away from the city and into higher elevation, Christine had felt like one of those stuffed Garfield cats that had suction cups on all paws stuck to a car window. She was all wide-eyed and excited.

She may have been all around the world due to her career, but she'd mainly only seen the inside of hotel rooms. She'd lived in two giant cities, never the country or anything even close to it. The car passed miles and miles of open land, some with remnants of snow on it. They passed itty bitty little towns and the random homestead off by itself. One thing that was always present were the majestic, snowcapped Rocky Mountains.

"How far to go?" she asked her driver.

"About eight minutes," he responded.

She was feeling excited and anxious. She thought back to the previous winter when she'd made this very same drive in a rental car. How on earth had she gotten out this far? She had no memory of the drive, which was even more terrifying.

The car slowed slightly as it neared an old, rickety bridge. Christine leaned forward in her seat. Though she wouldn't be able to visually recognize the bridge in a lineup, she knew in her gut where they were. She held her breath as he drove easily over it, the driver completely unaware of how that very bridge had changed her life forever.

Bridge crossed, the car continued, and she exhaled. A handful of minutes later, he slowed, turn signal clicking away as the car made a left-hand turn onto a long dirt road. Christine's excitement was palpable as she knew in her gut it was Willow's property. Somehow—she couldn't explain it—she could feel her.

The car pulled up in front of an absolutely enchanting farmhouse, a few outbuildings that she guessed were for storage or had been intended for animal care standing nearby. Always preferring to tip with cash, Christine gave the driver a generous one, grateful for the ride. Climbing out of the car, she grabbed her small roller bag and guitar case off the seat before closing the car door.

As the car drove away, Christine took a moment to look around, again taking in the fresh air. She noted a big Dodge Ram parked nearby and wondered if that was Kevin's truck. She didn't have long to contemplate as the front door opened and Willow came charging out of the house, flying across the large, wraparound porch and down the stairs, nearly bowling Christine over with her squealed greeting.

"Hey!"

Surprised, Christine released the handle of her roller bag and opened her arms, engulfing the other woman in an equally enthusiastic hug. She gave her a tight squeeze before releasing her and presenting her with one of the two bundles of flowers she'd bought.

"These are for you," she explained, giving her the larger of the two. "And these"—she held up the smaller bouquet—"are for us to drop in the river off of the bridge." She gave Willow a sheepish grin and shrug. "Kinda want to say goodbye to that awful night."

Willow was quiet for a moment as she buried her nose in the flowers, eyes closing as she took in their fragrance. Looking up at Christine again, she smiled. "Thank you," she whispered. "And," she added, "I'm very okay with that. The bridge." Then she smiled, big and bright. "You look amazing, and I'm sorry I look like crap. Just got home from work."

Christine looked her over, noting not for the first time just how dangerously gorgeous the nurse really was. She especially thought so as she took in her dark green scrubs, fresh face, and hair piled up in a messy bun. "You, my dear nurse," Christine said. "Are stunning. Meanwhile, I look like a high school kid let loose on a field trip."

Willow's smile was genuine and sweet. Without a word, she stepped back into Christine's personal space and took her into another hug. She wrapped her arms around Christine's neck, resting her head on her shoulder.

Christine's instincts told her that Willow really needed her physical presence right now, so she held fast. She didn't know what was going on, but she had a feeling it was more than just the pregnancy.

"I'm so glad you're here," Willow said softly.

"Always," Christine responded. "You're stuck with this high school traveler." She smiled when she heard a little chuckle followed by a contented sigh.

"Not complaining." Willow grinned up at Christine. "Come on, let's get you in and settled. Hungry? Was the flight okay? I'm so sorry you had to pay for a ride here. I would have picked you up."

Christine was amused at the questions fired off at her before she could even answer. As she opened her mouth to respond, Willow grabbed her bag and was zipping on up the stairs toward the front door. Christine watched for a moment before shaking herself out of her surprise and slinging her guitar case over her back and hurrying after her, managing to grab the screen door and pull it open for her.

"Please forgive the disaster that would be the dining room," Willow said, nodding to the side as she headed straight for the staircase to the second floor.

Christine glanced in that direction, but all she saw was a wardrobe screen and what looked to be a computer monitor peeking around one side. "I will forgive but I never forget," she teased in response. She was a bit distracted, though, as she was faced with an incredibly shapely behind, even in baggy medical scrubs.

"Good to know." Willow laughed, turning and, to Christine's horror, catching her staring at her ass.

The singer quickly looked away, elevator music playing in her head. *Nothing to see here.* Grateful that her hostess said nothing, Christine was a good girl and kept her eyes on the wooden stairs.

"This is where you'll be staying," Willow said, leading them into the first bedroom to the left. She grunted as she lifted Christine's bag to the full-sized bed. "This, I am happy to inform you, was the bedroom I spent a lot of my childhood in."

Christine looked around. It was a small room, not surprising considering the age of the old farmhouse and how differently earlier generations saw space. It kind of made her feel sick to think that the size of this perfectly respectable bedroom was about the size of her closet in Malibu. Americans were so wasteful, she thought.

"Is this original to the house?" she asked, walking over to the bed, noting the brass headboard and footboard.

"It is," Willow said with a smile, her hand wrapped around one of the brass bars. "It was my grandfather's when he was a kid." She grinned. "Passed down from his parents. Pretty sure he was conceived in that bed."

"I see," Christine murmured, leaning over with both hands flat on the quilt that covered the bed. She tested the bounciness. With a quirked eyebrow she nodded, glancing over at an amused Willow. "Get some good height on that."

Willow buried her face in her hands. "Oh boy," was muffled behind them. "Anyhoo." She laughed, moving them out of the room and across the hall. "This is the bathroom you'll be using for the next few days."

The bathroom was small but had an amazing clawfoot tub, obviously antique. "This place really has some serious potential," she said, noting the stained woodwork around the doors and original floors that looked like they could be salvaged with a good sand and restain.

"What do you mean, 'potential'?" Willow crossed her arms over her chest. Christine worried she'd said something very wrong until a smirk quirked the corner of Willow's lips. "Aren't you into seventies' chic?" she asked dryly. "All the rage."

Christine met her smile. "I think you're off a decade or two." She raised her eyebrows. "No shag rug and not a lick of avocado green anywhere."

Willow chewed on her bottom lip and eyed the singer. Finally, she playfully stomped away toward the stairs. "Fine."

Amused, Christine followed. Downstairs, they went into the kitchen where Willow set the flowers on the counter and searched through cabinets until she found a crystal vase. She looked at Christine, who stood nearby watching. The vase was covered in dust. Clearly, it hadn't been used in a very long time.

Willow gave her a bit of a shy look, almost embarrassed as she turned to the sink and washed it. "What are your absolute favorite flowers?" Christine asked conversationally, leaning on the breakfast bar as she watched Willow do her task.

The nurse seemed to think it over as she dried the vase. "I guess the purple rose," she finally said, glancing over at Christine. "A doctor at the hospital got them once for her birthday, and I thought they were absolutely beautiful."

Christine nodded. "Those are really beautiful."

"What about you?" Willow asked, carefully setting the vase down on the counter as she began to unwrap the bouquet of flowers from their plastic.

"Well, you're talking to the blackest of black thumbs," Christine said, sending a grin her way. She pulled her phone out of her back pocket. "I have no idea what any of this is called, that's why I have a gardener. But, I love it." She brought up a picture of her gardens back home, turning the phone to show Willow.

"Oh, wow," Willow whispered, taking the phone and bringing it up closer to her face. "This is exquisite." She spared a glance to the singer. "This is at your house?" Christine nodded. "Wow. I'd never come in." She handed the phone back. "Really beautiful, Christine." She grabbed a pair of scissors and snipped the tips of the stems diagonally before placing the bouquet into the vase. "So, I was thinking," she said. "How about I place the smaller bouquet that you brought for the bridge in some water for the night, then we stop by tomorrow on the way to Woodland?" She shrugged. "Tonight we can have some dinner and just relax."

Christine nodded. "Sounds perfect."

❧❧❧❧

Later that night, Christine was showered and dressed in a T-shirt and flannel pants. She sat up in bed, looking over some emails on her phone. A soft knock sounded on the closed bedroom door. "Yeah?" she called out.

The door opened and Willow appeared, hugging a folded blanket in her arms. She, too, had showered and was dressed for bed. Christine marveled at her hair, light brown waves flowing over one shoulder and down to about her shoulder blades.

"Hey," the nurse said, entering the room. "I wanted to make sure you'd be warm enough." She spread the blanket out across the foot of the bed. "It's supposed to be cold tonight."

"Thanks, I really appreciate that." Christine set her phone aside.

"Do you have everything you need?" Willow asked. "Are you hungry? Thirsty? Hot, cold?"

Christine grinned and shook her head. "No. All good." She patted her stomach. "How about you and little one?" she asked, indicating Willow's own belly, far from showing.

Willow shrugged. "Good, I suppose. At least the nausea is beginning to ease up a bit." She walked over to the bed and perched on the side. "Almost through the first trimester, so here's hoping all goes well."

"Did you want kids?" Christine asked gently, not wanting to upset her, knowing what a touchy subject it was in her situation.

Willow looked down at her hands, which rested in her lap. "My answer might be a little confusing." She met Christine's gaze again. "I did. I've wanted to be a mother since I was little. Well," she clarified. "Knew since I was little that *someday* I wanted to be a mother. But I knew what it took to have children, and somehow that didn't exactly appeal to me."

"You mean, the sex part?" Christine asked. She scooted a bit farther onto the bed, pulling up to sit cross-legged atop the quilt. "Yeah. I know it's stupid, but sex used to scare me. The thought of it." She shook her head, again looking down at her hands. "Just wasn't a pleasant thought."

Christine considered those words for a moment before responding. "That day on the phone when you told me about the baby, you mentioned that you guys don't have sex. You and Kevin. Is that because of you? And," she added quickly. "If I'm being too nosy, tell me to shut it."

Willow shook her head, reaching over and lightly squeezing one of Christine's hands. "No, you're fine." She picked at some lint on her pants as she began to speak softly. "It's both of us, I suppose. Kevin, he just doesn't really have a need for it. Just kind of the way he's built. And, in my own way, neither do I, I guess."

"So, you never do?" Christine asked, a bit confused considering the pregnancy. Her eyes widened as a thought occurred to her. "The baby—"

"Is his," Willow confirmed. "Somehow, it's gotten too complicated, Christine." Again, she looked down at her pants. "I'm changing and I don't know what to do about it." She looked up at the singer. "Julie said you're a lesbian icon. Is that true?"

Christine shrugged, studying her friend, trying to figure out what was just beneath the surface. She felt like something was about to explode out of Willow but couldn't quite make out what. "I guess," she answered. "I mean, I have a ton of lesbians in my fan base."

"So," Willow asked slowly. "You're a…lesbian, then?"

Christine nodded. "Yes."

"Did you always know?"

"Sex had a very, very twisted start for me, Willow," she said. The engine that was her brain was turning, trying to decide how much to say. She could see Willow was curious but wasn't going to push. Perhaps this was the right combination in the right person she needed in order to feel safe enough to share some of her truth. "My parents were both addicts," she began, her voice flat. "We moved around constantly. Guessing now to avoid the law, I don't know. Anyway, when I was about eleven, we move into this piece-of-shit apartment in Queens. Half the time they didn't bother to register me for school, and this was one of those times. I played with the kids in the neighborhood, which was where I met Adam."

"Your best friend," Willow said.

Christine nodded. "Yeah. So, one day I get home after playing and they're gone. Place is empty, except for some trash and a partially drunk half gallon of orange juice. I thought maybe we were moving again and they'd moved all the stuff and would come back for me. So, I sat there on the floor, drinking juice." It was her turn to look away. "To this day I can't stand orange juice," she whispered.

"Did they come back?" Willow asked, a bit of dread in her tone.

Christine shook her head. "Nope." She blew out a breath, surprised at how much it hurt to say that. She felt a soft, warm hand wrap around her own, so she laced their fingers. "I stayed with Adam and his mom, who was almost as much of a train wreck. That lasted about a year and her newest boyfriend decided that Adam and I were playthings. One day, we decided to leave."

"Oh, Christine," Willow whispered. "How old were you by then?"

"Almost thirteen, I think. We met this old lady in the neighborhood who let us sleep on her floor. We helped her out," she said, finding the courage to meet Willow's eyes again. She almost had to look away when she saw the compassion in their beautiful green depths. "We went shopping for her, cleaned, all that. She was a little crazy, but good to us. Then," she blew out, seeing it all over again. "One morning she didn't wake up."

"Oh, no," Willow said. "I'm so sorry." She scooted closer until they were shoulder to shoulder, backs against the headboard, holding hands.

"So, we didn't know what else to do, so we looked for any money we could find, thinking, hey, she doesn't need it anymore." She spared a glance at Willow. "I know. We were thirteen. But we managed to scrounge about two hundred bucks and some food. Locked the place up and left a note for the super before we got the hell out of there."

"You did what you had to do," Willow said gently.

Christine nodded. "Used the money to get a cheap hotel room. We did odd jobs, whatever we could to earn money." She smirked. "Even tried to sing in the subway." She shook her head. "Didn't work too well. I had a lot of learning to do."

"I would have loved to hear a busking thirteen-year-old you." Willow rested her head against Christine's shoulder.

"Trust me, no," Christine said, resting her head against her. "Anyway, so, I don't remember whose idea it was, but we decided we only had one other option to make money. I mean, George had thought he'd won the jackpot when he could get it for free, so why not make the rest of 'em pay for it?"

"Wait, you…You…"

"Yeah," Christine said, squeezing Willow's fingers lightly to let her know it was okay, they'd survived. "We took turns. While one was busy making money, the other hid in the closet with a baseball bat we found in the trash, in case things went sideways."

"Did you ever have to use it?"

"Couple times. One guy, though, a regular, was decent. He thought I was sixteen. I know, not much better. Anyway, he'd leave extra money, sometimes even food. I told him I wanted to sing, so he brought me a guitar he'd given his kid a couple Christmases before that. Kid never touched it, so he gave it to me. I was playing that in a total dive the night Knowles discovered me."

"How old were you?"

"Fourteen."

Willow sat up, looking at her. Pain painted her eyes, which brimmed with tears. "That's just a baby," she whispered.

Christine nodded. "Yeah." She reached a hand up and gently wiped a tear away as it began to fall. "Don't cry for me, Willow," she said softly. "I'm not worth it."

"Are you kidding?" Willow exclaimed, more tears following, slowly rolling down her cheek. "God, how could they do that to you? You're so wonderful, how could they do that? All of them."

Christine shook her head. "Don't know. But it's over now. I'm okay. I survived."

"But, have you?" Willow asked. She took the hand that had wiped her tears away in her own. "Have you, Christine? You tried to kill yourself." Her voice broke on that last sentence.

Christine's heart broke at the pain she'd caused the woman she was beginning to care for far more than she had any right to. "Come here," she said softly, pulling Willow to her, hugging her close. She cradled her head with the back of her hand. "I'm so sorry," she whispered into her ear. "I'm so sorry I put you through that."

Willow said nothing, simply pulled away a bit, her eyes closed as she stayed in Christine's personal space, her breath hot and mint-scented from her toothpaste. Christine's heart was racing, her hand still on the back of Willow's head. Her own eyes fell closed when she felt the touch of Willow's lips against her own.

The kiss was shy, uncertain, but so warm, so soft. Willow pulled away just a hair before returning. This time, there was a bit more pressure, though Christine followed Willow's lead. She suspected this was about a profound need to connect, assure and be assured that someone cared.

Willow placed her hand on the side of Christine's face, leaving a third kiss lingering before she eased away. "I'm sorry," she whispered.

Christine shook her head. "Don't apologize," she said gently. She brushed long strands of wavy hair away from W. She gave her an encouraging smile to let her know she understood.

"I..." Willow looked down, her eyes closing for

a moment before they reopened and focused on the singer. "I should go."

Christine nodded. "Okay." She dropped her hand and leaned back just a bit to break that physical bubble that had surrounded them. "Sleep well, Willow."

Willow nodded and scooted off the bed. "Sweet dreams." With that, she left, closing the door softly behind her.

Chapter Fourteen

Willow pulled the truck to a stop, glancing over at her passenger, who was looking out over the bridge's edge to the river below. The morning was overcast and cold, which she figured was appropriate for the somber event they were about to pay tribute to.

She'd awakened after a surprisingly good sleep, but the moment she'd opened her eyes, they'd squeezed shut after she remembered what she'd done. She'd been terrified to face her guest that morning, but leave it to Christine, the woman quickly becoming a close person in her life, to be light and drama-free.

She'd greeted Willow with a kiss to the forehead, which had sent a flurry of emotions and sensations through the nurse. The look of affection in Christine's eyes and the lopsided grin on her lips put Willow at ease: *We shared an intense personal moment, but don't let yourself be upset by it.*

Willow took the silent advice and had allowed herself to enjoy her morning with the celebrated singer. They'd had coffee and gotten ready for their day, planning to eat breakfast in Woodland.

Now, parked on the bridge where it all began, Willow turned off the ignition of the truck, her hand falling back to her thigh. She wanted to follow Christine's lead on this one. If she got out of the truck and wanted Willow with her, she'd join her. If she never decided to get out and instead got lost in her own mind, Willow would sit quietly beside her.

After a few minutes, Christine blew out a breath and met her gaze. "Ready?"

"Absolutely."

The two climbed out into the cold morning. Willow pulled her jacket close as she walked around the front of the truck to join Christine at the railing.

"It all looks so different during the day," Christine said, standing about six inches from the rail, looking at it as though it were a snake that would strike at any moment.

"In a few ways, I'd imagine," Willow said softly.

Christine smiled and nodded, never taking her eyes off the turbulent, frigid waves below.

"I'd like to ask you something before you throw the flowers in."

Christine looked over at her. "Okay. What?"

"Why did you do it?" Willow asked simply. "I mean, I know you were under the influence, but that simply lowered your inhibitions. What was behind you wanting to end your life?"

"Margaret," Christine said. "My counselor in rehab, helped me to understand that I hadn't really dealt with the trauma from when I was younger, I just kind of bolted from that life into the music world with Bob, never fully accepting what had happened and what I'd been forced to do to survive."

Willow nodded in understanding. "I can only imagine."

"So, between that and Bob…" Christine shook her head and let out a long, heavy breath, which came out in a puff of white steam.

"What about Bob?" Willow asked. She noticed

there was a tightness in Christine's jaw whenever she mentioned her manager and would-be savior, but she didn't know the details of their relationship.

"He was good for me in the beginning," Christine said, looking back to the water. "I'll always give him credit for getting me out of the slip-and-slide Adam and I were on. But, and I didn't realize it then, he was weaving a carefully crafted web to trap me."

"Trap you, how?"

Christine didn't respond for a moment but then finally looked over at her. In lieu of a direct answer, she said, "You're the only other person I've told any of that stuff to." Her voice was soft, sad.

First, Willow was stunned at the amount of trust that had been placed in her the previous night. Before she could fully appreciate that fact, a feeling of rattlesnake-level furor took over. "Wait, you're saying he'll use your past against you? Tell the media, or whoever, about what you went through?"

"That's the not-so-veiled threat."

"Fuck him!"

Christine's eyes widened as she took in Willow's uncharacteristic flash of vulgarity.

"I'm sorry, but fuck him, Christine." She met the singer's gaze with fire in her own. "He may have gotten you out of a horrible situation, but it's your talent that keeps him looking like Guido from some student-film mobster movie." The look on her friend's face would have been amusing if she weren't so fired up. She turned to Christine, hand on hip. "You know what you should do?"

"I'm afraid to ask."

"You should go on friggin' *Dr. Phil* and tell your story. Christine," she said, grabbing the singer by the front of her jacket, shaking her lightly. "You have a right to your story. Frankly, you have a right to your privacy, but unfortunately you're in an industry where, as a public figure, that no longer applies. Be preemptive. Take the wind from his sails and take back your life and your music. It's yours," she whispered passionately.

Christine turned away for a moment before looking back at her. "Maureen Conifer's people have actually contacted me."

"*Conifer Talks* Maureen Conifer, you mean?" She gasped, eyes wide at the mention of the woman at the helm of the most popular talk show on television. When Christine nodded, Willow smiled, gently releasing Christine's jacket as she began to relax. She felt she was being heard. "Even better. She's fair and not salacious."

Christine lightly tapped the small bouquet of flowers against her denim-clad leg. "Bob says my fans will be disgusted by what I did, who I am."

"Okay, stop right there." Willow rested a hand against the singer's jaw. "Who you *are* is a survivor. What you *did* was survive. How many of us could have ever made it through what you and your friend did?" She gave her an encouraging smile, lightly caressing her cheek before allowing her hand to drop. "As for your fans, I was there. They love Swann. And, part of what they love about her, besides her excellent music, is who Swann is. She's dark, she's a rebel, she's dangerous. She's all those things because of what she lived through to sing another day."

After a long moment of contemplative silence, Christine turned her attention to the bouquet. There were four flowers in the bundle, and she gave two to

Willow, who accepted them.

Willow watched as Christine took one of her two and, with a slight pause, took the final step to the railing. Willow stayed where she was to give her space. Christine held the yellow flower above the water.

"With this flower, I release all the demons that have held me captive for so long," the singer said. She let the flower go, both women watching as it fell straight down, the waves immediately consuming it. "And this one," she said, holding out the red flower. "Is for the little girl who didn't get to be a kid. The little girl I've tried to protect and the little girl I'll always love, even when she hates herself," she finished softly. The flower went.

Moved, Willow stepped up beside her and placed her arm around her waist. They stood in silence for a long moment before Christine looked over at her with expectant eyes. Her turn. Willow looked down at the white and pink flowers she held. She took the white one between her fingers, twisting the stem back and forth as she considered what was first.

"With this flower," she began. "I'm going to accept the fact that I'm worthy of the life that I want and worthy enough to have what I need to be happy." She felt a wave of release wash over her as the flower dropped from her fingertips and down into the water. She glanced over at her companion to see a look of approval on her face.

"One more," Christine urged.

Willow nodded and looked at the final flower. She stared at it for a long time, willing courage into her own heart. "I'm not going to hide anymore," she said quietly. She watched the flower until it disappeared, taking all her masks with it.

⁂

Once Remmy had garnered some self-control and stopped staring, the foursome had a wonderful meal, prepared by their hostesses, for an early Thanksgiving dinner. The food was amazing and company was even better.

Willow had been very curious to see how her friends would react to Christine. Yes, Julie had met her the night of the concert, but that was under very specific circumstances—Swann in full glory. How would they do with Christine, who Willow was learning was *very* different from her stage persona? She shouldn't have been worried.

"What did you think of Woodland?" Julie asked, sitting back in her chair, the feast eaten and now the four of them miserable and too full to leave the table.

"I loved it," Christine said, one arm draped back over the top of the chair with her hand dangling forward at the wrist. "I think this town is charming." She cleared her throat and rubbed the back of her neck dramatically. "And, uh, I may or may not have joined The Coffee Shop's frequent brewer club."

Willow laughed. "She bought like fourteen thousand bags of coffee today."

"It was only sixteen, thank you," Christine corrected with a quirked brow.

"And, I'm guessing, you tried their muffins too?" Remmy grinned.

Christine met her gaze, brow still quirked. "No comment."

Willow held up three fingers, using the fingers on her other hand to tick off each one. "Lemon poppy seed, blueberry, and chocolate chip.”

“You lie, wench!” Christine exclaimed. She cleared her throat again, looking at the other two women who were watching them closely. “It was uh, chocolate peanut butter chip,” she muttered. She tilted her head just a bit. “Wonder what it looks like at Christmastime here. All snowy and festive.”

“See?” Remmy added. “You need to see Willow’s ranch during that time. Oh man, so beautiful! Just a field of beautiful, pristine snow,” she said softly, moving her hand slowly across in a straight line, indicating the landscape. “And then you’ve got the gorgeous mountains behind it.” She shook her head. “Nothing like it.”

“Didn’t you get enough snow growing up in New York?” Willow asked, feeling that mentioning public knowledge was fair game and wouldn’t violate any trust.

“Well, yeah but it wasn’t the Oreo cream stuff,” the singer said, face scrunched up.

“Oreo cream?” Willow repeated. “Please explain.”

Christine grinned. “Ya know, all smooth and white. Growing up in Queens, by the time we got to it, it had been driven through, walked through, peed on, garbage thrown onto it, and God only knows what else.”

“Okay, understood.” Willow laughed. “Maybe it’ll snow before you leave.” She absolutely hated the thought of her going, but it was inevitable, and happening Friday. “We’ll have to get you here over Christmas, too, so you can see it in all its fabulousness.”

“Oh yeah?” Christine said, a little flirtation in her tone.

Willow just gave her a little smirk and flirt of

her own. "Maybe." Willow could feel the eyes of her friends on her and knew they were wondering what on earth was going on. She knew there would be questions later, but she didn't care. She was determined to enjoy the moment and let herself just feel for once, no matter what tomorrow brought.

※ ※ ※ ※

It was a cold morning, Willow shivering as she hurried from the warm, steamy bathroom to her bedroom to get dressed for her early shift at work. It was Thanksgiving Day, and it was going to be a very long one. She'd offered to take an Uber into work and leave the truck for Christine the night before, but the singer had refused. She'd said she planned to use the quiet of the ranch to work on songs for the new album.

Shivering, she quickly dried herself and pulled on fresh panties and bra before putting on a white, long-sleeved T-shirt under her scrubs top, then the matching pants. Glad to be warming up a bit, she grabbed her wet towel and was heading back to the bathroom when she glanced out her bedroom window.

It was just after four in the morning, and the scene that met her eyes was magical. It had snowed overnight and a pure, pristine blanket lay across the land. It was turned silvery by the moonlight above from a clear sky.

"Wow," she whispered. She thought for a moment about how excited Christine would be when she woke up, but then thought that maybe it wouldn't look like that later in the morning. For one, the sun would be up, and for two, animals or sun could tarnish the perfection.

Hoping she wouldn't make her angry, Willow hurried from her bedroom down the hall to Christine's. She listened at the closed door, only to hear silence on the other side, as expected. Considering again just leaving her alone, she decided she couldn't. She knocked lightly on the solid wood, not sure how deep a sleeper her friend was.

She turned the knob and pushed the door open to find Christine asleep on her side, the covers pulled up to her shoulders. For a moment, she stood there and watched her, never wanting to get into a bed more in all her life. It was so easy to imagine spooning up behind her and closing her eyes.

Pushing that very appealing thought aside, Willow hurried over to the bed. "Christine," she said softly, lightly shaking her shoulder. "Christine."

Dark blue eyes slowly opened, blinking several times before they focused on her. "You okay?"

"Yes. Come on, I want to show you something," Willow explained, gently tucking long bangs out of Christine's face.

Christine nodded and pushed herself to sit up. "'Kay."

Willow waited as the singer dragged herself out of bed. She thought she looked absolutely adorable with baggy flannel pants and a T-shirt that was slightly twisted from movement in sleep. When Christine walked up to her, she grabbed her hand and led her out of the bedroom and down the stairs to the front door.

"Okay," Willow said, excited. "Close your eyes." When Christine complied, Willow unlocked the big wooden door and pulled it open to reveal the wonderland beyond. She moved behind Christine and gently urged her to take a step forward, then maneuvered her to stand directly in front of the glass storm door. "All right, open." She smiled when she heard a gasp.

"Oh, my god," Christine whispered, planting her hands on the glass door. She looked back at Willow with a look of childish wonder. "Look at that!"

Willow nodded. "Ordered it just for you."

Christine grinned before turning back to look. "It's magical."

"Exactly what I thought. With the moon and everything."

Without another word, and startling Willow, Christine flipped the lock on the door and burst out into the cold night with no shoes. She whooped as her bare feet hit the snow that had blown up on the porch but didn't stop until she was out front on top of what would be the grass. She turned and faced Willow, a huge grin on her face, then fell backward.

Willow burst out laughing as the singer began to make a snow angel, arms and legs slowly flapping through the thick "Oreo cream." She held open the door as Christine popped up and bolted back to the house.

"Always wanted to do that," she said, teeth chattering. "Cccold, cold, nneeed shower!" she managed as she bolted up the stairs, the entire back side of her body painted in a layer of snow.

※ ※ ※ ※

Willow's stomach was in knots as they waited for the Uber to arrive. She hated not being able to take Christine to the airport, but like her arrival, she understood. As it was, when they were in Woodland, a woman at the coffee shop had kept staring at her, looking as though she were trying to figure out if she knew her or not.

"What'cha thinkin' about?" Christine asked, walking down the stairs. After a load of laundry the day before, she was back in her "high school field trip" getup.

Willow glanced over at her over her shoulder. "Just the time you've been here," she responded. She turned to the singer who walked up to her, stopping a foot away. "It went so fast. Too fast."

Christine nodded. "I know." She looked down at the toe of her tennis shoes. "I'd be lying if I said I wanted to go home."

Willow smiled. "I'd be lying if I said I wanted you to." Their gazes met and held for a long moment before Willow turned away. "Um, I need to give something back to you."

"Back? What do you mean?" Christine followed her to the kitchen, where Willow placed her hand on the check Robert Knowles had given her. She slid it across the breakfast bar. "What's this?"

"Knowles gave this to me that night, along with an NDA," Willow explained. "I told him right away I didn't want it, and now I don't want it even more."

Christine picked it up and looked at it, raising her eyebrows. "Guess my stupidity is worth thirty-five grand, huh?"

"I never saw it that way," Willow said, worried Christine would think she was part of his ploy. "I swear to you."

Christine looked at her. "I know." She slid the check back over to her. "Keep it."

Willow shook her head. "Absolutely not."

Christine met her gaze for a long moment, Willow holding firm. "Then I'll tell you what I'm going to do." She tapped the check with a finger. "I'm opening an account for your baby."

Willow stared at her, mouth falling open. Finally, she shook her head. "No, I can't let you do that. You've worked so hard for this, and—"

"And it's mine to do with as I please." Her look was soft and understanding as she continued. "You and I both know how hard life can be, how tough it can be to get going. If I do something with this now, by the time she or he is of age, they'll have a nice head start."

"I can't believe you," Willow whispered, so deeply touched.

Christine smiled. They both looked toward the front door at the sound of a car driving up. Willow felt like she was going to throw up. "I'm going to keep this in my name for now," she quickly explained, looking into Willow's eyes. "That way, you don't have to worry about it vanishing or being split in two if you decide to change things in your life."

It took Willow a moment to figure out what the singer was alluding to, but then it hit her. Her and Kevin. She nodded. "Okay."

Christine took the check and ripped it up into strips. "Burn these?"

Willow nodded. "Of course." Confused initially, she realized that since the check was never cashed, the money was still in Christine's account.

Together they walked to the front door. Christine took Willow into an all-encompassing hug. Willow's eyes squeezed shut as she held the singer close. She didn't want her to leave and was doing everything she could to hold back the tears until she left.

"I'm gonna miss you," Christine whispered into the hug, squeezing a little tighter.

All Willow could do was nod, as she knew her voice would fail her. She was surprised when Christine pulled just slightly back from the hug and cupped her face.

"Forgive me," Christine murmured right before she took Willow in a kiss.

It only took a moment for her to snap out of her startlement and respond. She grabbed Christine's jacket in her fists, holding her as close as possible. The kiss was deep and passionate and desperate. It seemed Christine, too, was feeling the loss already.

Both left breathless, Christine rested her forehead against Willow's for a moment. Willow was trying to recover, but her heart hurt too much. "Promise me you'll come back," she whispered.

Christine nodded. "I promise." She left final kisses to Willow's forehead, then her lips, before without a word she grabbed her bag and her guitar and hurried from the house.

Chapter Fifteen

Well," she explained. "You couldn't split royalties totally, as those also go out to the band members. But your personal royalties for the song, sure."

Christine nodded. "Okay. We're recording this week, so I wanna set something up with you for that."

"All right." Mona, the singer's longtime accountant, jotted down a few notes. "Now, money comes in from several different sources," she said, looking over the top of her glasses that sat toward the tip of her nose. "Are you wanting just royalties coming in from album sales, uploads, merchandise…" She shrugged in question.

"Everything to do with 'Safe Harbor,' be it a T-shirt, upload, whatever. For the album, just apply its sales relative to the other songs to get a percentage per album sale." She brought her hand up, mimicking scissors. "Cut my share of that in half."

"Got it," the older woman murmured.

"Excellent. And I need to chat with your hubby about investing some money for future use."

Mona nodded. "Can do that, too. I'll get you and Albert set up."

"Excellent. Thanks, Mona."

Later that night, Christine lay in bed thinking over the last few weeks that she'd been home. She'd been busy, sitting at auditions to replace Eddie. It was a long and grueling process.

After leaving Willow and the discussion about the check and doing something for the baby with the money, it had gotten Christine thinking. The fact that Bob's signature was on that check reminded her that they had an account in common. It had been set up years ago when he'd told her he wanted to help her learn how to manage her money. Fair and legitimate reason.

That was no longer necessary. Before leaving Mona's office, she asked her to essentially do a deep dive into her finances over the years. Had Bob left fingerprints that shouldn't be there? Such as thirty-five thousand dollars to pay hush money. What Mona found would help guide her next steps.

Lying there in a huge bed that had never felt lonely until then, her mind went back to Willow. They were in touch daily, and the nurse had sent her a picture two days before in her clown costume and makeup, sans a dip in the river. Still creeped out, Christine had to admit she was the sexiest clown she'd ever seen.

She smiled, thinking back to some of their time together Thanksgiving week. It had only been a couple of days, but she'd loved every second of it. How was it possible to feel so comfortable with somebody you didn't even know? Every time she touched her, no matter how innocent or subtle, it sent a shockwave through the singer. And, that kiss.

Closing her eyes, she wasn't sure whether to feel guilty or aroused. Perhaps a bit of both. Willow was still a married woman, and there was no getting around that. She cared too much to let herself lose all integrity over the situation. She knew Willow would hate herself for it, no doubt beating herself up for the little that had happened when Christine was there.

She'd been asked to return for Christmas again just the other day, and Christine wasn't sure what to do. Yes, she wanted to go. With everything in her, she wanted to go. Would Kevin be there? She wasn't sure what would be better: there or not there.

She knew ultimately she wouldn't be able to say no, so they'd figure it out then, she supposed. For now, she needed to focus on tomorrow's trip. She was heading to New York to talk to Adam. She'd given a tremendous amount of thought to Willow's impassioned plea that she open up about her past. Not just for her fans, but for herself, to know that she no longer had anything hanging over her head, no dark secrets to dog her steps.

She had no idea what Adam would say about it, as it was his story too. No, he may not be a public figure, but it could still very much affect his life and that of his wife, Camille.

With visions of Willow's beautiful face in her mind's eye and the memory of the softness of her skin and hair on her hands, Christine turned onto her side and curled up.

❧❧❧❧

"Hello!"

Christine welcomed the enthusiastic hug from Camille, who had been Adam's rock for more than nine years. She returned the squeeze and was released so she could accept one from her best and oldest friend.

"So glad you're here," he said, pulling back and

looking her in the face as he held her by the shoulders. "My god, you look so good! I've never seen you look this good, Chris."

She gave him a sheepish grin. "I'm just not sure how to take that."

He laughed, slapping her on the shoulder. "Come on. Dinner's ready."

Their Queens apartment was small, a two-bedroom, one bath in an eight-story walk-up. The pre-war building was like many in the area, though theirs had a tiny "balcony," as Adam liked to refer to it. In other words, a deep window ledge to hang out on when the huge window was opened.

More than once Christine had offered to buy them a place anywhere they wanted to go, but Adam had always declined, seeming almost insulted. He and Camille were determined to make it on their own, and she respected them both for it.

"Looks good, Camille," Christine complimented, her mouthwatering at the fragrant dishes that were being brought out from the kitchen, one by one. Enchiladas, which she knew would be homemade from the ground up. Homemade Mexican rice and Mexican black beans.

"Good, you better eat up, woman. Spent all day cooking for you," she said, eyeing their guest with the no-nonsense attitude of a woman who'd raised five kids on her own, including a set of twins.

Most of Camille's kids were already out of the house when she and Adam had met. Initially, Christine had been worried about the eighteen-year age difference. But Camille's strength and nurturing nature was exactly what he'd needed, and somehow, they fit like puzzle pieces. Not to say that they hadn't had their problems, as Christine had witnessed some of their epic fights, but they always came back together stronger than before.

She'd asked him once what their secret was to making it work. Adam's simple response had been, "She understands I'm learning how to be human, and I understand it's not her job to fix me. It's mine."

The three of them sat down at the table, Christine licking her lips as Camille dished up a generous plate for her. "Thank you," she said, eyes wide and hand already reaching for her fork.

"So, what did you want to talk to me about?" Adam asked, sipping from his beer.

"I've been doing a lot of thinking about a lot of things," Christine began. "And, since everything that happened in February, I've had to do some soul searching. Willow has helped me with that too." She glanced over at her friend who was quietly eating his food, but she knew he was hearing every word she said. "I want out from under Bob."

That made him glance up at her, a heavy brow raised. "Oh? Finally?"

She nodded. He'd been after her for years to do just that, but she always stubbornly declined. "Willow said I should be preemptive and tell my story my way."

"Willow sounds like a very smart lady," Camille said, scooping beans onto her own plate.

"I never understood how he had you so trapped, anyway. Not like he had anything on you," Adam said. "You weren't in prison or anything."

"He held her captive by her trauma, sweetheart," Camille responded. "Her whole childhood was about being left, abandoned. In his own twisted way, he was threatening to do the same by ending her career if the truth came out."

Adam shook his head. "Always hated that man."

"The thing is, if I tell *my* story, it means I have to tell *your* story," she said to him. "You have a reputation you've worked hard to build as a freelance writer." She shook her head. "I don't want to hurt that."

Adam eyed her as he took another sip of his beer, setting the bottle down gently on the table and swallowing before speaking. "About three years ago I told Camille I wanted to write your story for you."

Not expecting that, it took Christine a moment to catch up. "Wait, what?"

He nodded. "I want to write a book about what happened. Get it out there. You have an entire legion of fans, a lot of young people, who may be or have been in a similar situation. They look up to you. Plus," he said with a shrug. "I think it would do you some good." The smile that followed was pure evil. "And, if Knowles gets the boot in the process, all the better."

"Well, that was easy." Christine smirked. "And here I thought I'd have to twist your arm a little."

"Chris," Adam began. "When you were born, you were essentially forced to be five years old. When you were five, you were forced to be ten. At ten, fifteen, and at fifteen, twenty-five. Now, you're in your early thirties, and you deserve to live life in this moment, not years beyond. What I want to see is for you to just enjoy what you've built. What you've accomplished. I want to see you truly breathe it in, and," he added, holing up a finger for emphasis. "I want to see you happy as well."

"We watched the footage of you in Denver," Camille said. "When you first sang that song to the woman, Willow. First of all, you two look amazing together."

Christine was surprised by her words, glancing over at her best friend to see him nodding vigorously as he stuffed his face with food.

"Very sexy. Anyway, but I think when you were singing to her," Camille said, her voice soft, dreamy. "I saw true joy on your face. I've seen you perform so many times over the years, so I know it wasn't because you were debuting a new song."

"It was moving as hell," Adam agreed. "This one was a mess." He grinned, nodding toward his wife.

"Yeah, so was *that* one," Camille said, nodding right back.

Christine laughed. "It was a moving moment."

"You gotta figure out what was it about that particular moment that gave you such joy," Camille said, using her fork to point at the singer before stabbing a bite of enchilada. "That's the key. Find what gives you joy and seek it."

Christine studied her for a moment then looked down into her plate. *Indeed.*

❧❧❧❧

The night was cold, both Christine and Adam huddled in heavy jackets, scarves, and gloves. The singer had tugged a beanie down over her head. She looked at the street before them, cluttered with cars at the curb and traffic in between. Though she'd visited Adam and Camille many times over the years, she hadn't allowed herself to venture beyond their building and direct neighborhood.

They strolled through their old stomping grounds. She felt like she'd been transported back to a time that was all about survival, quick thinking, and pushing down the fear monster, as it had no place. She felt nauseous as those instincts were trying to kick in, but she was doing her level best to stay in the moment. None of it could hurt her anymore. She had to remember that.

"Number four," she said softly, looking up at the building they'd stopped in front of. She looked over at her friend. "Do you remember that her place constantly smelled like cat pee even though she didn't have cats?"

He grinned and nodded. "God, yes. You on the floor one night, me on the couch, then swap the next." He looked at her. "Do you ever wonder what she died of?" He shook his head. "Never forget waking up that morning and finding her."

"In her bed," Christine murmured. "Don't know. She had us get her meds all the time, so obviously something was wrong. Maybe heart issues or blood pressure. Stroke. Diabetes." She met his gaze with a shrug.

Without discussion, they moved on, walking farther down the street, commenting on this or that. Suddenly, Christine stopped dead in her tracks. Adam hadn't realized it and had continued on. He returned to her.

He looked down the alley that Christine stood at the head of. "What?"

"Don't you remember?" she asked him. She nodded in the general direction. "This is where that guy picked me up. Well, tried to." She met his gaze. "That guy who was killing girls."

"Oh, damn. Right." Adam rubbed the back of his neck nervously. "That was so scary. Thought I was going to lose you that night."

"You almost did," Christine said flatly.

"I've been thinking," he said as they began to move again. "Maybe you should hire a private investigator to see what happened to your parents."

She felt an instant tug at her heart and her guts. It was almost like pulling on the string that was holding her emotions together as they made their way through their childhood. "Why?"

"Don't you want to know what happened?" he asked as they trotted down the stairs into the warmth of the subway tunnels.

She considered the question for a long time. "I suppose. I think I'm afraid of the answer, though."

They passed a guy, young, maybe twenty, sitting on the floor with his guitar case set open for tips. He strummed and he sang. She stopped and listened, a small smile on her lips. That, too, brought back a flood of memories. Reaching into her inside jacket pocket, she retrieved her wallet and pulled out a hundred dollars in various bills, tossing them into his case.

He nodded at her before his eyes widened in recognition. He stopped playing and popped to his feet. "Can I have an autograph, Swann?"

She smiled at him and nodded. "You got it." She had learned long ago to carry a Sharpie with her, as she never knew what was going to be shoved in front of her. "Gimmie that," she said, nodding at his guitar. She wanted to give the kid a memento, but also something to sell if he needed the cash. It wasn't an easy path to be someone trying to make a living on a passion and a talent.

He handed her his guitar without question, and she signed the body, making sure it wasn't in a place that could be rubbed off through play. She capped her marker and handed it back to him. The young man looked down at it in awe before looking at her again.

"Um, can we do a picture?"

She grinned. "Got a phone?"

Christine sat in a chair in her hotel room in Manhattan. She didn't stay with Adam that night because she had some business meetings early and wanted to get into the right headspace, and that usually required time alone.

True to his word, Jed had gotten her in touch with retired Broadway dancer and current choreographer Christian Scott, who had gotten the singer in touch with some pertinent people in New York. So, while she was there, she was taking some meetings to find out if it was even a direction she wanted to go.

She was also there to meet with a woman named Riley. She was a veteran manager in the business, and she wanted to hear what she had to say. She'd made her mind up on Robert Knowles. It was time to move on, in so many ways. That last unexpected meeting at her Malibu home had been kept tightly under wraps; she hadn't shared it with anyone, not even Adam or Willow. She wanted to get all her ducks in a row before pulling the trigger.

Willow. She had thought long and hard about what Camille had said, and her observation. That night in Denver had been amazing—Christine couldn't deny that. When sitting on that piano bench next to Willow, singing to her, it had felt like she'd done it a thousand times. It had felt so natural, so completely intimate, and better than any sex she'd had.

Had the joy Camille and Adam seen come from that? From the feeling of an intimate connection that she just didn't have in her life? Or was it specific to Willow? By that point, they hadn't really known each other, and it had been only the second time they'd met or been in the other's presence. What had Adam and Camille seen that she hadn't?

"What is it about you?" she whispered, absently strumming. She began to sing, her voice soft as the words came to her.

What is it about you, why do I find peace
Sitting here alone, my life is up for lease
Go again, start anew, where do I sign
Choices I made fermented into wine
All I know …

Metal bar cages tryin' to hold in smoke
Emotions run wild, the zoo is closed
Wonderin' where you are, how you do
Seeing your smile and grace, I smile, too
All I know …

Moon rises, sun abates
Silvery glow can't erase
My heart guilty
You don't know what you bring
Never get what it means
Your quiet beauty

You touch my face and touch my soul
You tell me I must let go
Which do I hold on to

This crazy past or the dream of you
All I know ...

Let's fly away where rules don't apply
We can make love above the sky
Just you and me.

Moon rises, sun abates
Silvery glow can't erase
My heart guilty
You don't know what you bring
Never get what it means
Your quiet beauty
Your quiet beauty
You don't know what you bring
Never get what it means

Her voice fading into the night, Christine's eyes slowly opened as she hugged her guitar to her, staring out into the night.

Chapter Sixteen

Willow opened her locker, reaching in to grab her purse and phone. It had been a long, difficult day at the hospital. Her heart was heavy, and she just wanted to go home and curl up under the quilt and go to sleep.

"You okay?" Rachel asked gently, walking up behind her.

Not looking at her, Willow nodded, though she wasn't. "I've been doing this a while now," she said quietly, softly closing her locker door and locking it. She shook her head and let out a heavy breath. "It doesn't get any easier."

"No, sweetie, it sure doesn't." Rachel rested a hand on Willow's back. "Especially when they're so young. They shouldn't be dying."

Willow shook her head. "No. No, they shouldn't." She shrugged into her jacket. "She was only twelve."

"I know. But, hey, at least we're going to go out tonight and enjoy ourselves, huh?" Rachel gave her an understanding look. "You and Kevin and me and Andrew. Hot cocoa and seeing some Christmas lights."

"Rachel, I need to tell you something."

"Sure. What up?" Rachel's smile faded with the serious tone of Willow's words.

"I'm pregnant."

Rachel stared at her, eyes wide with excitement,

but then she seemed to clamp down on that enthusiasm. "You're not happy about this?"

Willow thought for a moment before answering. She'd told her friend because she needed somebody in her everyday life to know, somebody who would be on her side. But, she didn't know how far she wanted to go regarding Kevin's reaction. Finally, she nodded. "I'm very happy about this," she said, meaning every word. "Very."

"But Kevin's not."

She shook her head. "No, he's not." She hugged herself, almost as though protecting the tiny little being inside of her. Something she'd noticed she'd been doing a lot lately. "He won't even let me talk about it. Hasn't gone to any of the doctor's appointments."

"How far along are you?" Rachel asked.

"Thirteen weeks."

Rachel stepped toward her and took her in a long and warm hug. "I'm very happy for you, sweetie. You'll make an incredible mother." She smiled at her as she pulled out of the hug. "Maybe we can talk some sense into Kevin tonight, hmm?"

Willow shook her head. "No. Please don't say anything. You can tell Andrew at home or whatever, I know he won't say anything. But leave Kevin out of this."

Rachel nodded. "Okay. I promise." Another quick hug and the two women left the locker room. "Let's go tonight and have a good time, okay?"

Willow nodded. "Okay."

❧❧❧❧

Since Kevin's return from Maryland after

Thanksgiving, things between the two had been friendly, though a bit of tension was in the air. Willow thought it was coming mostly from her, as his indifference toward the baby was beginning to truly make her realize her situation. Their marriage— good, bad, or other—was between them, but if he was already this apathetic toward his own blood while in the womb, what would happen once it was born?

Willow had driven them to Woodland in her truck as it was clean. Kevin's back seat was filled with computer stuff. Always computer stuff. When they pulled up, Rachel and her husband Andrew headed out of the house to meet them. Kevin opened the passenger side of the truck.

"Honey, go ahead and scoot," he said to Willow. "Girls in back and guys up front."

She looked at him and, for some reason, that pissed her off. This time last year, this time last month, she wasn't entirely sure she would have let it. "I'm fine where I am, Kevin," she said. "Ladies up front, boys in back," she said, hitching her thumb toward the back seat of the extended cab truck.

He stared at her, a look of irritation and surprise in his eyes. "Honey," he bit out. "We have longer legs. We'll get up front."

"We'll pull the seat up, won't we, Rach?"

"Absolutely!" Rachel stood next to the open door, waiting for Kevin to vacate. Andrew was already making his way to the back driver's side.

With an annoyed sigh, Kevin finally moved, leaving the door open for Rachel as he joined Andrew in the back. Rachel climbed in and pulled the door closed, belting herself in. She glanced over at Willow, the two women sharing a smirk before working together to move up the front seats.

"Next stop," Willow exclaimed. "Coffee and hot cocoa!" Willow could feel Kevin seething from the back seat, but she was determined to ignore it, ignore him. She pulled up to the drive-thru of the commercial coffee shop and collected orders. Kevin, of course, was acting like a child and refused to join in the fun.

"Come on, dude," Andrew muttered, slapping him on the shoulder. "Let's have a great time." He leaned over and stage-whispered, "I love it when my woman is in control." He slapped him again in "bro" camaraderie.

Willow shook her head, amused at her friend's husband, whom she had always liked.

❧❧❧❧

When they arrived home, Willow was in a wonderful mood, certainly far better than she'd ended her workday. Kevin, however, remained quiet and pensive. As she'd done the entire night, Willow ignored him. She wasn't going to ask, wasn't going to play his passive-aggressive game. Instead, she headed upstairs to get ready for bed after shrugging out of her jacket and hanging it in the coat closet.

When they'd entered the house, Kevin had gone to the kitchen to start a pot of coffee, which was usually the silent cue they had both used in the past to indicate they were angry or needed to work something out. She'd bypassed the kitchen altogether and gone straight to the stairs.

The thing was, there was nothing to work out, in Willow's mind. Well, other than Kevin's bruised ego, and that wasn't her problem. She was resigning her position as Consoler in Chief. Instead, she headed to the bedroom that she sometimes shared with her husband, as he pinged back and forth between their bed and the one in the guest bedroom, the one Christine would be using when she arrived in two weeks.

That thought brought a true smile to her face and light to her heart. She switched on the bedroom light then went on through to the bathroom, switching that one on, too. The woman that looked back at her in the mirror startled her for a moment. There was a fire in her eyes that she wasn't used to seeing. There was light, there was *life*. She'd been told her whole life that she was beautiful, but it was never a word she affixed to her personal resume.

As she looked at her reflection now, for the first time she wondered if, just maybe, there was something there. Just maybe she had something to offer. Something to offer to someone like Christine?

"What the hell was that about?" Kevin asked, screeching Willow's train of thought to a screaming halt.

She looked at his reflection in the mirror. "What was what all about?" she asked, tugging her fleece off over her head. She tossed it across the closed toilet lid so she could begin her nightly routine.

"That business with the ladies in the front and the boys in the back?" he clarified, standing in the doorway of the bathroom.

"As opposed to the girls in back and guys up front?" she retorted, eyebrows raised in challenge.

Kevin rolled his eyes and stepped into the bedroom, tugging his hoodie off over his head. "That's just my way, and you know it."

She turned and walked to the doorway, watching

him. "So, condescension and then hypocrisy about it is your way…is that what you're saying?"

"Don't twist my words, Willow," he said angrily, tossing his hoodie to the bed before tugging off his button-up, it, too. landing on the bed. "You embarrassed me. You made me look like an idiot and totally emasculated me."

"Tell me you did not use that pathetic word." She took a few steps into the room, crossing her arms over her chest and putting her weight on one hip. She was not in the mood for nonsense. "Do you know what the word emasculate means, Kevin? It means some man got his little feelings hurt because somebody told him no, usually a woman. In other words, I took your control away by insisting on driving *my* truck," she said, hand moving to her own chest.

"So what?" he said, sitting on the side of the bed to untie his shoes. "We're married. I can drive your truck."

She studied his back for a moment, the picture becoming clear. "You're pissed that I stood up to you," she said softly.

"That's absurd," he muttered, tossing one shoe off before moving to the other.

"No," she said, shaking her head. "It isn't." She turned to head back into the bathroom, her hand on the door before closing it. "Get used to it, Kevin," she said. "My days of complacency are over."

❧ ❧ ❧ ❧

"So beautiful out," Julie said as the two walked along the trails in the foothills above Woodland. "The sun is out, air is fresh." She took a deep breath, then smiled at her companion.

"It is," Willow agreed. Though there was snow on the ground, it was nearly fifty degrees, so it was very pleasant. "I love wintertime."

"Is Christine excited to come back for Christmas?" the teacher asked.

"She is," Willow said with a smile. Just the mere mention of the singer sent butterflies beating against her insides.

Julie was quiet for a long moment as they strolled before said asked, seemingly out of nowhere, "I fought it too."

Willow glanced over at her. "What?"

"I fought too," Julie said again. "My attraction, my feelings." She shrugged. "After all, we were friends. Best friends, but friends."

Willow was quiet for a moment, allowing Julie's unexpected words to sink in. Finally, she asked, "What did you do about it?"

"I asked her to move in," Julie said simply.

"As a couple? You were straight, I thought. Or, am I wrong?"

"No, you're not wrong. I was straight until I wasn't." Julie chuckled. "And, no, I asked her to move in because I wanted her close to me all the time. I didn't fully understand it, honestly, and my brother nearly had a coronary."

"I bet." Willow laughed, knowing Julie's brother and what a conservative voice he could have, though he loved his little sister dearly. "What was it?" Willow said, stopping their progress and looking her friend in the eye. "What was it that did it?"

"One night I realized I was hurting her by denying my own feelings." She shrugged. "It was literally as simple as that. I gave in, pushing away my fears and doubts, and kissed her."

Those plain words sent little shivers through Willow. "How was it?"

Julie smiled. "Best kiss of my life, and best decision I ever made. We've been together ever since."

"No regrets?"

"Absolutely none."

Willow considered her words for a long moment, looking off in the distance, her mind racing. It was Julie's question, so gentle and understanding, that made her turn back to look at her. "We kissed," she responded. "That's all. But, both times were on the heels of an emotional situation, so it wasn't sitting on the couch making out or anything."

"Could you?" Julie pushed. "Could you lie on a bed with her and kiss, touch her, be touched by her?"

Willow didn't need to think long on that. She looked down at the toe of her hiking boot as it kicked lightly at a large rock. "Yes. In fact, I feel horrible about something." She met Julie's gaze. "The night I got pregnant." She blew out a breath, surprised she was sharing something so deeply personal, even with her best friend. "I had an erotic dream about her. I woke up, shocked. Didn't know what to do." She spared a glance at the teacher, expecting to see disgust, but all she saw was understanding.

"You had sex with Kevin to scratch an itch he didn't cause?"

"More like, I had sex with Kevin to prove to myself *that* was what I wanted." She buried her face in her gloved hands.

"Oh, sweetie," Julie whispered, taking her in a hug. "Let me ask you something."

Willow nodded into the hug. "'Kay."

"If Christine weren't an option, would you find yourself wanting to stay with Kevin?"

Willow looked at her, confused. "What do you mean?"

"Well…" Julie looked around and saw something. "Okay. See that woman over there sitting on the rock taking pictures?" She pointed to an attractive young woman thirty yards away.

"Yes."

"Okay, she's very cute. Can you imagine yourself kissing her? Or, her kissing you?"

"Julie, she's like twenty years old."

"Forget about that for a minute. Just focus on the fact that she's cute and a woman. Could you kiss her?"

Willow studied the young photographer, noting her face, her lips, the way her short, brown hair blew in the slight breeze. Very cute. Finally, she nodded. "I could." She looked at her friend. "Why?"

"Because you need to know if it's an attraction to Christine or a broader attraction to women."

Willow considered the statement. "If something happened between you and Remmy tomorrow, you wouldn't go back to men?"

Julie shook her head. "No way. Remmy is my person, my wife, but if something happened and we couldn't be together, no. If I were ever with somebody else, it would be a woman."

Willow nodded, understanding. She wished she could fast forward through all this and be so self-assured. She blew out a breath and looked up into the robin's-egg-blue sky.

"I know it's hard," Julie said, as though reading

her mind. "Trust me, I know. But whether your path is with Christine or not, Willow, there isn't anything you can do. You can't move forward or backward until you figure out who you are and what you want. You owe it to yourself, and to my little niece or nephew," she added, patting Willow's tummy.

Chapter Seventeen

Hands on hips, Willow looked around the out-building closest to the house, which she'd always called the "other house" or "summer kitchen." Back before the days of air conditioning, the long, hot work of canning would heat up the entire house, and in the summer months, that made for pretty miserable living conditions.

So, a separate building was often built on farms or homesteads that was basically just a kitchen to accommodate that work. It had a stove, a sink, and plenty of space for a table or other work surface. For her grandparents, when technology evolved so it was no longer a necessity, they'd used the other house for storage.

When she was a teenager, her grandparents had remodeled it a bit, laying carpet and installing a sleeper sofa and insulation so that Willow could have a little privacy when she stayed. She would sit out there and read, or just watch TV by herself.

Now, she looked around to see what could be done to turn it into a space for Christine to work. She knew she was writing, and from what she'd been able to gather from their daily communication, usually via text, she needed a quiet space where she could play her guitar and not disturb anyone or be disturbed by anyone.

The sink and counter were still there, though

the stove had been removed years before. The couch remained, as did the TV, as well as many stacked boxes, which she would need to move to another outbuilding to store. She looked down at the carpet and determined it was in good shape, though it needed to be cleaned. All in all, it seemed like it could work with a little elbow grease. She'd just have to be careful about what cleaning products she used so as not to hurt the baby.

She headed back to the house to gather her things and get to work. Kevin was in the kitchen making his coffee when she stepped back inside, the frigid mid-December morning chasing her in.

"Damn," she whispered, a shiver passing through her. "Cold."

"Supposed to snow," he commented. "Do you want me to pick you up from the hospital if it gets too bad?"

"No," she said. "Thanks. I think I'll be okay." She grabbed her keys and phone from where she'd left them on the breakfast bar. "I'll probably head home early today. I want to get going on the other house so Christian will have a place to write."

"Write?" he asked. "I thought she was a singer or something."

Willow looked at him as though he had two heads. "How do you think songs get written to be sung?"

"Oh," he muttered, focusing on his task. "Got it. How long is she staying?" His tone was that of genuine curiosity, but she knew him well. Though the situation the night of the Christmas lights fiasco hadn't been brought up again, she knew that didn't mean he was over it.

"As of right now, a week," Willow said, shrugging into her winter jacket

"As of right now?" He looked over at her.

"Yeah. I told her that if she needed to get away from the crazy of LA she could use the ranch." He simply nodded but said nothing. "See you later," she said, leaving.

⁂

Kevin had texted to find out when Willow was leaving work, and when she'd responded with the time, he'd told her to head to Pizza Madness and pick up the order he'd called in for them. She was confused, as he wasn't due to get off work for another four hours after her, but she agreed.

Located in a large old building with exposed brick walls and pipes along the ceiling, the pizza joint served great food in a fun environment. It was a little pricey, but worth it for a treat. As she stood off to the side, out of the way of other customers trying to pay for their lunch, she looked around at those sitting at the tables and booths enjoying their meals. She noticed a group of women over by the restrooms, four of them all around the same age, perhaps late twenties. They wore similar work badges, so she assumed they had all taken lunch together from the office.

She regarded one of them, and noticed the woman's beautiful facial structure and complexion. The woman next to her was talking, and her melodic voice reached Willow's ears, putting a small smile on her lips. Another of the women was cutting her pizza into small bites with a knife and fork, and Willow's gaze settled on the woman's hands, so delicate, lovely.

She looked away from the group of women, feeling as though she were being rude. She saw a woman walk by her, a waitress at the restaurant. She wore a T-shirt with the name and logo splattered across the front, but Willow also noticed how the women's shirt held her breasts. They weren't particularly large or small, just beautifully shaped.

She was grateful when her name was called out for her order, as she was beginning to feel like a creeper. She accepted the large pizza box and a bag of garlic knots, then weaved her way through the maze of tables to the door and out. She stowed the food in the back, then climbed behind the wheel.

She thought for a moment about her experience. For just a second, she wanted to berate herself for being disrespectful. But then she stopped her conditioned thought response and considered why exactly she was looking, and what exactly she was looking at. She wasn't ogling, she wasn't sexualizing. She was appreciating the beauty that were women, all their pieces and parts.

She noticed a woman, all bundled up in the next parking lot, who was working diligently to scrape her car windows. It was clear her car had been parked there the entire morning and into the afternoon, as the falling snow had accumulated on it.

She watched her power through the snow and ice, and it hit her just how amazing women were. Not so much for clearing some snow, but just in general. Their beauty was so much more than skin deep, it was about their motivation, their tenacity, and drive.

Looking away from the woman, she inserted her key and turned on the ignition for her truck, allowing it to warm up for a moment on the bitterly cold day. She felt different, as though blinders had been removed from her eyes. She felt like she could give herself permission to see what had always been there.

Now, what she did with that permission might be a whole other story.

She took the drive slow, but finally reached the ranch, grateful that their neighbor, the owner of the horses, had used his plow-endowed truck to clear not only the main road, but also the one on her land leading up to the house. She'd have to bake him and his wife one of her banana cream pies that they liked so much as a thank-you.

Kevin's car was parked at the house already, which surprised her. She figured he'd had her pick up food because he'd be coming a bit later. She gathered her belongings, shoving them into the pockets of her coat so she'd have free hands for the food. She climbed out of her truck and grabbed lunch/dinner and headed toward the house.

"Hey!"

She looked over to see her husband coming out of one of the outbuildings, wiping his hands against each other as he did. "What are you doing?" she called back, noting his flannel shirt and old, worn jeans. Definitely not work clothes.

He walked over to her, leaving a kiss on her cheek as he took the pizza box from her. "I was putting the last of those boxes in there," he explained. "Come see."

She followed him into the summer kitchen and, sure enough, all the boxes had been removed as well as some random items like the old kerosene heater and some old metal truck toys. The couch was still there, as was the TV, and a couple plastic shopping bags with unknown items in them.

"I got you some more of that cleaning stuff that you said won't hurt the…the…"

"Baby?" Willow offered dryly.

"Yeah. The baby." He looked at her, eyes bright and looking rather proud of himself. "Come on," he said, heading toward the door. "One more thing to show you."

They entered the house. Willow noticed immediately that all the computer junk was gone from the dining room. She was stunned. "My gosh, you were busy!" She looked at him. "Where did all this stuff go?"

"Upstairs. I need to get everything organized, but it's up in that third bedroom." He set the pizza box down on the counter. "And," he added, nodding toward a vase of daisies on the breakfast bar. "Picked those up too."

She looked at the flowers, a little confused. "Daisies?"

"Yeah," he said confidently, again looking mighty proud of himself. "Your favorite."

Since when? But she simply smiled. It was a nice gesture, so no need to totally blow up his bubble. "That was sweet, Kevin. Thank you."

He grinned, moving over to her. "So, I was thinking after we eat dinner, we might spend a little time together."

She looked up at him, no idea what to say. Six months ago she would have been delighted, but now all she felt was sadness. She wasn't ready to talk about it, so she smiled. "Let's eat."

They sat at the newly cleared dining room table, though looking around she could see a lot of cleaning needed to be done. All his junk had sat there for two years; it hadn't been swept, baseboards were filthy. However, she was just glad all his crap was out of there. She dreaded seeing the state of the third bedroom.

"So I told him, these goddamn kids keep causing loops in the network…"

Willow nodded now and then as she picked off mushrooms from her pizza, tossing them with disgust onto his plate.

"…too many group policies took for-fucking-ever for things to boot up…"

She looked out the window, watching as the snow began to fall in earnest. There was the storm the weather guy had mentioned that morning.

"…oh, and the printers! Jesus. Don't even get me started on the printers…"

She thought it was supposed to be around twenty that night for a low. Maybe she'd pull out the electric blanket for Christine's bed.

"Don't you think?"

Wide-eyed, Willow's head jerked up to meet his expectant gaze. "Hmm?"

"I think we should get some more firewood. I asked if you agree." His face looked a bit like a combination of confusion and irritation.

"Yes," she said. "Definitely. It's already snowing."

※ ※ ※ ※

Later that night, Willow lay in the darkness of their bedroom. She'd pulled her pajamas on after, as had Kevin, who snored softly next to her. She glanced over at him, wishing she could be so at peace just to fall into slumber. Sleep was far from coming for her.

After dinner, they'd gone and bought some firewood, then started a fire in the fireplace and had watched Christmas movies on TV. Well, that is to say, the movies had been playing while Kevin stretched out on the couch and played golf on his phone while Willow spent time on social media, hoping that Christine would jump on. She hadn't. Disappointed yet knowing she was busy, she'd sent her a message, wishing her a good night.

When it was finally time for bed, true to his word, Kevin had initiated "some time together." Her instinct was to rebuff his advances, but she decided she needed to try one last time to see if sex with her husband was something she enjoyed or wanted.

Kevin wasn't the worst lover she'd ever had, not that she'd had many, but there wasn't a lot to it. Perhaps that was all sex was? She'd had sex with three people in her entire life. She'd lost her virginity to her first boyfriend late in high school and that was it— just the one time. Nothing to write home about, for sure. She'd dated another guy in college for about a year and she wasn't much more impressed with him. When she found out he was cheating on her, she'd happily let the other girl have him.

Then there was Kevin. She studied the back of his head as he slept facing away from her. She felt no need to reach out to him, to touch him, even just to connect for a moment. She felt no need to spoon up behind him just to feel his warmth.

Their intimacy earlier had been essentially coordinated. You undress yourself, I'll undress myself, and then assume the position. Very little kissing, no touching just to touch—other than him squeezing her right tit like he was looking for a good melon. She was still sore from that, especially with her breasts being extra sensitive from the pregnancy.

It was clear from that "foreplay" that there would be absolutely no orgasm in her future, so she'd waited for him to finish, which hadn't taken long, then tugged on her pajama pants and T-shirt to get warm beneath the covers. Was that what it was supposed to be like? She couldn't imagine that was the case. She had watched Rachel and Andrew.

They were cute together, and he was so considerate of her. She'd seen the way they looked at each other, even if they were seated away from each other in a large gathering. They always seemed to know where the other one was. And, though she and Rachel didn't talk all that much about sex or their respective sex lives with their husbands, she could see a connection between those two, an intimacy.

That had never existed with her and Kevin. They cared about each other, and she did believe that Kevin loved her and she did love him. But it was more of a fondness, not a passion.

Then there was Julie and Remmy, the gold standard for her. They were best friends, deeply passionate about each other, and deeply connected in a way Willow hadn't really seen before. They finished each other's sentences and were so amazingly solicitous of the other, almost anticipatory of the other's needs. She'd never seen them fight, though had seen them disagree. It was always handled with love and respect.

She wanted that.

She thought of the exercise Julie had had her do the other day on their walk, trying to imagine the young woman taking pictures. Could she see herself kissing her or being kissed or touched by the young woman? She decided to repeat the exercise, but flip the coin over.

She thought about some of the men she worked with. Tried to think of one she found particularly attractive or really liked as a person. A doctor came to mind, Allen. He was just a little older than she was and was kind, smart, had a great smile, and was just an all-around good person.

She tried to imagine them in an intimate situation. Kissing. She closed her eyes and tried to bring it to mind. She could see it, could even imagine a little what his lips would feel like, but then it all evaporated in her mind's eye, leaving her feeling empty. She tried again, thinking of good-looking actors, athletes, models—anybody to try and get a reaction from her body.

Nothing.

Her mind turned to Christine. She gasped at the instant arousal that nearly made her clench her legs together. Any and all juices that her brief encounter earlier had failed to produce were leaving her panties utterly saturated now.

Unbidden, images of the singer came to mind, her face, her mouth, her beautiful hands as they'd so gracefully made their way across the piano keys. She imagined those hands being so graceful across her body. What would Christine's hands feel like on her breasts? A new kind of ache cinched her nipples into hard pebbles.

She thought of the two kisses they'd shared. Though quick and certainly not meant to arouse, they had given her an idea of what it could be like to kiss her. Her lips so unbelievably soft, not chapped. No bristly hair on her upper lip to make Willow wince and wipe at her face.

Softness. Curves. Gentleness.

Willow stared up at the dark ceiling of her bedroom. Again, she forced herself to return her thoughts to the man lying next to her, the one she was legally bound to and who was the father of the baby she was carrying. Could she continue with him? Could she swallow her own wants and desires, that she had only recently discovered she had at all, and simply be the dutiful wife and just live for her child?

"No," she whispered into the darkness.

Chapter Eighteen

"I understand you have a big interview coming up with the American TV show, *Conifer Talks*," British TV host Gerard Walsh said with a boyish grin. "Give us a little taste of what you'll be talking about?"

Christine laughed as she looked out at the live studio audience who was cheering her on. "Now, now, Gerard," she scolded dramatically. "You know I can't do that."

"Fine." He pouted. "But I do know what you can do!" Gerard rose from his seat. "Ladies and gents, let's give Swann a huge hand as she sings her new song, 'Safe Harbor!'"

Grateful to get away from the talking, Christine pushed up from the couch and walked over to where the piano had been brought out for her. A back wall in the set rose to reveal the twenty musicians she'd rehearsed with before taping began.

As she began to sing, she found her soul. She thought of the woman who had inspired the song, and who had begun to inspire more and more of her decisions. That scared the hell out of her, but she couldn't help it. She wanted to make Willow proud of her, and felt herself leaning into that bright light, like a plant in the darkness seeking the sun.

As she sang, she felt Willow's spirit with her, felt her strength. Willow was quickly becoming her muse, and it made her extremely nervous, yet there was nothing she could do to stop it. Her entire career, pain and anger had been her muses. She was now learning to refocus, a new perspective.

The song came to an end and the studio audience was on its feet. She turned on the piano bench and smiled. The reaction she was getting to these new feelings, new perspective through the reaction to the song that embodied it, validated how she felt, and it meant everything to her.

She bowed in deep gratitude.

⁂

Jet-lagged and exhausted from two weeks' worth of appearances packed into about four days, freshly showered and wrapped in the fluffy robe provided by the hotel, Christine plopped down into one of the chairs in the living room portion of the suite, phone in hand. She hadn't had a minute to catch up on emails or messages or even voicemails for two days.

She wasn't in the mood for voicemails, so went to messages, as she knew only those that were deemed pertinent by her team ever got to her. She dealt with those, then signed into her dummy account on social media, created with one purpose and the one single friend on it. She smiled when she saw that one single friend had messaged her.

Willow: Hey, you. I hope you're doing okay. Haven't talked to you in a couple days. Miss you.

She was surprised to see that Willow was online. Glancing at the clock, she did the mental calculation of what time it was in Colorado. It was only 3:12 in the afternoon. She went ahead and sent a video call. She knew if Willow could answer she would, if not, she wouldn't. Her smile was instant when the call was picked up and she saw the beautiful, smiling face of her faraway nurse.

"Well, hey, there. Looks serious." Christine laughed. Willow had her hair pulled back in a ponytail and a bandana Rosie the Riveter style. She had smudges of dirt or something on her cheek and forehead.

Willow grinned, a little sheepish. "Yes, well, I'm cleaning the summer kitchen for you."

Confused, Christine quirked an eyebrow. "Summer kitchen? As opposed to…?"

"Oh. Right." The phone's camera was reversed to show the room Willow was in, revealing a space that was the size of a medium bedroom with a counter and sink setup, which she found confusing. There was also a couch and a TV on a stand that were shoved over to one wall. The camera refocused on Willow again. "These little buildings were built for the canning to be done during the summertime," she explained. "Thus, 'summer kitchen.' Didn't heat up the house when air conditioning wasn't available and it was too expensive to run fans."

"New one for me," Christine said, turning sideways in the chair so she was resting against one arm and her legs were flung over the other. She was glad Willow wasn't there, as her robe fell open. She grinned to herself and made herself somewhat presentable again. "Why are you doing that? I mean, if you're that bored and want to clean, I've got an entire house in Malibu…"

Willow's smile washed away all of Christine's

stress and weariness. "Bring it," she teased. She grew serious quickly, though. "You look very tired. I can see tension in your face. Is everything okay?"

"Yeah, it's great," she said, trying her best to sound upbeat, but she could see on Willow's face that she wasn't buying it. "No," she finally admitted with a tired sigh as she ran her hand through her damp hair. "Very tired. Very stressed. Very nervous about Wednesday."

"The talk show?" Willow asked gently. At Christine's nod, Willow got the cutest little look of confusion on her face. "Where are you? Doesn't look like your house."

The singer shook her head. "It's not." She held the phone up and moved it around to show Willow a quick view of the hotel suite. "I'm in London," she said, bringing the camera back to her again. "I'm sorry I didn't have time to tell you. I had about two hours to pack and get to LAX before this whirlwind circuit of talk shows and mini-concerts here."

"Oh, wow." Willow sounded almost wistful. "I think that would be exciting," she said, "Being wanted on both sides of the pond."

Christine grinned. "How do you know you're not wanted on both sides of the pond?"

The look on Willow's face could be described in two words: pure sex. "Oh?"

Christine was left speechless for a moment. If she'd flirted so brazenly like that before, Willow would have smiled shyly or looked away. But this woman… not only did she catch the ball, she threw a curve ball back. She felt a little moisture trickling between her legs.

"Oh, yeah," she murmured.

She knew that her robe was open a bit, both from her relaxed position on the chair and from moving earlier. She decided to send a spitball back. She subtly adjusted her phone, allowing a bit of her cleavage to come into frame. One thing she'd always been told was that she had great legs and great breasts. She was fine with using that to tease the woman that she suspected was pure tiger beneath that sweet, compassionate demeanor.

Willow glanced down at the exposed flesh before her gaze flickered up to meet Christine's through the screen. There was fire in those green depths, now turned emerald. "I see," she said, her voice dropping an entire octave. It was time for Willow to look away, the camera falling for a moment as her hand readjusted. Christine could see she was flushed, like a teenage girl seeing a little flesh for the first time. She cleared her throat and looked back into the camera, seeming to gather herself. "How long will you be there?"

Christine decided to give her a break and readjusted her own phone, more centered on her face than down her partially open robe. "I leave tomorrow." She blew out a breath, running her hand through her hair again. Sexy play over, her nerves were coming back. She stared off into space for a moment as she considered the next hectic twenty-four hours.

"Christine?" Willow said softly.

The singer's gaze returned to that in the screen. "Hmm?"

"What can I do?"

She smirked. "Other than hold my hand and tell me everything's gonna be okay?"

Willow was quiet, then her head tilted just slightly to the side. "Do you need me?" she asked softly.

Christine met her gaze and held it for a long moment. Finally, she let out a heavy breath. "What's good for me isn't good for you, sweetheart," she murmured.

Willow gave her the sweetest smile. One thing Christine was learning: a little vixen one minute to melt your panties and the sweetest person on the planet a minute later to melt your heart. "I didn't ask that now, did I?"

Christine chuckled, shaking her head. "No, no you didn't. As much as I feel like a loser to admit it, yeah, I need you. Your strength in all this."

"Tell me when and where, and I'll be there."

"No," Christine said, shaking her head as she sat up in the chair. She let out a heavy breath and brushed her long bangs out of her eyes. "I can't let you do that, Willow. You have a job and…a husband to deal with." She hated herself for feeling such jealousy at that word.

"I have plenty of personal time to take at work, so don't worry about that," Willow assured. "As for Kevin, don't worry about that, either. If you need me, I'll be there."

❧❧❧❧

She held the phone to her ear as she paced back and forth in the kitchen, Mona on the other end of the line. She was dressed for the interview with Maureen, Swann toned down a bit. She wore her signature leather pants but a simple white top, fitted but tasteful. Her hair was her normal all over the place, but her makeup would also be toned down by the studio's makeup people. She needed the day to be about what she said, not what she wore.

"How much," she asked, eyes falling closed as her hand went to her forehead. "Jesus Christ," she whispered. "How the fuck did he get away with nearly twenty-two million dollars, Mona?" She wasn't accusatory toward the accountant, but angry nonetheless. "I'm the primary, right? Okay, then take the fucker off the account. Shut him down, and I want copies of *everything* sent to Jake," she said, referring to her new attorney, hired specifically for this case.

She heard a car drive up, so she walked over to the window near the front door. Her stomach did little nervous flops when she saw the black town car pull up, a very special passenger inside. Turning back to her phone call, she said, "I have to go. Please keep me posted, okay? I'll let you know when I make my move. Thanks again, Mona. Bye."

Ending the call, she took a deep breath, set the phone down on the small table just inside the entryway, and pulled open the big, wooden door, all smiles despite her inner turmoil. The driver got out of the car and opened the door for Willow, as well as pulled her bag out of the trunk. He tipped his hat to them both before climbing back into the luxury sedan and driving off.

Once he was gone, she hurried down to collect the duffel bag Willow had with her. She didn't need much, considering she'd be flying back to Denver the following afternoon. It was a quick trip, but so very much appreciated. And to Christine's delight, she'd be heading to Denver herself three days later.

Duffel bag heaved over her shoulder with one hand, she grabbed Willow's hand with her other one and tugged her toward the house. They didn't have long before the limo would arrive to take them to the studio, and she wanted her friend to have a chance to breathe after the two-hour flight.

They ended up in the guest bedroom, where she deposited the duffel bag on the bed. She'd had Milly freshen the bedroom for Willow's stay, as short as it may be. She turned to Willow, who stepped right into her awaiting arms. Neither said a word, simply absorbed. Willow was so warm and felt so good against her.

Closing her eyes, she buried her face in wavy, light brown hair. She inhaled her scent, able to smell her perfume and shampoo. "I'm so glad you're here," she whispered.

Willow nodded. "Me too." In the hug, she cupped the back of Christine's head, turning her own so her face was buried in her neck. "Are you okay?"

Christine smiled. "Yes," she said. "Now." Still holding the smaller woman, she said, "We've got about fifteen, twenty minutes before the limo gets here, so not sure if you need or want to do anything before we go. Pee, whatever."

"Limo?" Willow asked, pulling away just enough to look up at her.

"Yes, ma'am," Christine said, pushing some hair out of Willow's face, tucking it behind her ear. "The studio will send one to get us back and forth. A bit of a perk for agreeing to bare your soul on film." She gave Willow a disarming grin.

"Good to know." Willow stepped out of her embrace and looked around the space. "Is this your room?"

"Nope," Christine said. "Guest room."

"This is ridiculous," Willow muttered. "This guest

room is larger than my entire living room back home." She looked at the singer as if for an explanation.

"Hey now," Christine said. "I didn't build it."

Looking rather amused, Willow tugged playfully on the hem of Christine's shirt. "You need to leave so I can change. Don't want to look like a local yokel in the land of broken dreams."

"Do I have to?" Christine pouted, giving her a sexy little side-eye. When Willow raised an eyebrow, the singer chuckled. "All right, all right." She stole a kiss, giggling as she scurried from the room.

❧❧❧❧

The studio had sent Christine and Willow out to dinner after the taping, which had seemed to take forever. She honestly wasn't sure she would've been able to get through it if she hadn't been able to glance over at Willow in the audience from time to time, just long enough to gather her thoughts, emotions, or courage.

Maureen Conifer had been fair, her questions reasonable yet certainly not softballs. The audience had their share of questions, as well, and that hadn't been easy. The strange thing, she had to admit to herself, was she felt even closer to her fans during that time taping the show than she did at any one of her concerts. She was sharing something with them that was deeply personal and painful. And, just as Willow had predicted, they'd been warm, understanding, and incredibly protective.

Now, she gave Willow a tour of the house, needing distraction. Plus, she was proud of the house and wanted to share it. She was amused by Willow's comment that her bedroom suite was bigger than Willow's college dorm and first two apartments put together.

"You must think my farmhouse is pretty pathetic," Willow said, glancing over her shoulder at Christine as her fingers wandered over the smooth, cool wood of the giant four-poster bed.

"Not at all." Christine leaned against the doorway to the bedroom part, arms crossed over her chest. She knew she had to keep some distance from her guest or she'd do something she may just regret. "I love that farmhouse. This place is big and it's beautiful, but it lacks the warmth and feeling of family that your house has." She gave her a lopsided grin. "Though, I have to wonder how much of that warmth comes from the woman who lives there."

Willow smiled. "Nah, it's always felt like that there." She wandered from the bed to her dresser, looking at this or that. She picked up her bottle of perfume and spritzed just enough to smell the scent. "I like this on you," she murmured.

It was torture watching Willow touch her things. Not because she didn't want her to, but because she was envious of those hands, those fingers, running across those objects when she very much wanted them on her.

"My grandmother was a tough lady, but the most loving person I ever knew," Willow said, her circuit of the room bringing her back toward Christine. She stood in front of the singer, head slightly cocked to the side as she studied her. "I think she would have really liked you," she said softly.

"Yeah? Why's that?"

"Because you're honest," Willow said simply.

"Don't pull any punches. What you see is what you get, if you understand what you're looking at."

"I like that. Do you think you understand what you're looking at?" Christine asked, a bit afraid of the answer.

"Oh yes, very much so."

"What?"

Willow studied her for a long moment, so long it almost made the singer uncomfortable. When finally she began to speak, her voice was soft, soothing. "What I'm looking at is a woman who has been underestimated her whole life. Misunderstood. Because of that, you closed your heart. But," she added. "It's a heart that has bottomless depths for love, caring. You've given to those around you all your life. Yet, you don't know how to accept what others want to give you. You question it. Wonder if they're sincere, and if they are, are you worthy?"

Christine looked down at her fingers, which tapped lightly on her biceps. Finally, she met Willow's patient gaze. "You understand a lot."

"I watched you today," Willow said. "You were so charming, funny even, as you told this horrible story. And, why? Because you wanted everyone there to feel okay, to not be sad or feel uncomfortable." She placed her hand on Christine's arm, a gentle touch which sent a bit of a jolt through the singer. She was on emotional overload as it was. "You come off as so tough," Willow almost whispered. "You in your leather pants, so goddamn sexy. Your muscles and wild hair." She smiled, reaching up and running her fingers through said hair. "But at heart, you're a sensitive, gentle soul. I understand you very well."

Christine wasn't sure whether to cry or beg

Willow to marry her right then and there. Her choice was made up for her when she heard her phone ringing. She was expecting a phone call from the private investigator she'd hired per Adam's suggestion.

"I have to get that," she said, brushing the backs of her fingers down Willow's cheek and along her jaw before dropping her hand and heading to the other room where she'd left her cell.

Chapter Nineteen

Left alone in Christine's bedroom, Willow turned and took everything in once more before she decided to head to the guest bedroom and change into more comfortable clothes for the night. She'd dressed up for the show, never in her life having an experience like that. All the cameras, lights, crew, and everything that went into making the show run smoothly…it had been something to see.

She'd meant what she'd said to the younger woman moments before. She'd watched her during that show, watched how she reacted to the audience. She watched as Christine noticed a woman who was having an emotional reaction to something Christine was saying. Willow wondered if perhaps it had hit a personal nerve on some level for her, or if she was simply feeling a great deal of empathy for her favorite singer.

Either way, Christine literally changed her tone, becoming more upbeat, a little bit lighter, in order to comfort that woman sitting forty feet away. Willow had always suspected the true heart that beat in the chest of a rebel, but seeing that sealed the deal for her. No doubt every performer was good at reading their audience. It was probably a talent every bit as much as singing or playing an instrument or acting was.

The woman sitting on that dais today wasn't a singer reading her audience to see where she needed to put a little more sex or a little more attention. She wasn't performing, she was a woman baring her soul to a group of strangers that she was more worried about than herself.

As Willow swapped her blouse for a tank top and her skirt for a pair of cotton pants, she looked at her reflection in the mirror. Dressed, she grabbed her brush and brushed out the long, wavy strands of her hair. She was in trouble, that she knew more than ever.

Face washed and teeth brushed, she decided to go look for her hostess. She didn't hear her speaking on the phone anymore, so had to navigate the silence to find her in the massive oceanfront house. She ended up outside in the beautiful place that was the Japanese gardens. Christine sat on a bench near the fountain. Her feet were spread and her forearms rested on her thighs, hands dangling between her knees and her head down.

"Hey," Willow said softly, placing a tentative hand on Christine's back. "Everything okay?"

Christine lifted her head and the silent tears that slowly rolled down her cheeks glistened in the moonlight over the ocean. She shook her head. Willow slowly lowered herself to the bench to sit next to her, her hand continuing to rub slow patterns across the singer's back.

"What happened?"

Christine sat up a bit, her hands resting on her knees. "That was Tony, the private investigator I hired to find out what happened to my parents," she said quietly.

Willow stopped rubbing her back and grabbed one of her hands, their fingers lacing as their hands rested on Christine's thigh. "Okay."

"They're dead," Christine said, her voice little-girl-quiet. "Been dead this whole time."

"Oh, sweetheart," Willow whispered.

Christine looked up into the night sky, her tears turned silver. "Dad was involved in some drug dealing," she explained. "Messed with the wrong people, Tony surmises. Probably either tried to keep the money or keep the drugs. That day somebody came a callin'. When Dad didn't have the goods, they took them both. I think Mom was just collateral damage."

"And, if you'd been there?" Willow asked.

Christine's head fell again before she turned and looked at Willow. "Then I wouldn't be here." She gave the saddest smile Willow had ever seen. Her heart hurt for her. "I'm not entirely sure what's worse. Thinking they were out there somewhere, alive, and maybe better off without me, or thinking, what would my life have been like had he not done whatever he did to piss off the wrong people?"

"Who knows," Willow murmured, brushing Christine's bangs out of her face, some of the strands sticking to the tear trail. "All I know is that I'm so grateful to whoever made you leave that apartment that day. So grateful you're still here."

"Willow," Christine whispered, more tears falling down her cheeks. There was so much pain and loss in her eyes.

"I'm here."

"I need..." She swallowed, no more words following.

"What?" Willow's hand moved from her hair to rest on the side of her face. "What do you need, Christine? If I can do it, get it, or have it, it's yours."

Christine looked Willow in the eyes, leaning her cheek into her touch. "I need…" she said again.

Looking into her eyes, Willow saw it. It was a desperate need to connect, to feel something other than the heavy grief she'd had on her shoulders for so many years. She knew in that moment that she had a decision to make. One would deny the woman she was falling in love with what she needed, a woman who asked for so little. The other would end her marriage.

No more thinking to do, she held Christine's face with her hand as she leaned forward, lightly pressing her lips to hers. She could taste the saltiness of the singer's tears on her own lips as she just barely pulled away. She went back, pressing her lips to hers again, though this time she didn't pull away.

Christine responded, tilting her head just slightly as she deepened the kiss, her lips moving against Willow's, softness against softness. Willow sighed as the barest touch of Christine's tongue caressed her own. She welcomed the intimate caress, her hand sliding from the singer's cheek to the back of her dark head.

Willow sighed into the kiss as it became a bit more passionate. Christine was an amazing kisser, even during a time of such emotional tumult for her. Willow's heart raced and her body pulsed. She wondered if Christine was feeling the same as she ended the kiss and pushed to her feet. She looked down at Willow, extending a hand to her.

Looking at the hand for a moment, such beautiful fingers, she took it and allowed herself to be pulled to her feet. A look passed between them, almost as though Christine were asking one last time for permission, which Willow gave freely and willingly.

Without a word, Christine led the way back into the house and to her bedroom.

Willow's heart was about to pound out of her chest when they reached the side of Christine's bed, but she knew this was right, for so many reasons. Looking into Christine's tormented eyes, she tilted her head slightly, cupping that proud jaw that, in that moment, seemed so out of place in the lost little girl she was looking at.

"I'm here," she whispered.

Not entirely sure what to do, she decided to allow her instincts and her own needs to guide her. She stepped away from Christine and pulled down the covers of the bed before returning to the singer, who hadn't moved. She caressed her face again before leaving a lingering kiss on her lips.

Taking a deep breath for courage, Willow took a slight step back and reached down to the hem of her tank top, tugging the garment up and over her head. Left topless and feeling vulnerable, Willow continued. She hooked her thumbs into the waistband of her pajama pants and panties and pushed them both down her legs, kicking them off and to the side.

She glanced shyly at Christine, who was looking intently at what had been revealed. The amazing thing was, Willow didn't feel like a piece of meat or cheap, she felt worshipped, appreciated, and adored. Definitely a new feeling for her.

She took a step closer to the singer and gently tugged her fitted shirt up and over her head, revealing a white lace bra—not what she expected to find. She found   it sexy and, somehow, endearing. It depicted the dichotomy that was Christine Swann. Her gaze settled on the beautiful breasts that had haunted her ever since that cruel peek over video chat. In person, lovingly cupped in the bra, the creamy flesh of her cleavage sent a thrill of arousal through her. She wanted to touch, taste, and experience.

As she reached around Christine's torso to unhook the bra, her mouth found the soft warmth of Christine's neck. She heard a long, soft sigh from the singer, so figured she was doing it right. In her relatively few sexual encounters, she hadn't been wholly participatory. She'd often let him do whatever and she was largely Gumby, taking on whatever position she was nudged into.

The one time she'd initiated anything was the night she got pregnant, and it had been the woman she was loving at the moment who had inspired that desperate need. Now, she felt a passion swelling within her that was foreign yet somehow familiar. She felt like she was being allowed—and encouraged by Christine's fingers in her hair—to fulfill her fantasies, curiosities, and to explore.

When the bra fell away, Willow gasped softly as their naked breasts touched for the first time. She rested her hands on leather-clad hips as her mouth found Christine's again. This kiss was different than the others they'd shared. It was slow, wet, and breathy, and held a very different meaning. It wasn't about comfort or desperation, but about adding logs to a fire that was already lit and needed to be stoked.

Christine's hands trailed down the length of Willow's spine, making her shiver a bit at the sensation that nearly burned her. Her behind was cupped in warm hands, Willow's hips pulled tightly against Christine's as the kissing continued. She felt that gave her permission to do some touching of her own.

Her hands moving from Christine's hips, she trailed her fingers up the singer's sides, feeling the rounded sides of her breasts before reaching strong shoulders. Again that wonderful dichotomy, the strength of her shoulders and biceps covered in such soft skin.

After several moments, Christine eased the kiss to an end, resting her forehead against Willow's as they both were breathing hard. "Get on the bed, baby," she whispered.

Willow nodded, doing as asked. She crawled to the center of the large mattress, the sheets beneath her soft and cool. She watched as Christine quickly removed her boots and peeled the leather pants down over her hips and muscular thighs before stepping out of them, leaving her in a black thong.

At Willow's quirked eyebrow, she grinned. "Can't have panty lines with leather."

Those, too, went, leaving the singer gloriously naked. She climbed onto the bed, her gaze fixed on Willow, who thought her reminiscent of a panther slowly creeping up on her prey. Christine was magnificent. She reached for her, a need for her growing by the second.

Willow accepted Christine's body as she lay herself down atop the nurse, gently nudging Willow's thighs apart. Though it was a position Willow was very familiar with, it felt so different with Christine. It wasn't about the boring same ol', same ol', let's get this over with. It was intimate and deeply arousing to feel Christine's breasts press against her own. And, when the singer adjusted her hips so that her clit was pressed against Willow's, white-hot lightning of sensation hit Willow squarely between the legs, so much so she gasped.

Willow moaned into their renewed kiss as she opened her legs a bit wider, bringing her knees up closer to her body as Christine began to slowly move against her, hard slick clit against hard slick clit. She could hear how wet they both were with every small movement of their hips together.

Soon it became too difficult to kiss with their heavy breathing, but Christine stayed in her personal space, Willow looking into her eyes as they made love. And, for Willow that's exactly what it was. She'd had sex before, even with her own husband. But she'd never made love, never understood just how different the meanings truly could be.

Pleasure began to grow, and even as Willow wanted Christine to quicken her pace, the singer refused, instead keeping her movements slow and steady. To her surprise, that brought on an orgasm that was almost numbing from the absolute explosion of it. It may have started in her clit, but the intensity and power flowed through her entire body like a shockwave from a bomb.

She cried out, long and loud, as she clung to the woman on top of her, who followed moments later. She held Willow tightly to her as she ground her hips into Willow's, a small second cry erupting as Christine's body shuddered.

Unable to speak, unable to see as her eyes were squeezed closed, unable to even think, Willow buried her face in Christine's neck. Her own quick, hot breaths warmed her face as they blew back off the soft cocoon she'd found.

Finally, Christine moved off of Willow to settle beside her. She braced her upper body with her forearm and used her other hand to cup Willow's face as she kissed her, soft, comforting, loving. She sat up and grabbed the sheet and blanket, pulling them over their bodies as she nestled with her head on Willow's shoulder, Willow's arm tucked around her, fingers in her hair.

"Is this okay?" Christine asked, uncertainty in her voice.

"It's perfect," Willow responded, absolutely loving the feeling of Christine's naked body snuggled against her side, her hand cupping Willow's right breast almost possessively. She left a kiss on Christine's head. She could honestly say she'd never felt more content. "I always dreamed it could be like that."

Christine settled in even closer, seeming to need to be as close as possible. "Me too." She snorted derisively. "I like sex, certainly enjoy a good orgasm," she said softly. "But I now understand that it was just that, sex, an orgasm."

Willow listened, her fingers absently wandering from the softness of Christine's short hair at the back of her head to the even softer skin of her shoulder and upper back. She wanted to ask questions but sensed that Christine needed to just talk, think out loud.

"Early on I learned how to separate the body from the heart," she continued softly, fingers lightly stroking the rounded outer side of Willow's breast, as if just to feel, not to seduce. "So, because of that, sex has never been an emotional experience for me. I never tied the two together. Does that make sense?"

"Makes absolute sense," Willow said, resting her cheek against Christine's forehead. "I can relate. It's always been a means to an end for me, typically an end for the guy whining that he was horny." She smiled at her own words. "God, that sounds awful, doesn't it?"

"No." Christine was quiet for a moment then asked, "You once said that you and Kevin don't have sex that much. Why?"

"Neither of us wants it, but for two different reasons."

Christine lifted her head, resting it in an upturned palm as her elbow pressed into her pillow. She looked down into Willow's face. "What are they?"

"Kevin is asexual—at least that's what he calls it," Willow explained easily. "It's just not something he needs in the traditional way, I guess. And, I didn't want it from him."

"Are you asexual too?"

"No," Willow said, shaking her head. "I did, however, think there was something wrong with me. I had a sex drive, needs, all that, but I just took care of it myself for the most part. The men I was with didn't do it for me."

"No?" Christine murmured, her fingers trailing to Willow's nipple, eliciting a little gasp from her as they lightly tugged at it, gently twisting the sensitive flesh until it began to harden. "Why not?"

Willow's eyelids were growing heavy as fresh arousal began to lay its warm blanket upon her body. "The larger reason is because they were men," she said, her voice becoming deeper as she was getting wet all over again. "But," she managed, eyes closing as Christine's head dipped, her mouth replacing her fingers on her breast. "I think part of it, too, they weren't you."

Christine groaned her approval at that around the hard nipple, which she batted with her tongue. She held her upper body up on her forearms on the bed on either side of the nurse as she focused her attention on her breasts.

"Christine," Willow whispered, head falling to the side as she was licked and lightly sucked. The attention was as gentle as it was arousing, making her body move of its own accord like a slow wave of desire. She was so wet, her clit pulsing and aching.

After a generous amount of time spent on both breasts, Christine began to kiss her way down Willow's gently writhing body, humming against the skin of her stomach, yet to show much of her pregnancy beyond a small pooch.

She was sure where Christine's mouth was headed, and it filled her with both excitement and nervousness. She'd never had anyone put their mouth on her before, so had no idea what to expect. What she knew right now was that she felt unbelievably erotic.

Christine settled herself between Willow's legs, strong arms wrapping around her thighs, holding her open and lowering her mouth to the volcanic heat of Willow's greatest need. Willow's neck and back arched back a bit at the first long, slow lick of Christine's tongue through her folds, from her entrance to her clit then back down.

One of her hands made its way down into Christine's hair as the other gripped the sheet beneath her. Her hips rolled with Christine's tongue, whimpers beginning to escape from her lips as she grew lost in the pleasure. Much like when she'd made love to her before, Christine's ministrations were maddeningly slow, but the amount of sensation that they drew out had Willow's breasts heaving with her, breathing and random cries and gasps flowing from her.

Finally, she couldn't take it anymore. "Baby,'

she whimpered. "Oh my god, please make me come."

Christine growled deep in her throat as she held her thighs tighter as she acquiesced. Her tongue became relentless as she sucked Willow's clit into her mouth.

"Oh my god." Willow gasped, her body straining as her orgasm creeped up on her, little tendrils of promise vining out into every part of her until finally, she came hard. Her upper body was thrown slightly forward with the intensity of her release. Her mouth opened and eyes squeezed tightly closed, though she made no more sound as her body shuddered violently with the last of the wave that hit her.

Panting, she fell back to the bed, limp, her legs splaying open uselessly as Christine released them. She felt lightheaded as she'd been nearly hyperventilating. Her brain could just barely detect Christine making her way back up her body, leaving little kisses along the way. When she kissed her mouth, Willow groaned when she realized the slick, warm tanginess on Christine's tongue was her own desire.

"Holy cow," she managed when Christine lifted her head from the kiss.

Christine chuckled, reclaiming her former position snuggled up next to the nurse. "I agree," she said softly, once again pulling the covers up and over them.

Chapter Twenty

Since she'd only been gone two days, Willow had left her truck in short-term parking. She'd been in such an emotional state, worried about Christine when she'd left, that she'd just jumped in her truck and driven like a mad woman to catch the flight that had been booked for her, not even thinking about a ride to or from.

Now, on the long drive back to the ranch, she was glad that she was alone and had some time to contemplate the previous twenty-four hours. Everything was different for her, her perspective on every aspect of her life irrevocably changed. It had gotten harder and harder for her and Christine to say goodbye, even from a phone or video chat. But, after spending the entire night and morning making love in between what amounted to be naps, it had been a lot of hugging and even more tears to finally get into the black sedan that would take her to LAX.

The entire flight home, she'd relived their moments together. Yes, they'd made love, but they'd also talked and laughed, they'd touched, endless kissing. She loved kissing Christine, even if it simply led to another nap. Her lips were so soft, her touch so gentle yet deeply sensuous.

The one thing they hadn't talked about was… now what? Christine's life was in California and around the world, Willow's in Colorado. Then, of course, there was Kevin. Willow, however, had a pretty good idea what was going to happen with that. Christine or no Christine, Willow had discovered the part of herself that had been missing, the part that she'd been too afraid to recognize. She was now ready to face that part of herself head-on.

Pulling onto the property, she saw Kevin's car was there, as well as the smattering of snow that remained from the last storm. He'd threatened that if she left he may not be there when she got back. Well, there he was, yet she had no idea what awaited her inside.

Pulling into her parking spot, she cut the engine and unbuckled before climbing out of the truck and grabbing her duffel bag from the back seat. She eyed the house as she walked up to the porch, seeing no movement inside. The door was unlocked, so she let herself in. The house was quiet save for the distant tick-tock of her grandmother's clock that still hung in the living room.

Heading to the kitchen, Willow let out an irritated sigh and rolled her eyes. She allowed the strap of her bag to slide down her arm before the bag landed on the floor at her feet. The room was an absolute pigsty with food containers left open or empty on the counters, dirty dishes in the sink, and a half-drunk glass of milk on the breakfast bar.

"Goddamn it, Kevin," she muttered.

She went about cleaning up the disaster that was her kitchen. She was tired, had a lot on her mind, and the mess was the last thing she wanted to have to deal with. What got her was, she'd been in that house the day before. How on earth had he made such a mess in such a short amount of time? Not like she'd been gone a week.

"Thought I heard you drive up."

She turned to see her husband walk up to the entrance to the room. He was wearing a white undershirt that was slightly stretched out from wash and wear. His flannel pajama pants were a little twisted around his hips and his hair was sticking up in crazy spikes.

"Were you sleeping?" she asked, noting that it was nearly six thirty at night.

"Yeah," he muttered, padding into the room and opening the fridge.

"Why were you in bed so early?" she asked, gathering his mess, starting with the trash and the food.

"What do you care?" he asked, taking out the milk jug and removing the cap before taking a huge swig from it, the white liquid spilling down the corner of his mouth and onto his shirt.

"Jesus, Kevin," she exclaimed, slamming a Styrofoam container down on the counter. "Can you please act civilized?"

He lowered the jug, wiping his mouth with the back of his hand before looking at her and opening his mouth, a long, loud belch erupting. Disgusted, she turned away from him, stuffing his trash into the garbage can, which needed to be taken out.

"Classy, Kevin. Real goddamn classy," she muttered. She indicated the kitchen. "What the hell, Kevin? You know I can't stand the house to be such a disaster."

"Yeah," he said, shoving the milk jug back into the fridge. "And you knew I didn't want you to go, but you went anyway." He smirked at her. "Ain't life a bitch?"

Willow nodded, using her booted foot to compact the trash in the can so she could add more to it. "I see," she said, shaking her head, her irritation growing. "Very mature."

"You owe me some answers," he said, arms crossed over his chest, feet planted wide apart in an aggressive stance.

She added more trash to the can and considered what he'd said. Truth was, he was right. *Here we go.*

"What the hell was so important that you had to run to California?" he asked. "Irresponsible to me and irresponsible to your job."

"She needed me, Kevin," Willow said, her voice filled with the annoyance she felt. She wasn't so annoyed at him, as he had every right to ask the questions he was asking. She was annoyed at the situation, which she wished she could make go away. She hated confrontation, but this was going to be the biggest moment of confrontation of her life thus far.

"For what?" he asked. "She's a grown-ass woman."

"She needed my emotional support, Kevin," Willow said, feeling defensive.

"What? Then she needs to get a shrink or a dog. Why did she need you? Why you?"

Willow looked at him. Such a loaded question. She needed to be honest with him. All their years together, she owed him that. She owed herself that. "I went there to support her while she did an interview with Maureen Conifer," she explained. "For the first time she was going to divulge the events of her very traumatic childhood. Nobody knows about it, and it was very difficult for her to do."

He studied her, his face like stone, all expression

carefully guarded. He said nothing, so she continued, her heart in her throat.

"I slept with her while I was there," she said, voice flat as she swallowed her emotion and fear. She saw his jaw muscles begin to bulge and pulse, but other than that, he didn't move. "That was absolutely not my reason for going to Los Angeles," she said, not entirely sure how true of a statement that was. "But it did happen, and I want to be honest with you."

He looked away, almost as though he couldn't stand to look at her anymore. He reached a hand out, bracing himself on the breakfast bar. "I've known something was wrong for a bit now," he said quietly, still not looking at her. "I could feel it." He slapped his hand down on the counter hard, making Willow jump. "I'm losing you, aren't I? To her."

She leaned back against the counter closest to her, hugging herself. "You're not losing me to her, Kevin," she said softly, and it was true. "But you are losing me, yes. You're losing me to myself."

"What does that even mean?"

"It means that I've been a shell for a long, long time. Hiding from myself, and therefore hiding from you."

"Is it because of my sexual situation?" he asked. "Not really being into it?"

"No," she said, shaking her head. "It's because of *my* sexual situation. The fact that you're asexual isn't the problem. The fact that you're a man is the problem. The fact that I'm a lesbian is the problem."

"So I was right to not trust spending so much time with Julie and Remmy?" he accused. "They got to you, didn't they?"

"What? Kevin, what are you—"

"They talked you into this, didn't they? And then that singer, rich, influential, all that LA bullshit, she made you do this, didn't she? You want to be like her, so you gave in—"

"Kevin!" It was her turn to slam the counter with the heel of her hand. "Goddamn it, listen to me!" She placed her hand on her own chest. "I am a lesbian."

He looked away from her, shaking his head.

"Do you honestly think that I'm that much of an invalid that I can't think for myself? That I can't figure things out for myself?" When he still refused to look at her or respond, she turned her back to him, hands braced on the counter as she leaned on them, silently asking for strength to not kill him. "You know, I'm wrong. The biggest problem with you for me isn't just that you're a man, but also the fact that you can be so damn entitled." She turned back around to face him again. "Who do you think you are?"

He still remained silent, but he met her gaze at least. His jaw was tight, arms crossed so tightly across his chest the muscles in his forearms stood out in relief.

"Do you have so little respect for me that you think I need others to guide me?" She snorted. "But then, I guess you've had that job for thirteen years, right?"

He ran a hand through his hair, his hands going to his hips. "So, what does this mean, then?" he asked. "For us? For me?"

"I want a divorce," she said quietly. "Neither of us can give the other what we need."

"You mean, I can't give you what *you* need," he said bitterly.

"That's right, you can't," she agreed, doing her

level best to not get bitter or nasty in return. She had her own hard feelings in all of this, but none of that mattered anymore. "I can't give you what you need either, Kevin. I can't just go along to get along anymore. Something in me has changed, woken up."

"Are you saying I'm controlling?" he asked, again taking the aggressive posture.

"Yes, I am. But I allowed it. I didn't fight you on much, and eventually, it just became the way things were. So, you want to know what's happened lately, why you've felt threatened or that something was wrong? I started standing up for myself. Simple as that."

He looked as though he wanted to argue with her, mouth opening then closing. He shoved his hands into his pants pockets, a sign she recognized as him knowing she was right but would never admit it.

He cleared his throat. "Tell me the truth. Have you been fucking her all this time? These last few months?"

Willow shook her head. "No. That's the truth."

He nodded, chewing on his lip. "Are you going to be with her now?"

She let out a heavy breath and a shrug. "I honestly don't know. I'd be lying if I said I didn't want to. But, this," she said, indicating the two of them. "Has nothing to do with her. Christine or no Christine, this would be happening."

He nodded. "Well, I'm going to stay at a hotel." He turned toward the kitchen doorway.

"Kevin," she called out. He stopped but didn't look at her. "I'm sorry I hurt you. That was never what I wanted."

He stood there for a moment, nodded, then continued on to the stairs.

⁂

After a full day back at work, Willow came home, the ranch eerily quiet. She usually got home before Kevin, but somehow his essence and energy was still there even when he wasn't. He was off for winter break with the school district, and he'd come the previous day to get some things while she'd worked a half day. She wondered if he'd been back today too.

Using her key, she let herself into the house, yet again noting the eerie silence. She tugged her neck scarf free before unzipping her heavy winter coat, which she hung up in the coat closet. All of his stuff was gone from there, leaving a perfect center line between her things and empty space. She scooted the hanger head across the bar, spreading out her coats and jackets. She was sure the same would need to be done upstairs too.

She walked into the kitchen in her scrubs, setting her purse and keys down on the counter. Curious, she checked cabinets and the pantry, wondering what he'd taken. She'd already decided that unless he took something that had belonged to her grandparents or was absolutely hers, she wasn't going to fight him.

Though she knew it had been the right move for her, and ultimately for him because of that, she still felt guilty. When you weren't used to fighting for what you wanted, let alone getting it, victory came with baggage.

She noted a few things he'd taken, mostly duplicates of this or that, though he had taken her bread maker. She wasn't thrilled about that, but a hundred-dollar appliance was worth peace of mind.

Willow glanced toward the direction of the front door when she heard a knock. She headed to the door and opened it to see a man standing there holding a gorgeous crystal vase filled with a massive amount of purple roses. She gasped, eyes wide as she took it all in. The poor man holding the massive bouquet could barely be seen.

"Willow Bowman?" he asked.

"That's me." She accepted the vase, which was surprisingly heavy.

"Have a nice day." With that, he turned and hurried down to his flower delivery van.

"Thank you, you do the same," she said, closing the door and carrying the huge arrangement to the kitchen.

Setting it down on the counter, she looked it over, marveling at what three dozen purple roses looked like. Absolutely gorgeous. She was sure she knew who was behind the delivery but plucked the card from the little plastic holder anyway.

Sending some purple until I get there tomorrow and I can say, "I'm here" – Christine

Willow smiled, her fingertips caressing the card, even though she knew the singer had never touched it. She also understood that she'd kept the message short and in a code that had developed over the past week. *I'm here* had begun to suffice as a message between the two of them that, certainly from Willow's point of view, neither was ready to say yet, but the feelings were there, the intent was there.

She decided to break up the bouquet and place

a vase in the living room and then a third upstairs in her bedroom. A beautiful, fragrant reminder of the new life she had chosen to fight for and was forcing herself to open up to. She did, however, have to wonder how much money Christine had spent on those flowers. Not just the number of them, but as it was late December, there was certainly nowhere locally that just had those on hand.

Shaking her head, she smiled as she arranged the flowers in their original vase for their photo op. She grabbed her phone and got to their social media messenger thread, hitting the video button. She swept the camera slowly over the flowers before turning it on herself.

"They're absolutely beautiful," she said to the women who would receive the video. "Just like you. I can't wait to see you tomorrow. I have a lot to tell you. Many changes have happened in the last twenty-four hours. I hope you're having an amazing day, and I'll talk to you later." She blew her a kiss and ended the video before sending it.

She felt light and happy, and honestly, the timing of the flower delivery, no doubt planned to arrive just after she got home from work, helped to boost her confidence that yes, she'd done the right thing.

As she made her way upstairs to grab a quick shower and change into warm, comfy clothes for the evening, she thought about the consequences as well. It would be difficult financially, she knew. The farmhouse was long paid off, but costs like property taxes still existed and were substantial.

She tugged off her scrubs top and tossed it into the laundry basket, followed by the long-sleeved shirt she wore beneath and then bottoms and undergarments.

As she made her way to the bathroom, a thought returned to her that she'd actually been considering for a while: selling off some of the land.

She turned on the water, a little more cold, then a little less, until the temperature was perfect for her to step beneath the spray. As she smoothed her hair back from her face, the water beating down the waves, her thoughts switched to her upcoming time with Christine. She didn't want to tell her about her and Kevin until Christine was there in person. They had a lot to talk about. Willow needed to know where the singer stood and what she wanted.

Which brought to mind, what did *she* want? That was a terrible habit she needed to break herself of, always considering the other person's wants and needs first. They were certainly important, but she couldn't allow herself to fall back into the soothing rhythm of complacency.

She knew for a fact that she'd never go back to men. Even if she were alone for the rest of her life, that was no longer an option she ever wanted to entertain again. She was tired of stuffing who she was into a trunk shoved into the dark recesses of the attic of her soul.

All that said, was she strong enough to take on a relationship with one of the biggest rock stars on the planet?

Chapter Twenty-one

ook at him," Christine whispered, accepting the tiny bundle into her arms. She couldn't help but smile, looking down at the tiny little nose and lips, his eyes closed as he slept in peaceful slumber. No doubt already tired of this strange new world he'd literally been pushed out into. "You're so tiny," she said, her smile growing when his little lips puckered for a moment before they stilled again.

"Isn't he beautiful?" Bug asked, a large hand running gently over the forehead.

"He is. This grandchild, how many?" she asked, meeting his gaze.

"Four." Bug looked every bit the proud grandpa. "First boy, though."

Christine rolled her eyes. "Girls are better," she murmured to the baby. "Don't you forget that, Gareth."

"You tell 'em, sister." Bug's wife Bonnie walked up to her and reached for the infant. "It's time for Mama to feed him," she said as the two women gently exchanged the week-old from one set of arms to the other.

Christine watched the bundle in his grandmother's arms and her mind went to the life growing inside of Willow. She knew she had a doctor's appointment while Christine was there for Christmas, and she wanted to go with her.

"Come on, Chris," Bug said, slapping the singer

on the shoulder. "Let's go listen."

He led her through the beautiful house in Redondo Beach he shared with Bonnie. He took her to his recording studio downstairs, which was a small affair with soundproofing on the walls, a small recording booth for an artist, an engineering booth, and his office just beyond. On the walls were all their records that had gone platinum or gold, framed and hung proudly. She had hers, too, but they were in boxes. For some reason, she'd never displayed them.

"So, what do you think of my boy?" he asked, plopping down behind his desk while Christine sat in a chair across from him.

"Cute as can be." She slung her arm over the back of the chair.

"He looks like his grandpop."

She smirked. "He's not hairy enough."

"When you gonna give in and have some kids?" he asked. "Settle down?"

"Well, I actually wanted to ask you about that," she said, feeling a bit shy. "How did you and Bonnie do it? You've been together forever, you in music the entire time."

"Shit, I was in music even before we met. But really, what it's boiled down to is communication. I never left her in the dark about nuthin' we were doing. Hell, she even went with us on a couple tours once the kids were grown."

Christine nodded, remembering that. "Makes sense. But, what about if she had her own career? I mean, I think Bonnie was mostly a mom and housewife, right?"

He nodded, reaching into the ever-present candy dish on his desk, snagging a handful of jelly beans before sliding the bowl toward her. She grabbed some, holding them in the palm of her hand as she cherry-picked which flavor she wanted. "Yeah, but she had stuff she was involved in, Chris. Groups, causes, stuff for the kids. She was a busy lady."

"What about you?" she asked. "How did it affect you, being away from the family?"

"I love my job, Chris," he said, tossing a few jelly beans into his mouth. "But my family is where my heart is. Always will be. It ain't easy, but it can be done. All about priorities, and keeping it straight in your head," he said, tapping his head with his finger. "Keep your ego in check, which you do overall, 'cuz that ego is what gets people in trouble."

She nodded, chewing on the candy thoughtfully. She met his gaze when he spoke again.

"One word of warning, kid," he said softly. "If you're gonna bring a lady into the life who isn't used to it, you have to protect her. Find you two a little nest somewhere." Eyes twinkling, he added, "Like Colorado."

She smiled, looking down at the remaining jelly beans in her palm. "If you weren't already from California, would you guys have left?"

"Oh, yeah. We talked about it. Gettin' a place in Arizona where Bonnie's sister lives. Ultimately, we decided to stay put. But, if all you got to do here is record…" He shrugged. "Fuck LA."

She studied him but said nothing. She was surprised by his somewhat veiled support of her situation with Willow. "Thanks, Bug," she murmured.

⁂

Christine didn't even need to don the Swann, as Bug would say, as she entered the downtown Los Angeles skyscraper where Robert Knowles's office was located. All smoky, mirrored windows. How appropriate, she thought. Smoke and mirrors, that was Bob Knowles.

She made her way up to his floor and, not bothering to speak to Gerta, his receptionist, she marched right on through to his office. The poor woman at the front desk knew better than to try and stop her. Christine simply gave her a nod of acknowledgment and went on her merry way.

Finding his closed office door unlocked, the singer barged in dramatically, the heavy door banging against the wall. Bob, who sat at the glass conference table with his attorney, nearly jumped out of his seat.

"You can go," she said to the attorney, whom she'd never liked. She'd always thought him slimy and toxic.

The man looked to Bob but then gathered up his belongings, shoving them into his leather satchel and got out, closing the office door behind him. Alone with her soon to be former manager, Christine eyed him as she walked around the table, making her way over to him. He followed her progress with his eyes, looking rather uncertain as she shark-swam her way to her prey.

Finally, she reached the chair to his left, bypassing six other chairs, wanting to extend his level of discomfort. She cocked her head as she studied him, the man who was dressed impeccably as always. Hair slicked back from his face, grown more bloated over time with age and a great love of scotch and bourbon.

"Mind if I record this?" she finally said, placing

her phone on the table. It was a practice they'd both long employed during important meetings with lots of information.

"Nope," he said. "As long as you don't mind that I am."

"Nope." She smirked at the joke that only she knew the punchline to. They sat in silence for a moment, eyeing each other. "So," she finally said, her voice like a gunshot in the silence. "I have some questions for you, Bob." She reached into her pocket and pulled out a thumb drive, tossing it onto the glass top. "You see, Mona did a little investigating for me, and wouldn't you know it, a whole buncha money is missing."

Bob looked down at the thumb drive, then over at her. As much as he was trying to keep his facial expression guarded, she could see he was squirming inside. "No idea what you're talking about," he finally said.

"No?" She gave him a saucy little grin that, depending on the intended audience, could look like she was about to eat you alive and give you the best orgasm of your life, or eat you alive and leave you for the vultures. Bob knew which was his fate. "We'll get back to that. So, I did a thing," she began conversationally.

He looked at her. "What 'thing'?"

She reclined in her chair, bouncing slightly on the springy back. "I went on Maureen Conifer's show."

"You what?" he said, finally coming alive. "I didn't arrange that, nor did I okay that. Her producers didn't contact me."

"Nope, they didn't. Turns out, I met and fucked one of her people at a party a few years back, and she still had my number. Go figure." She smirked. "Guess it's not just Kevin Bacon who can play connect the dots, huh? Anyhoo, Maureen called me personally."

"That's a breach of contract," Bob growled.

"Which I can dissolve at any time. No doubt that slimy piece of shit out there has his portable printer and can print you out a copy to peruse." She gave him a strange look. "What is it with that dude and his printer, anyway? Creepy. So, in essence, you're fired."

His jaw muscles tightened, but he didn't react otherwise. She knew him better than that, though. Inside that worm-filled mind of his, he was already planning revenge and trying to think of the best way to get back.

"Oh," she continued. "And don't bother with your plan to, as a friend put it so succinctly, 'trap me with my own trauma.' You see, I told Maureen, and the world, everything."

He smirked. "You told her how much of a little slut you were?" he asked, trying to get a rise out of her. At one time it would have sent her into a spiral of self-hatred and dependency on the one person she believed would rescue her—him. Too bad he hadn't realized the woman she was becoming. She was molting.

"If you're asking if I told her what I had to do to survive a horrible situation as a child with limited options, yes, I did." She didn't tell him how terrifying it had been, though. "Honestly," she said instead, revealing a truth that came later. "It was liberating." She was deeply pleased when she saw actual fear in his eyes. They both knew that was all he had on her, a weapon which he'd wielded to great effect.

"So, what does that mean for me?" he asked, voice low, and for once sounding a bit scared.

"That depends on you," she said, reaching and grabbing the thumb drive again, tapping it lightly on the glass table as she turned it round and round in her fingers. "Do you return my money, or don't you?"

"I was on that account legally, Christine."

"You were," she agreed, nodding. "But you're no longer. Incidentally, it was set up for a minor with the stipulation that it be used by you to help procure shelter for a fifteen-year-old breadwinner who couldn't legally do it for herself and other such things that a 'trusted' adult needed to do for her."

He glared at her, beginning to breathe heavily through his nose. "Without me you'd be nothing," he growled.

"No," she said evenly, refusing to take the bait. "Without you, I wouldn't have gotten to California as quickly as I did. Without *me*, you wouldn't have the successful career you've had. You rode *my* coattails, Bob, not the other way around. When you walked into that bar, you saw a meal ticket, and you cashed it in."

She placed the thumb drive flat on the table and, with a single finger, slid it over to him.

"To help jog your memory," she offered. "Now, with it being Christmas week and all, I'll be generous. You have until January first, New Year's Day, for that money—twenty-one million, eight hundred and seventy-two thousand dollars and thirty-five cents—to find its way back to me, no questions asked. Don't care if you deposit it back into the account or if it shows up on my doorstep in a cashier's check with a little bow on it. Whatever floats your boat."

"If I don't?" he asked, voice low and daring.

"If you don't, what?" she pressed. "Return the money you embezzled?"

"Yeah," he said, his bluster returning just in time.

She smirked and pointed to the thumb drive.

"Then my attorney will turn over a copy of that to the police." She reached over to her phone and made a show of turning off the recording app. "Along with this." She pushed to her feet, feeling mighty pleased with herself. She walked over to the door of the office, pulling it open. She glanced back over at him. "By the way, you're officially fired."

She didn't bother closing the door as she held her head high and shoulders squared, feeling better than she had in a long, long time. She felt strong, assured, and in control of her own life. She walked to her car and headed home. She had some packing to do.

⁂

At home, Christine quickly sent the audio file to her attorney before setting about to get ready for her trip. Milly had done laundry, and she was able to easily find everything she wanted to pack. The current plan was for her to stay until New Year's Day, then fly back. She wasn't sure what the situation was like with Kevin, and in a way was nervous to face him. She'd never met him, though after the time she'd spent with Willow when she'd been in California, she wasn't sure how successful she'd be at pretending like they were just friends.

Or, were they just friends? Yes, they'd made love, yes, it had been mind blowing, but yes, Willow was married. She was having his baby. That's a whole lotta reasons to stay, she thought. But she also had to keep in mind that she knew that going in. The moment she'd turned to Willow, needing her touch, needing her warmth and comfort, she knew she could very well be setting herself up for serious heartbreak.

Luggage packed and guitar chosen out of the many she owned, she carried or pulled everything to the front door of the house. It was quiet, as Milly was off for a few days to spend time with her sister in Anaheim.

Nothing else needed to be done, so Christine wandered the house, looking at this and that. She tried to see it through Willow's eyes, through some of the comments the nurse had made when she'd been there. Yes, it was large, yes, it was beautiful, and yes, Christine's own thoughts added, it felt so very empty.

Looking back at it now, no doubt the purchase had partially been driven by ego: look what I can do! Look how successful I am. It had been many years since she'd needed that sort of personal boost. Now, the money, the fans, the travel—all old hat. Just part of her life.

She ran her fingertips over the fine marble countertops in the kitchen. Took in the huge appliances that she never even used. Normally when she had time to waste, she was in the music room composing, usually just for her. But now she had nineteen hours before her flight, and all she could think of was getting to Willow.

"Fuck it."

She hurried to her bedroom, stuffing her phone charger and other last-minute items into a carry-on bag. Zipping it up, she shrugged into the straps and headed to the front door. She didn't want to be there. If home was where the heart was, well then she'd be catching the first flight she could that would take her seventeen hundred miles to the northeast.

Landing at DIA, Christine decided to rent a car for this trip. She knew Willow had to work during some of it, so she wanted to be able to explore. And, arriving a day early, Willow wasn't expecting her. From their conversation the night before, she knew she wasn't getting off work for another three hours. Some of that would be eaten up with the drive from the airport, but she had decided to spend a little time in Woodland.

As delighted as she was by the snow, she wasn't delighted as she had to figure out how to drive in it. Sitting in her rental SUV in the Hertz parking lot, she watched a few videos on how to do just that. Blowing out a nervous breath and removing her baseball cap in order to run a hand through her hair, she nodded.

"Okay," she muttered. "I got this."

She kept the radio low to keep her concentration high as she got on the road. Things were pretty clear on the main roads, which she was grateful for. She found it ironic that she'd grown up in a region where winters could be brutal, only to spend her early adult life in a region where sixty was considered a cold-ass day. And here she was, in her thirties and wanting to be nowhere else but back in a region with heavy winters again.

One thing she had to say for Colorado that New York could never rival was the mountain view. As she drove, she was left breathless by the snowcapped Rockies. She could only imagine how beautiful they'd be come spring and summer. She'd seen pictures, of course, and had little glimpses when in the area for concerts, but mountains and views weren't exactly her focus when visiting somewhere to perform.

She loved the wide-open spaces. It was so strange to her after the congestion of the city. So many people crammed into every nook and cranny, paying out of the ass for a tiny speck of space. She'd heard that Denver was getting expensive but knew it had yet to catch up to either coast, the places she'd called home thus far.

Pulling into town, she was again charmed by the main street of shops, some local, others part of a chain. She couldn't help but smile when she spotted Willow's hospital off to the right, the taller building seen over the tops of single- and double-story buildings of town.

She felt such a massive sense of pride at what Willow did with her life. It put her own life as an entertainer to shame. Willow should be the one making millions, not Christine. Perhaps before she left to go back to California she'd see if there was anything she could do by way of donations.

She watched the people walking along the sidewalks, some carrying bags with the logos on them from whichever store, no doubt last-minute Christmas shoppers. She'd done hers before leaving for Colorado. Well, truth was, she'd done hers weeks ago and was excited to watch Willow open her gifts.

She pulled to a stop at a red traffic light. She saw a pizza place to her right, and just beyond was a Mexican food place. Her stomach letting her know exactly what it thought of that after a long day of traveling, she pulled off to the shopping center where both places resided and found a parking space out of the way. Feeling a little naughty, she brought out her phone.

She pulled up her contact list and sent a video

call to Willow. She knew she wouldn't answer if she couldn't, but she still hoped she could. After a couple rings, the call was answered, and the absolutely beautiful face of her nurse responded, all smiles.

"Hi! I was just thinking about you as I finished up some paperwork."

"Oh, yeah?" Christine teased, careful to keep her surroundings out of the frame. "What were you thinking about?"

Willow grinned. "Can't say or I'll get myself fired."

Christine chuckled. "Well, then I'll stick to a good-girl topic. I'm hungry and can't decide what I want."

"What are your options?"

"Pizza or Mexican. At least, that's what I'm looking at." She grinned.

"What? What's that grin for?"

Christine turned the phone so the two restaurants could be seen by Willow before turning the camera back on herself. She chuckled at a very confused Willow.

"Wait, those are restaurants here" Her eyes flew open wide. "Are you here?" she exclaimed. When Christine gave her a slow nod and a shit-eating grin, Willow squealed, something that the singer found utterly adorable.

"Couldn't wait." She gave her a winning smile. "So, what is little you in the mood for?"

"Little me." She laughed. "Well," Willow said, looking at her watch. "I get off in thirty-five minutes. Can you cool your heels that long and I'll meet you at Jose's?"

"I'll be here."

Willow looked to her right, as though somebody were there or coming. Sure enough, somebody passed behind her. Once they were gone, she turned back to the camera. "I have to go, but I can't wait to see you," she said, so much in her eyes reflecting all that Christine felt.

Chapter Twenty-two

Willow glanced into her rearview mirror, her stomach fluttering with butterflies when she saw the headlights a little ways back. She almost felt giddy to know that Christine was behind those headlights. They obviously had to play it down at the restaurant, but she had been so excited to see her, and shocked that she'd come a full day early.

As they sat there across from each other enjoying a good meal, she felt how incredibly comfortable they were with each other. It seemed that now that the sexual tension had been not only acknowledged but also addressed—many times over—they were able to settle into just being themselves. They talked, they laughed. She absolutely loved Christine's personality. She was intelligent, witty, yet entirely willing to make fun of herself.

She hadn't told her about Kevin yet, feeling a public place wasn't exactly the right venue for that. She was nervous to tell her, as she didn't want the singer to think she had left Kevin for her, didn't want her to think she was making any assumptions or trying to put emotions into her mouth.

They crossed the Dittman Bridge, then soon after reached the turn for her ranch. Christine followed in her rented Explorer, unwittingly pulling up into Kevin's old parking space. She unbuckled herself and grabbed her belongings before climbing out of her truck.

"Am I in Kevin's way?" Christine asked, opening the door to the SUV.

"Nope," Willow said. "Not anymore." At the singer's confused look, she smiled and said, "Let's get your stuff in, it's cold."

They headed upstairs, Christine's backpack on Willow's back and her beloved guitar in her hands as Christine carried the bigger, heavier roller bag up to the second floor. At the doorway to the guest room—thank god she'd already put clean sheets on the bed—she stopped and looked at Christine, who stopped a foot away.

"So, Kevin no longer lives here," she explained.

Christine stared at her. "What? Why?"

Willow took a deep breath, then said, "I asked him for a divorce."

Christine fell back against the doorframe. "Wow," she murmured.

Willow felt a bit of panic wash over her. "I don't want you to think I did that because of you," she hurriedly added. "God, that sounded horrible. I mean, whether you were in my life or not, it was time for me to stop living a lie. Kevin, or any other man, isn't what I want, can't give me what I need. I know that now."

Christine looked down at the floor for a moment before she met Willow's gaze again, her own unsure. "Do you still want this?" she asked, indicating the two of them. "I mean, now that you figured everything out, and—"

"Oh my god, yes!" Willow stepped up to her, a hand going to her face. She looked deeply into her eyes. "Yes. I just didn't want you to think that I'd left Kevin because I was presuming anything." She stroked the softness that was Christine's cheek, finally resting her hand against her jaw. "You helped me find my truth, yes. But in so many ways, you *are* my truth."

Christine held her gaze for a long moment. Finally, she leaned in and left a lingering kiss on Willow's lips, a kiss that felt like it was full of promise.

"I do have one question, though," Willow said. "You can sleep in there with me," she said, indicating the bedroom she once shared with Kevin. "Or, you can sleep in here. Totally up to you."

Christine glanced past Willow down the hall, then into the darkened bedroom they stood in front of. "Which bed is bigger?" she asked.

"Mine," Willow responded. "But," she said, wanting to be totally honest. "It's where Kevin used to sleep. I understand if it's not exactly your idea of where you want to be."

Christine gave her that little lopsided, sexy grin. "I say we christen the shit out of it tonight, then go look for Christmas sales tomorrow and get a new bed."

Willow threw her head back and laughed, relieved. She trailed her fingernail along her jaw. "I like the way you think."

❧❧❧❧

Hours later after making love, getting up to lock up the house, making love again, then passing out, Willow awoke. She was snuggled in Christine's arms, head resting against her shoulder. Her body buzzed, content and sated. After her sexual past, either not wanting to be with the person or Kevin's asexuality, she was slowly coming to terms with the fact that perhaps she could have a sex life that she'd heard about from friends or read about in books.

She couldn't help but be haunted by the thought that when Christine got there, the passionate magic that had burned bright between them in LA would be gone, Christine either getting what she wanted the first time or simply seeing no reason to continue now. She couldn't have been more wrong.

Christine's passion for her seemed to match her own. Though Willow knew she had a lot still to learn, she was a very willing student. She was nearly obsessed with Christine's body, couldn't get enough of her. And the way she kissed, holy cow! She felt like at age thirty-five, she was only now discovering sex and passion.

This was ironic, of course, considering she was almost four months pregnant. It was also ironic that she'd always been so grateful Kevin had preferred to sleep in pajamas, when now she'd throw an all-out holy hell fit if Christine dared put on clothing of any kind in bed. Same for herself. She loved the feel of their skin together, so warm, so soft, especially as it was so cold outside and the old farmhouse, which needed to be reinsulated, could be drafty. Bring it, she thought. If it meant more naked cuddling under the blankets, she was all for it.

"You awake?" Christine murmured sleepily.

"Yeah," Willow whispered. "Did I wake you?"

"Hmm, must be the smoke coming from the hamster wheel," the singer said with a little chuckle. "Y'okay?"

"I'm perfect," Willow said, meaning it. She'd never in her life felt like she was exactly where she was supposed to be exactly when she was supposed to be there. Well, except perhaps that February night on

Dittman Bridge.

"I'll agree with that," Christine said, holding Willow a bit tighter and leaving a kiss on her forehead.

Willow smiled, letting out a happy sigh. "I have my doctor's appointment tomorrow," she said. "She's going to do the fetal DNA test. So, I was thinking, I have plenty of food here for you while I'm gone, then I'll hit the grocery store after the doctor—"

"Or," Christine said, brushing her fingers through Willow's hair. "I can just go with you to the doctor, then we can go grocery shopping together after."

Willow felt a bit emotional for a moment. They'd discussed the doctor before and the singer had shown interest in going, but Willow figured it was just out of politeness.

"Is that okay?" Christine asked, uncertainty in her voice. "Or, if I'm overstepping, if Kevin will be there, or you'd rather I not—"

"No." Willow raised her head, looking down into the singer's face. She smiled. "No, I want you to go. I didn't want you to feel like I was pushing anything on you."

"Baby?" Christine said softly, looking up into her eyes. "Please know that I'm very vocal about what I do and do not want to do. I don't offer unless I mean it. I don't say yes unless I mean it. I don't say no unless I mean it."

Willow smiled, nodding. "Okay," she whispered.

"And," Christine added. "I expect the same from you. I'll always only ask if I truly want to know what you think or feel. No bullshit from me." She grinned. "To my detriment often."

Willow leaned down and left a kiss on her lips.

"I'll work on it," she murmured. "And yes, I want you to go. And no, Kevin won't be there." She rested her head back on her shoulder, sleepiness beginning to hit her again. "Thus far, he's shown absolutely no interest in this baby, and honestly?" she added with a loud yawn. "I'm glad."

"Me too," Christine whispered, barely audible, almost as if to herself.

❧❧❧❧

It was the most awesome feeling in the world as Willow drove them around for their errands in her truck and Christine, belted into the passenger seat, chatted away with her hand planted firmly on Willow's thigh. It was everything she'd always dreamed of, what she'd always been so envious of in Julie and Remmy. A connection, a true connection.

"Are you excited to be a mother?" Christine asked, her voice light, happy. They'd just left the doctor, who had taken blood to run genetic testing and to determine the baby's sex.

"I am," Willow said, glancing over at her passenger. "I think that I'd known for so long that kids weren't an option being married to Kevin, I kind of numbed myself to the want. But now that I'm pregnant, I'm very much beginning to regain feeling again." She smiled at her own analysis.

"Gettin' the little tingles as they're waking up?" Christine offered.

"Tingles somewhere," Willow teased, tweaking one of Christine's breasts. She laughed when her hand was batted away. "What about you?" she asked. "Kids?" She was a bit nervous about the answer.

"Here's the funny thing about me," Christine said, her hand absently rubbing Willow's thigh. "Because of where I came from, my history, I thought I'd be terrible for kids, a big kid myself, but not in the good way, you know?" She looked over at Willow, who briefly met her gaze before returning her focus to the road. "Like, didn't know anything about anything, had a chip on my shoulder, all that stuff."

"I can understand that," Willow said with a nod.

"But when my band members began having kids…well, Bug's oldest is older than I am." She smirked. "I loved when they brought them around. Used to love to play with them. Loved their energy."

Willow nodded. "I completely understand. That's why I love the babies at work. It's so hard to see them hurting, and it kills me when we lose one, but I love it. Which," she said, slapping her hand lightly on Christine's on her thigh. "I'm going in tomorrow, Christmas Eve, for a bit to try and brighten their holiday."

"Um, baby, Pennywise the Clown is not gonna brighten their day. You're gonna scare the crap out of them."

Willow laughed, shaking her head. "Nooooo. I'm going as an elf." She pulled her truck into the parking lot of the grocery store, finding a space. Truck stopped, she glanced over at her. "You wanna come?" she asked.

"Can I bring my guitar?"

Willow's smile was slow and bright. "What a wonderful idea."

The grocery store was crazy busy as people bought last-minute holiday preparations. People were running around the large grocery store, muttering,

Excuse me, and, *Can you hand me that?* Holiday music was piped in through the sound system.

"Would you mind pushing the buggy?" Willow asked.

Christine chortled. "Buggy?"

"Well, what do you call it?"

"Um, a shopping cart. But yes, I will push the buggy," Christine said, stepping into place behind the rolling cart. "What do we need?"

As Willow looked for her list on her phone, she couldn't help but smile at the *we*. It certainly had a nice ring to it. "Well," she said, "I promised you some good, homecooked food over Thanksgiving but I had to work, so I'm going to fulfill that promise to you on Christmas."

Christine's eyebrows rose. "Really?" she said, a little suggestiveness in her tone.

Willow rolled her eyes and playfully swatted at her as they continued into the store. "Okay, I figure we can start at the front of the store and work our way to the back." She looked at Christine. "Good with that?"

"Where you lead, I'll follow."

"Good," Willow murmured. "You remember that." She walked away, an extra little sway in her hips as she did so, knowing full well she had a pair of deep blue eyes riveted to her ass.

As the cart began to fill, Willow glanced over at Christine, who was looking down at their treasures with a bit of confused sadness on her face. "What's wrong?"

Christine chewed on her bottom lip for a moment before meeting Willow's concerned gaze. "It just hit me," she said. "I've never done this."

"Done what?"

Christine indicated the cart and the two of them. "Never shopped for holiday dinner before, and never bought groceries with the person I…the person I'm involved with."

Willow met and held her gaze, something passing between the two, straight to her heart. She smiled, lightly squeezing Christine's arm. "Same here," she murmured. "Though I have bought holiday dinner before, just always myself…and the buggy." She delighted at Christine's scrunched-up face when she used her colloquial term. "Come on. Let's finish up and go home."

Christine smiled. "I like that. Home. Oh, hey," she said, a hand to Willow's arm. "I noticed you don't have a tree up. Is that something you do tomorrow, Christmas Eve, or…?"

Willow looked down, a bit ashamed. "Kevin didn't like the mess."

Christine used two fingers to lift her chin. "I'm not Kevin."

※ ※ ※ ※

Big, fat flakes fell outside while a fire burned warmly in the fireplace and the newly purchased artificial tree had been assembled and decorated, sending colorful light over the two nestled on the couch.

Willow ran her fingers through Christine's hair as the singer lay with her head on a pillow in Willow's lap. She was singing Christmas songs softly. She'd just finished "Ave Maria," and Willow clapped lightly.

"It's not fair," she said. "You sing better lying

down than I do in the most acoustic shower stall." Christine laughed, looking up at her. Willow adored her, and she wondered if the woman looking back at her realized just how much. "When did you start singing?"

"I was about two or three, I guess," she said. "We were living in this house, and the next-door neighbor had a dog who liked to howl. So, one day, I started howling with him." She grinned at the memory. "Somehow, my howling morphed into singing to the dog, whatever song I could think of that I'd heard on my dad's radio. Anything from Guns 'N Roses to Frank Sinatra."

"Oh boy," Willow said, amused. "I can imagine a little you singing Ol' Blue Eyes."

"Quite the thing to see, no doubt. But once I started, I just couldn't stop. I often sang myself to sleep. My parents were gone all the time, no clue where, so, even at night, I was alone. I'd sing. Pretend there was a crowd watching, I'd sing to them. It made me feel safe."

"Like, that crowd was there with you? Watching you?"

Christine nodded. "I guess so, yeah." She looked up into Willow's eyes. "If you hadn't been a nurse, what would you have been?"

"A vet," Willow said, nodding. "Hands down. I love animals."

"I think we should get a dog," Christine said. "Or a cat."

"You do, huh?" Willow brushed long bangs back from Christine's lovely face. Without the trademark hair in her face, Willow was amazed at just how innocent and sweet Christine looked. Her features were beautiful, delicate, other than the proud jaw. Her face was pale, a contrast to the dark eyebrows, long lashes, and deep, deep blue eyes that in their current light almost looked black. "You're so beautiful," she whispered. "You could've been a model."

"Thank you," Christine whispered in response. "But not tall enough," she said with a smile. "Is it okay with you if in my mind I plan for us to put up this very same tree next year, but with a new ornament to represent the new year?"

Willow thought it was the sweetest question she'd ever been asked. "Do you see us as a couple?" she asked in response, wanting to understand where the singer's mind and heart was.

Christine nodded. "I don't wanna be with anyone else."

"Neither do I." She ran the backs of her fingers lovingly over a soft, smooth forehead, then down along her cheek. "Are you asking if it's okay to start making plans for us? Our future?" she asked gently, wanting to not only make sure she understood what Christine was saying, but also to put voice to it, give her permission to speak freely about it.

Christine nodded, eyes closed as Willow's tactile tour continued. "Yeah."

"It's very okay." Willow moved her hand away and leaned down, brushing her lips against Christine's. "Very, very okay."

Chapter Twenty-three

Christine let out a long, soft sigh as she came into the reality of what she was feeling. The soft, wet warmth around her nipple was delicious, the flesh becoming even more rigid as the cool morning air clung to the wetness from Willow's tongue. Her hand rose up to cup the back of her head, fingers burying themselves in long, soft strands.

"Hope you don't mind," Willow murmured as she ran her tongue all around the hard nipple before sucking it into her mouth again. "I wanted to break in our new bed a little more."

"Nope," Christine managed with a sigh. "Don't mind." Her eyes fell closed and her mouth open as Willow lightly ran her teeth over the tip. "Gotta love those doorbuster sales." She heard a small chuckle in return.

Since the first time they'd made love in Christine's house in Los Angeles, Willow had been like a little sponge. She was passionate, observant, and a very giving lover. The one thing she hadn't done was use her mouth on Christine, and Christine could tell she was nervous about it. Oral sex was something the singer loved to give and receive, but she knew it could be intimidating at first, and she certainly wasn't going to push Willow into anything she wasn't sure about.

This Christmas Eve morning, it seemed that the nurse had decided to face her fears as she loved every inch of skin she encountered from Christine's breasts on down her body.

Christine's head fell to the side as tiny kisses and nips were rained down on her inner thighs, Willow's hair tickling her flesh with movement. Yanked out of the depths of sleep into the heights of arousal had been somewhat disorienting, but she was all in now, feeling every kiss, every lick, and every touch.

"Baby," she breathed, her fingers gently running through her hair as Willow's mouth found the spot she was most needed.

Her tongue was tentative, almost trying to taste the landscape before really digging in. The soft, quick touches turned into a long, firm lick up and over Christine's clit, eliciting a guttural moan from deep in the singer's throat. Her legs fell open wider, offering more access while inviting her in, encouraging her and subtly letting her know that she was doing just fine.

Willow seemed to be gaining more confidence as she settled in fully on her stomach, wrapping her arms around Christine's thighs as Christine had done to her many times. Christine gasped as her clit was sucked into Willow's mouth and battered with her tongue before it was released, only for Willow to press on it hard again, moving her head quickly back and forth, her clit being rolled with each savage shake.

"Fuck." Christine groaned, pleasure swarming her body, only for the movement to stop as Willow lazily licked her again. "Baby." She was panting, her breasts heaving as her body was being put through its paces.

Willow hummed into what she was doing, sounding like she was loving it as much as the singer was. "So good," she murmured before diving back in with the rigorous head movements again, relentless.

Christine cried out loudly as she came, an explosion of pleasure erupting out of the tiny spot on her body, making her shudder with the intensity. She had to push Willow's head away, as she was trying to get her to come again, but she was spent, her clit to the point of almost painful sensitivity.

"Come 'ere." She reached for the woman who had just rocked her world.

Willow climbed back up Christine's body, taking her in an enthusiastic kiss, which Christine did her best to respond to as she tried to breathe. She loved tasting herself on Willow's tongue, the two of them sharing her desire in a deeply passionate kiss. She could feel how aroused Willow was, her hips straddling Christine's thigh. Her wetness painted her skin.

"Keep coming," she whispered, urging Willow to move up.

When Willow spread her thighs, a knee on either side of Christine's head, the singer was able to grip her hips and hold on as she lifted her head a bit and had her first breakfast of the day. She opened her eyes and looked up Willow's body, so sexy. Her breasts were full and nipples hard. She held on to the wooden headboard as her hips rolled with Christine's tongue on her clit.

Willow was so wet, had become so excited by what she'd done to Christine, it didn't take very long at all to push her that little bit over the edge. Christine groaned in approval at her loud cry as her head flew back, the very tips of her hair reaching her fingers in the process.

"Good god." Willow panted, moving off of Christine's pillows to slump down on her own next to it. She leaned back against the headboard she'd just been holding for dear life.

Christine chuckled, turning to her side as she looked up at the woman who had totally stolen her heart. "You okay?"

"Nuh-uh," Willow muttered, looking down at her. "Mornin'."

A burst of laughter exploded from her lips. "Come here, you." She was charmed and turned on by the naked woman who was scooting down into her arms. Willow's face was flushed, her hair had a just-fucked look, and she smelled of sex.

She buried her face in Willow's neck, holding her close, pulling her leg up over Christine's hip. She groaned into the warmth of the soft skin when she felt all that wonderful slick heat against her.

"I love how you taste, how you feel, how you smell," she murmured.

"I couldn't agree more." Willow sighed. "I think my body is confused."

"Why's that?" Christine asked, leaving a trail of kisses up to Willow's ear, playfully swiping at the lobe with her tongue.

"Because I think it thought I'd entered a monastery."

Christine grinned. "Yeah, but a nunnery might be fun."

"The sacrilege." Willow raised her head to give Christine access as her mouth moved back to her neck.

"So is not using this incredible body," Christine said, pushing the nurse to her back and moving on top of her.

"Is that so?" Willow purred, cupping Christine's face as she pulled her into a kiss.

"That's so," Christine whispered into the kiss.

Christine adjusted a bit so she was more centered against Willow's thigh, doing the same for the woman beneath her. As they continued to kiss, slow and deep, she kept her thrusts against Willow just as slow, both women getting purchase where they needed it against the other's flesh.

She knew she was in trouble. Every touch, every kiss, every breath, and every little whimper that Willow made was pushing her further and further over the edge into an abyss she knew little about. It felt comfortable, soothing, warm, but it scared her to no end. She was falling deeply in love with her, if she wasn't there already.

The two of them moved together while they continued to kiss, hands roaming, fingers trailing. As they slowly brought each other to deep orgasms, Christine felt it was the physical manifestation of the words her heart was crying to say.

She was trying to show Willow how much she was beginning to need her, how much she wanted this to be their life, not a visit. How much she needed for her own world to slow down and be simplified, and how much she needed Willow to be the center of it.

She hoped Willow heard it in her moans, heard it in her quiet pleas for more, heard it in the very vulnerability she was allowing herself to display by truly showing her pleasure in every way. She didn't hide it behind the no-touch policy that many women had faced with her in bed.

She was always willing to do anything and everything to make sure her catch for the night had a mind-blowing experience, yet she never wanted anything in return. Somehow, she'd inherently known that no other woman could make her feel how she did with Willow.

Now, all she wanted was Willow's touch. Yearned for her voice to say her name, to hear *Christine* whispered from her lips, because only from Willow did it have meaning, did it become her identity. It wasn't a word, it wasn't a name; it was home.

Christine's orgasm hit her hard, leaving her speechless, unable to make a sound. She held Willow to her, shocked to discover she was crying. She felt ashamed, but Willow held her.

"It's okay, baby," Willow murmured. "I've got you."

Christine clung to her, her voice trapped in her throat, because she knew if she spoke in that moment, she'd lay her heart out, and she just couldn't. Yet. So, instead she allowed the tears to flow, the pure beauty of the moment to show in her emotion. She held on.

❧ ❧ ❧ ❧

Shower taken, Christine stood at the bathroom vanity in the master bedroom in bra and jeans, her new flannel shirt and her boots still to be put on. She looked at her reflection as she brushed her teeth, long, damp bangs hanging in her eyes.

She smiled around her toothbrush when she saw her little elf walk up behind her. She wore a green elf costume with red tights and pointed green elf hat. Bells dangled off the hat and from the little red belt that cinched her costume at the waist. She looked at Christine's reflection, and with a little shimmy, jingled her way into the bathroom and hugged Christine from behind.

Christine finished and spit and rinsed her toothpaste into the sink. She nearly choked on the water when Willow grabbed her by the hips and pretended to fuck her from behind.

"You are a naughty little elf," she said, reaching around and smacking Willow's shapely behind.

"That I am," Willow said into her ear as Christine stood erect again. "You've created a monster."

Christine wiped her mouth before turning around in the circle of Santa's Little Helper's arms. She cupped her ass and tugged her hips into her own. "You know," she purred. "We should get you something you could really use."

Willow looked at her, confused. "What do you mean?"

Christine grabbed her and, with a squeal from Willow, hiked her over her shoulder before dumping her on the bed and falling on top of her. She lay between Willow's spread legs, holding herself up on her hands.

"You know," Christine said with a devilish grin as her hips thrust against Willow, no question what she was pantomiming.

Willow gasped and realization filled her eyes. "Really?" she asked, hooking her legs over the backs of Christine's. "They make such a thing? I mean, obviously I know about dildos..."

"Ohhhhh, yes. They..." *thrust* "Make..." *thrust* "Such..." *thrust* "A thing."

Willow grinned, her hands reaching down and tucking into the back pockets of Christine's jeans. "I want one."

"We can make that happen." Christine was about to move off Willow when she froze, both looking toward the doorway.

"You home?" was called from downstairs.

"Are you kidding me?" Willow muttered.

Christine looked at her. "Kevin?" At Willow's nod, they got off the bed. "What do you want me to do?"

"This shouldn't take long." Willow gave her a quick peck on the lips, then left the bedroom.

Left alone, Christine felt a surprising amount of anger and jealousy rise up. She grabbed her shirt and tugged it on, looking out the window as she quickly buttoned it up with deft fingers. She tugged on her hiking boots and tied them. There was no fucking way she was going to cower from that son of a bitch.

"Kevin, I told you where it was, so go get it please and leave," Willow was saying, her voice raised somewhat in irritation when Christine reached the top of the stairs.

"And I told you I didn't put it there," he said, voice booming. "So, where is my kerosene heater?" He looked up at Christine, Willow turning to look up at her.

Christine wasn't sure what she was expecting, but this bloated Ken doll wasn't it. He looked unshaven, his hair hanging over his forehead making him look somewhat boyish. She walked down the stairs casually, her booted steps thudding on the wood. She didn't step up next to Willow, because the last thing they needed was for him to turn it into a pissing contest.

"So, this is what a rich singer slumming in Colorado looks like, huh?" he asked, a little smirk curling up his lips.

"Kevin," Willow warned.

He ignored her. "Is this where big stars go to get laid and get away from the limelight for a minute?"

Wanting nothing more than to punch the shit out of him, Christine held her instinct in check and instead smiled the smile she used to dazzle her critics. "Well, I guess it's better than slummin' at the house of the woman who kicked you out."

Kevin's smirk slid off his face. He glared at her before turning back to Willow. "I want my heater." With that, he slammed out of the house, the crack of the front door making Willow jump. She slowly sat down on the stairs.

Her own heart pounding, Christine again fought her violent urge to run after him and beat the shit out of him. He wasn't worth it, she decided. Instead, she walked the few steps until she could sit on the stair next to Willow. She wasn't sure what to say, so she just sat in silence, wanting Willow to know she was there.

"I've never seen him so hateful before," Willow said softly, her hands tucked between her knees.

Christine looked over at her, noting her profile and how lost she looked. "There's a thin line between love and hate, Willow," she said softly. "He loves you and hates me."

"I can't believe he'd just let himself in like that," Willow said, sounding unsettled. "He knew we were here, cars parked out front."

"Guessing that's exactly why he let himself in here. Show he has some control over a situation he has no control over."

Willow didn't say anything for a long time, then she asked, her voice little-girl quiet. "Is he right?"

"About what?"

"You. Am I just a nice distraction from all the crazy of your life? Your fans."

She wasn't sure whether she hated Kevin for making Willow feel this way, or wanted to hug him for making her finally speak her heart. "No," she said. "Look at me, Willow." She waited until the other woman did, her green eyes filled with confusion and suspicion. "I'm not here because I'm 'slumming' or because you're a distraction, or because Colorado is an escape from LA."

"Then why?" Willow whispered.

"Because you have become my sanity, my comfort, my happiness." She smiled at her. "You've become my everything." She took a deep breath. "I'm here because I've fallen in love with you. I've never said those words before and it scares me to death, but it's true. I love you."

Willow stared at her for a long time, so long Christine began to wonder if that had been a huge mistake. But when she was suddenly engulfed in a bone-crushing hug right there on the stairs, she knew she'd done the right thing by being honest.

"I love you too," Willow breathed into her ear.

Christine's eyes squeezed shut as she held her tighter.

Chapter Twenty-four

Willow's eyes slowly opened. They felt heavy and like they had sand in them as she'd been up and down all night to check on their Christmas turkey. Lying there, she took a deep breath, a smile coming to her face as the air smelled amazing. When she had been sleeping, she'd dreamed of food all night as the house filled with delightful aromas.

Opening her eyes again, she was surprised to see that she was alone. Vaguely, she thought she remembered hearing Christine's phone ring, though she had no idea how long ago that had been. Pushing the covers aside, she shivered as the cold morning air hit her warm, naked skin. She was surprised steam wasn't emanating from her. Getting the house reinsulated was definitely going to be on her agenda to save for in the coming year, as well getting the windows looked at.

She quickly dressed in the discarded pajamas on the floor and added her robe for more warmth before heading out in search of the singer. When she couldn't find her in the house, and saw no coffee had been made or any real sign that Christine was present, she began to worry that her worst fears had been realized, the very ones Kevin had touched on the day before. Despite their declaration of love, she still worried she wasn't enough.

Her relief was fierce when she saw the rental

SUV still parked next to her truck when she looked out the kitchen window. Her last place to look, without leaving the house, was the front porch.

There she was, standing at the rail. Willow's eyes closed for a moment as she took a deep, steadying breath. Getting her wits about her, she opened the front door and went out to join her. Christine gave her a brief glance as Willow stepped up to the rail before looking back out over the wintery expanse.

"It's so amazing here," the singer said, her voice quiet. "To look in every direction and see no other human being, only a handful of buildings, the land, the snow, the gorgeous mountains." A small, tight smile curled her lips. "To hear the distant animals. So special," she whispered. She looked at Willow. "Is this heaven?"

"I've always thought so." Despite Christine's calm demeanor and words of peace, Willow could tell that something was wrong. She could see a tempest of swirling emotions in her eyes. "Are you okay?"

Christine was quiet for a long moment before she responded. The whimsical tone of her earlier comments was gone. Now, her voice was flat, matter-of-fact. "Bug called."

"Is he okay?"

Christine nodded. "Fine. But he wanted to let me know that Bob Knowles's wife found him this morning." She looked over at Willow. "He'd hung himself."

Willow could only stare. It felt like the porch had fallen out from under her. "Oh no," she whispered. She absolutely did not like the man, largely for how he'd treated Christine for so many years, but he had still been the one to get her out of a horrific situation when she'd been just a child. "Why?"

"My guess is he didn't have the money he knew he owed me after embezzling for so many years, and knew he'd end up in prison."

"What?" Willow gasped.

"Yup. Found out he's been stealing money for quite some time. Little here, little there," she said, bringing her hand up with thumb and forefinger close together, "But over time, it added up. Told him he was fired and had until I returned on New Year's Day to make it reappear."

"Wow." Willow looked out at her property, trying to wrap her mind around everything. "I'm so sorry. Scoundrel or not, he was an important part of your life for a very long time."

Christine nodded and let out a long, heavy sigh. "Since there doesn't seem to be any foul play, the funeral will probably be in a few days." She met Willow's gaze. "I need to go back for that." She shrugged a shoulder. "Say my final goodbyes to that part of my life."

Willow nodded. "Of course, I completely understand."

"Is it okay if I come back?" Christine asked, looking unsure.

Oddly, the singer's insecurity made Willow's dwindle a bit. She'd imagine if she were being played, the cocky singer would be fully in charge, not this woman who looked so lost and, on some level, sad. "Of course, baby," she said again, brushing her fingers along a soft cheek. "As it is, you're going to have to force me to let go of your leg when you finally leave for good."

"Hey, now," Christine said, fully turning toward

Willow and pulling her to her, arms firmly wrapped around her lower back. "Hear me when I say this. I am *never* going to leave for good." She rested their foreheads together. "Got me?"

Willow nodded. "Good," she whispered. "My heart couldn't take that."

"I love you," Christine said softly. "And, it feels damn good to say that." She grinned, pulling away from Willow, who returned her smile. "But I can no longer feel my toes."

Willow burst into laughter, grateful for a break in the seriousness. "Come on, you," she said, taking Christine's hand. "Let's go get some potica and coffee and open presents."

"What's potica?" Christine asked. "I keep hearing you guys talk about it here. Is it like a buggy?"

Willow rolled her eyes, then gave her a sexy little side look. "It's magic in a loaf pan."

"Oh my…"

☙☙☙☙

"Baby?" Willow said, holding out the wrapped box, the process of playing Santa beginning, including her wearing the hat that Christine had worn when they'd entertained the kids in the hospital the day before.

Christine pointed to the huge bite of potica she'd shoved into her mouth. She took the box, speeding up her chewing and swallowing loudly. "Magic in a loaf pan," she murmured, licking her lips and taking a sip of coffee to wash it down.

Shaking her head, all the gifts got passed out and the childlike glee of ripping into boxes, bags, and parcels commenced. Oohs and aahs followed, complete with kisses of gratitude and surprise. Finally, a sea of boxes, bows, and ripped paper surrounded them as they sat on the floor in front of the lit tree, the crackling fireplace at their backs.

"This was amazing," Willow said, leaning over again for another kiss.

"It was. Thank you, baby. I do, however, have a few more for you."

"No, Christine, you already did so much—"

"I know, I know, but…" Christine shrugged shyly as she got to her feet with a little groan of exertion. She hurried up the stairs.

Willow began to gather the trash, shoving it into the bag she'd brought in for the very purpose of cleanup. She glanced up as her love trotted back down the stairs and into the room, a small wrapped box in her left hand and a manilla envelope in her right.

"Okay," she said, reclaiming her place on the floor as Willow moved back to where she'd been sitting. "I guess let's start with this," she said, handing her the box. When you see what it is, I'll explain. And," she added. "I bought this for you weeks ago, so know that the meaning goes far deeper than just us as a couple."

Willow took it and nodded. "Okay."

She unwrapped it, careful with the beautiful blue-and-silver paper and bow. It looked as though it had been wrapped professionally. Wrapping was not in her own personal wheelhouse of talents, so she was impressed. Inside was a jewelry box, dark blue and velvet. She opened the lid, tiny hinges squeaking as a satin-lined inside was revealed. Inside was a delicate lighthouse pendant made of gold and small diamonds, about half an inch in length.

A small gasp came from Willow. "So beautiful," she whispered. She looked to Christine for the promised explanation.

"Since that night in February," the singer said softly, taking the box gently from Willow's hands and removing the trinket from its moorings. She scooted behind her, moving her hair aside so she could put the necklace on her. "Which, by the way, the year anniversary is coming up in about a month and a half," she added. "But, you changed my life, Willow. You changed my perspective on so many things."

Willow lowered her head to give the woman behind her ample room to clasp the gold chain. Her heart was racing, chest about to burst with love.

"I've realized that I need to start taking responsibility for my own actions and stop blaming my past," Christine continued. "That I needed to take a long, hard look at myself, my life, and my own happiness, or lack thereof." She left a small kiss on Willow's neck before gently pulling the long hair back into place and scooting back around to where she'd been sitting.

Willow looked up again, meeting Christine's gaze, allowing her hand to be taken into that of the singer.

"I've looked at you, the person that you are." Christine smiled, head slightly tilted to the side. "The kind of person I want to be. You've been my guiding light back to myself, Willow." She snorted. "Hell, probably finding myself for the first time. My lighthouse, a light in the dark."

Willow's breath was taken from her, no idea what to say. So, she leaned forward and initiated a loving kiss. "I love you," she whispered against Christine's lips before slowly backing away, holding her gaze. She was so far gone, no turning back. "I absolutely love this," she said, fingers stroking the pendant that hung just below the hollow of her throat. "It's beautiful and it means the world to me. I'll never take it off."

"Whew," Christine said dramatically wiping at her forehead. "Okay, that's done." She grinned. "All right, so, next is the serious stuff." She held up the manilla folder and handed it over.

Fingers leaving her new necklace, Willow carefully unsealed the large envelope and pulled out some very official-looking papers. She looked to Christine for more explanation. "Help."

The singer grinned. She scooted to sit beside Willow, their thighs pressed together. "Okay, this grouping here is the agreement I signed with my accountant to split my royalties for any sales, in any form, of 'Safe Harbor' with you."

"Wait, what?" Willow asked, a little confused but shocked at what she thought she understood. Her eyes widened even more as the singer explained what it all meant for her, and why she'd done it.

"This, my love," Christine said, reaching into the envelope and pulling out something Willow had missed. "Is your first royalties check." She handed the business-sized check to her.

Willow looked down at the amount, then up at Christine. "This is insane. This is more than I make in a year at the hospital."

"Well," Christine said. "And again, I arranged this long before I thought there would ever be a 'we.' I just wanted to make sure that, no matter what, you and the baby would be okay."

Willow didn't know what to think. "Will this

kill my taxes?" she asked dumbly.

Christine chuckled. "It'll change some things, yes. Mona, my accountant, is gonna give you a buzz and help you through all of it."

"I don't even know what to say, Christine," Willow said, absently caressing her new pendant again. "It's too much."

"Listen." Christine put the paperwork aside and took both of Willow's hands in her own. "That night, sure, you saved my life. That's what everyone talks about. But what doesn't get mentioned enough is that *you* could have died, Willow. It was exceptionally stupid and selfish of me, and exceptionally dangerous for you." She nodded toward the papers. "The way I see it, I owe you this, at the very minimum. I can never repay the debt of my life or the risk you took with yours, but this is a tangible expression of the inspiration that night sparked in me. You made that possible, so you should share in its fruit."

Willow nodded in understanding. "I don't even know what to do with that," she said, tapping the check.

"Whatever you want. Pay off your truck, buy a new truck, make repairs you've wanted to here, sock it all in the bank, invest it." Christine shrugged. "Whatever you want."

❧❧❧❧

It had been a long day, made even longer because Willow knew she was going home to an empty house. Christine had left that morning to head back to California for Knowles's funeral, plus she said she had some business to take care of while there. Willow didn't ask for more detail, as she felt that Christine's life back in LA was none of her business, somehow.

Christine had done nothing to make her feel that way, just more of her own insecurities creeping up. Willow bundled up as she headed for the sliding glass doors of the hospital that would take her out into the post-Christmas world.

"See ya, Wills!" one of her coworkers called out as she headed to a different part of the parking lot.

Willow raised her hand and waved, digging her keys out of her coat pocket and clicking the unlock button for her truck, which chirped at the action. Climbing behind the wheel, she was glad to close out the cold. It was funny—when she and Christine were out in it together, it was fresh, crisp, enlivening. When she wasn't there, it was dull, gray, and just plain cold.

Annoyed at…well, just annoyed, she got the truck started and let the engine warm up for a moment. For about the eightieth time that day she checked her phone. No messages or voicemails from Christine. She knew she was being childish. The singer had a long day, a lot to deal with, plus traveling. The funeral was the following day, then she said she'd be back either late tomorrow or the day after.

"Get a grip, Willow," she muttered, putting her truck in gear and pulling out of the parking space.

She turned the radio on and, as if she was sending her an *I love you* from the West Coast, one of Swann's songs came on. Willow blasted the volume, allowing herself to become lost in Christine's voice. The song was about six years old, long before they'd met. It was one of her harder songs, fast-paced and a crowd favorite as there were plenty of parts for audience participation.

She remembered at the concert she and Julie had attended, they'd been on their feet with the rest of the crowd when Swann performed "Dirty Lullaby" to perfection. But now, something told Willow to really listen to the words, to *hear* them.

> *Needed fury, no jury*
> *Only me*
> *Lifetime tested, heart arrested*
> *Only me*
>
> *Prison bars trap these scars*
> *Every night I get paid*
> *Sin stains in your sweet car*
> *Tell Mama why you're late?*
>
> *We both see the darkness fall*
> *Skies are raw and rain is small*
> *Faces on a windowpane*
> *Childhood in refrain*
>
> *Say my name 'n I'll be there*
> *Pick who you are*
> *Say my name 'n I'll pretend to care*
> *Lies will take you far*
> *You don't care, you don't care*
> *You do not care*
>
> *Tied to the bed inside your head*
> *Can I come out and play?*
> *Who do you expect me to be?*
> *Anything called a she*
>
> *I wonder did you see the sky*

Roses and rainbows in my eyes
The grass is green the clouds are thick
In the garden am I to pluck and pick
Never you mind I will fall
When I hear the call

Say my name 'n I'll be there
Pick who you are
Say my name 'n I'll pretend to care
Lies will take you far
You don't care, you don't care
You do not care
Don't care

Hand to her mouth, Willow was stunned. With Swann's image as a sexy, almost androgynous sex goddess to any and all, she, no doubt like all her fans, had thought the song was about rough sex, or perhaps even a toxic sexual relationship with somebody.

Tears came to her eyes as she realized Christine was singing about her days on the street, her days forced to murder her own childhood in order to survive.

Chapter Twenty-five

The church was filled with Who's Who of the music industry. There were singers, musicians, songwriters, agents, managers, and just about anybody else in broad association, as well as some from the film industry.

Dressed in a black women's-cut suit, Christine imagined the scene in the film *The Devil's Advocate* when Al Pacino's character stuck his finger in the holy water and it began to boil. She wondered if the same would happen for her, as it had been a decade since she'd been in a church for any reason that wasn't naughty.

The last time she'd been inside one they'd been filming a music video, and she'd managed to get lucky with the makeup girl in a confessional. Not her proudest moment. She was certainly glad those days were gone.

Speaking of days gone by, it was the ultimate in gone. She sat up front, at Barbara's request. She had been married to Bob for twenty-seven years. She was devastated, and Christine felt like shit. She felt responsible, even though she knew she wasn't. She felt somebody grab her hand as the service went on. As much as she would have loved to look to her left and see Willow, she knew she'd see Camille. She was grateful for her love and support, but she so wished her love was next to her.

Her gaze settled on Bob's casket, which rested up front between the congregation and the clergy up on the dais. It was a black casket, shiny with highly polished chrome. How fitting. Even in death he was Guido.

She smirked, crossing one leg over the other at the knee. As the minister went on and on, her mind wandered. So many moments with Bob flashed before her mind's eye, and they weren't all bad. Especially in the early days, he taught her so much. He taught her about not only the business, but also life.

In the beginning, he protected her, helped her understand how to not fall for every conman/woman who crawled out of the woodwork and wanted a piece of her. He was a positive influence on a very impressionable young woman with a whole lot of money and power. So, where had it gone so wrong?

She didn't have time to think about it further because it was her turn to speak. She hadn't wanted nor intended to, but Barbara had asked her, and at this point, she couldn't deny the grieving widow anything.

Blowing out a breath, she pushed to her feet and made her way to the lectern on the dais. She pulled out her phone and brought up her prepared remarks. Clearing her throat, she looked up at those gathered. The saddest part was, Robert Knowles was hated by a large portion of the industry, and she knew in her heart that many had come to support her and the boys, as well as Bob's family, instead of paying their respects to him.

"I've known Bob since I was fourteen," she began. "Not sure how many of you knew that. Not sure how many of you knew, also, that we met because he was walking by a real piece of sh—uh, crumby bar in Queens." She gave a sheepish grin at the chuckle she got at her near faux pas. She made a show of looking up to the heavens and throwing a peace sign, garnering more laughter.

She waited for the laughter to die down and quiet to resume. She looked down at her remarks to get an idea of what she was going to say next, then looked back up and continued.

"It was a dive bar, and the owner never bothered to verify my age, and, hey, I looked a lot older than I was, so he let me play and sing. Bob said it literally brought him in off the street when he heard me." She smirked. "I initially thought he was trying to pick me up, and I told him he could go H-E-double-hockey-sticks, but clearly I believed him." She stared the audience down. "Eventually."

Again, she waited for laughter to die down. As she did, she read over more of what she'd written in the music room Willow had created for her on the ranch, the lines she hoped would exorcise and humiliate and condemn and heal. She decided that she didn't want to say any of it. She wanted to speak from the heart.

Tucking her phone back into her pocket, she braced her hands on either side of the wood structure before her. "Look, Bob and I had a love/hate relationship. Most people knew that. And earlier I was trying to think of when that happened. You see," she said softly, though her voice boomed in the microphone set before her. "I tried to really think about who he was to me, at one time." She let out a heavy breath. "He was my mentor," she said, meaning it. "He was my protector. He was my friend."

She was surprised she felt emotion trying to sneak up on her. She paused for a moment, getting her emotions under control, taking a deep breath before she was able to continue.

"I know what it feels like to think you have no other options, to be in that headspace. I don't know why Bob did what he did." She shrugged. "Not sure any of us will ever know. But, love him or hate him, Robert Knowles meant a lot to the music industry, shaped many singers, made many careers. Though he made a lot of mistakes along the way, I'll always be grateful to him." She looked up again, sending her own little, *Fuck you, asshole, but I hope you're okay.*

Without another word, she stepped away from the lectern and headed back to her seat.

❦ ❦ ❦ ❦

Still in her funeral clothes, Christine stood at the railing that overlooked the ocean from the balcony in her bedroom. She watched the waves come and go, her bangs lightly billowing from the breeze that came up to her. Once upon a time, the ocean had been her peace. After a long, trying day, or an even longer tour, she'd come home and walk along the beach by herself and just let the waves absorb her mental and physical exhaustion.

Somehow, despite the beauty of the Pacific before her, it didn't have the same magical effect that it used to. She knew, though, that the reason was because before it was just her. Her and her music, her and her pain.

The pain had been acknowledged and released to be forever recorded on the pages that held the story of her past. It wasn't just about her anymore; now Willow was her peace. It was time to turn the page, start not only a new chapter, but a new book.

Pushing away from the railing, she headed inside and stripped out of her clothing, wanting a shower, a symbolic act of washing away parts of her life that were over, that she was glad to be cleansed of.

As the warm spray fell upon her in the massive shower stall that could easily fit a small party, she closed her eyes and allowed a long groan to escape her throat. She raised her face to the powerful spray, using her hands to smooth her hair back with the water. Her mind began to wander, again thinking of the ocean, but it didn't take long for her to see a very different image.

The snow-covered pastures and property where her heart now lay. The old farmhouse, thinking of so many things that needed to be done to repair the old structure as well as simply make it more modern and convenient. She thought of the outbuildings and the work they required—to be shored up, remodeled, repainted.

But, as she washed her hair, she pictured something else entirely. Suddenly, she saw a large "barn" that had been constructed. It looked for all the world like the rest of the other updated and maintained buildings on the property, but this one had a special purpose. Inside was a state-of-the-art recording studio.

"Okay, here we go," she said. She was sharing the piano bench with Willow, who held a toddler on her lap. Christine, fingers on the keys, began to play a simple tune. "Yellow and blue," she sang.

"Makes green!" the little girl shouted.

"Good!" Christine laughed. "Annnnnnnnnnnnd,

red and blue make—"

"Purple!"

"She's a natural," Christine said to Willow.

"A Picasso in the making," Willow concurred, kissing the little one on her lap atop her wavy auburn hair.

"God help us," Christine laughed before continuing to play.

Christine gasped, eyes blinking several times as the very vivid image vanished. She looked around at her shower stall, feeling almost sick to her stomach to find herself alone.

※ ※ ※ ※

Her excitement built as the plane touched down, the now familiar surroundings of the wide-open spaces around Denver International Airport coming into view. She knew as she left the area she'd see the god-awful giant blue demon horse with glowing, red eyes. Whoever thought that was a good idea needed some mental evaluation, she thought.

She collected her carry-on and pulled her baseball cap low as she headed off the plane and back to what felt normal in her life: namely, Willow. She hadn't taken any luggage with her to LA, as everything she needed for Bob's funeral was at her house, so she only had her backpack to deal with. It was freeing to bypass the luggage carousel as she headed for the exit.

On her way, she passed by a brand-new car that was on the floor as an up-close-and-personal advertisement for a car dealership. She slowed as she passed the gleaming vehicle. She wasn't so interested in the car model itself, but it gave her a thought.

Stepping out into the cold, morning air, she walked to a taxi that was waiting at the curb. "Hey," she said, getting into the back seat and closing the door. "Can you take me to the nearest car dealership, please?"

An hour later, the singer was sitting at the desk where she'd just signed a billion different forms and was waiting for the man to return who had just sold her a brand-new Ford Explorer.

After signing her name about fourteen thousand times and the payment clearing, with a handshake and passage of keys she had herself a Colorado car. She played with all the gadgets as she drove toward the ranch, enjoying the new-car smell and feel. At one point she glanced into the rearview mirror to change lanes, and the back seat caught her eye. She could so easily see a car seat back there with a mini-Willow strapped safely inside. She grinned at the thought and cranked the stereo volume up that much more as she pushed the pedal to the metal and headed home.

When she arrived at the ranch, nobody was home, as was expected. Willow still had another couple hours at the hospital, but Christine had her own key. To her surprise and delight, it was the very first thing Willow had made her open on Christmas morning. She'd been told that if even though she wasn't expected to be but she wanted to be at the house, all she had to do was let herself in. She was always wanted there.

Parking where she normally would park the rental car, she grabbed her backpack and the few groceries she'd picked up on the way, locked up the new SUV, and headed inside. As soon as she crossed that threshold, she stopped, closed her eyes, and inhaled deeply. She could smell the room fresheners that Willow had plugged in all over the house. She could feel Willow's energy, so calming and comforting to her.

Closing the door behind her, she dropped her backpack at the foot of the stairs and headed to the kitchen to leave the groceries on the counter. She'd bought ingredients for Milly's lasagna, which was amazing, and she just hoped she could duplicate it.

She snagged her backpack again and trotted up the stairs to their bedroom. Everything was as it should be, nothing out of place or strange, the bed made to perfection with hospital corners, of course. She spotted a sticky note on the dresser.

She set the backpack on the bed and picked up the note, reading Willow's small, neat handwriting.

I made room for you, I hope you don't mind. Love you.

Setting the sticky note back on the dresser, she opened up some of the drawers and saw that, sure enough, Willow had emptied her roller bag and had neatly folded her clothes and put them all away in their own drawers on one side of the long dresser.

She ran her fingers over her T-shirt, a simple green T-shirt, a smile on her lips as she could feel how lovingly Willow had folded it into a perfect little square. She'd almost packed another suitcase filled with clothes while in LA, but she didn't want to assume, didn't want Willow to feel like she was intruding on her home. Though now, looking at that shirt, she knew that wouldn't have been the case.

Closing the drawer, she unpacked the toiletries in her backpack and found her roller bag in the closet, unzipping the empty piece of luggage and stuffing her backpack inside it before heading back downstairs.

She was happy to see that the Christmas decorations were still up, so she turned them all on, smiling when little ice skaters began their eternal figure eights on the tiny skating rink in the little village they'd created on the fireplace mantel. She noticed the wood supply on the hearth was low, so she grabbed her winter coat and gloves from the closet and went outside to the covered pile to bring in more. She wanted the house to be nice and warm when Willow got home in a couple hours.

She felt downright domestic as she replenished the wood inside, even got herself a nice splinter stacking it after she took her gloves off. Willow had taught her how to build a fire in the fireplace, so she got a nice blaze going. She replaced the glass screen in front of it and headed to the kitchen to start on dinner.

Turning on her favorite playlist on her phone, she sang along as she began to unpack the grocery bags. She'd checked, double-checked, and triple-checked the list of ingredients Milly had given her.

Butt shaking and feet tapping, she put the meat in the fridge until she was ready for it and went about grabbing the bowls and utensils she'd need before washing her hands and making the filling.

She glanced over her shoulder when she heard a vehicle pull up. It sounded like Willow's truck. A glance at the stove clock showed she was early, and she hoped everything was all right. Wrist-deep in ricotta, raw eggs, and mozzarella, she couldn't go check. She heard the engine cut, then a car door open and close. Footsteps crunched on the packed snow a few feet, then stopped.

Christine grinned to herself. If that was Willow, no doubt she was looking at her new ride, quiet and confused. She wasn't entirely sure what her reaction would be. She'd find out soon enough, as those footsteps finally continued onto the porch and then inside.

"Christine?" Willow called out from the front door, uncertainty in her voice.

"In the flesh, baby!" she called back, still standing at the counter in the muck of her mixture.

"Whose Explorer is that out there?" Willow asked, making her way into the kitchen, stopping just short of the singer.

"Mine," Christine said casually.

"Since when?" Willow stepped up beside her.

Christine met her gaze. "What time is it?" she asked with a lopsided grin.

"You bought that today?"

"I did." Christine's proud smile began to fade as Willow continued to stare, mouth open. She cleared her throat, suddenly feeling very, very unsure of herself. "Did I do something wrong?"

"No," Willow said, shaking her head. "Why did you buy that?"

Not sure at all what Willow was thinking or feeling, Christine became even more nervous, and her defenses began to rise. "Because it made little sense to me to keep paying daily on a rental car when I could just drop the money for a more permanent solution." She knew her tone was a bit biting, but her walls were slamming upward. "Is that a problem?"

Willow took a step back, shock in her eyes, like she'd been slapped. "Uh, no. I was just surprised." She wrung her hands together and turned away, as if to leave the room. "I'm sorry to cost you so much money, Christine. Never my intention. I'm sorry I've been selfish."

Crap! The signer gathered as much of the goop off her hands and her fingers as she could before wiping her hands on a wad of paper towel she snagged from the roll. "Wait," she said, hurrying after the small woman, who'd nearly reached the stairs. "Wait, Willow."

Willow stopped, one booted foot already on the bottom step, but she stopped, her back to Christine.

"I'm sorry," Christine said, moving up behind her and taking her in a hug. "I'm sorry," she said again, softly, into her ear. "I was nervous about buying the car because I didn't want you to think I was assuming you wanted me here all the time, so I think I was already halfway ready to run out and take it back to the dealership."

Willow was quiet, but at least she didn't pull away. After a moment, she took a deep breath and turned in her arms, looking up at her with guarded eyes. "Do you think I don't want you here?" she asked, her tone so uncertain.

"I think you do," Christine said with a sheepish grin. "I mean, you did give me a key, but it's your house and you're not even out of your situation with Kevin, yet. I...I don't want you to think I'm trying to push something on you, or take over."

"Do you want to be here?" Willow asked. "Like, here, in Colorado. I mean, would you prefer I was there in California?"

Not even having to think about the question, Christine shook her head. "No. I want to be here, with you, in this house on this property in this state." She gave her a small smile, trying to let her know that she was serious, but tried to ease up on her intensity of moments before.

"I know you have a craptastic amount of money," Willow said slowly. "So, you buying a new SUV is certainly different than me buying it. But, it's still a big step."

"Is it too big?" Christine asked, eyeing her. "Should I have gone with a compact car?"

Willow burst into giggles, swiping playfully at her arm. "You know what I mean."

Christine chuckled. "I do know. I want to be here with you. When I was in LA the last couple days, all I could think about was getting back here to you." She could see the doubt lingering in Willow's eyes. "I'm serious. I know my presence isn't some little thing or minor disruption to your life, and you've done so much to make room for me, make a place for me. So I want to do everything I can to make me being here as easy as possible for you. I thought having my own vehicle might help, but I should have talked to you first. I normally don't just blow money on cars or houses or extravagant jewelry." She tugged down on the neckline of her shirt. "See? No huge gold chains."

Looking amused, Willow played at peeking down her shirt, smiling when Christine playfully slapped her hand over it. "Okay. But I reserve the right to ask to see you in nothing but a gold chain."

Chapter Twenty-six

T hank you," Christine said, smiling at the waitress who gathered their menus after taking their orders. The waitress smiled shyly at her but left their table without saying anything.

Willow watched, amused. She'd noticed that the townspeople were becoming more and more aware of the new celebrity in their hometown, and it was interesting to watch their reactions. Some went all-out fan girl, even the men, while others, like the waitress, gave her a shy smile or look but left her alone.

"So, I was thinking," Christine said, looking bright-eyed and bushy-tailed after a wonderful night together on her first night back after the funeral. Lots of reconnecting by the fire, in the shower, in the bed… After all, she'd been gone two whole days.

"Always a scary proposition," Willow teased.

"Right?" The singer smirked. "You're off for the next two days, so I think we should go get a dog or a cat today." She steepled her fingers under chin. "That way we can spend some time with she or he."

"I so want a cat or dog," Willow said, feeling very wistful. "But with only me, Christine, it'll be tough to get it trained and all that."

Christine sat back in her chair, hand to her chest. "What am I, chopped liver?"

Willow gave her a sheepish grin and shook her head. "Of course not. But you're leaving in a few days.

You already have a ticket.”

"About that," the singer murmured, looking Willow in the eye. "Normally I take a little time after we finish a tour to chill, then I begin writing again, as you know. Already written some, but haven't really begun the true nose to the grindstone, which is what I intended to do when I got back to LA. Which is why I was leaving in the first place," she added.

Willow nodded, wondering where this was going. After their misunderstanding the day before regarding Christine's new SUV, she knew they needed to have a sincere heart-to-heart, really get to the core of what they had and what was steadily growing by the day, just like the baby that was starting to make her belly grow.

Christine had begun to speak but paused when the waitress arrived again with the singer's regular coffee and Willow's decaf, which she hated, but it was better than nothing. Once the young woman left, Christine began to talk as she prepared her coffee.

"I obviously have things I will need to do now and then back in California," she began. "My band lives there, our recording studio is currently there, all that jazz. But, I can write from anywhere. Often I leave the country and just go find a place to hide for six months or a year to work on the next album."

"Okay," Willow said, her heart beginning to race as she hoped she understood where Christine was going with this.

"I'd like to do all that here," the singer said, indicating the diner around them and the town beyond that. "Where you are." She gave her a lopsided grin. "Because I want to be with *you*," she said quietly, for Willow's ears only. "Not because I need a quiet place that isn't LA."

Willow looked away, feeling a bit sheepish, because that would have been her exact next thought. "Busted."

"I know." Christine reached across the table and covered Willow's hand with her own for a moment. "I think we need to talk, really get out our intentions."

Willow nodded, looking down at their hands. "I was thinking the same thing." Suddenly, Christine's eyes were on somebody just beyond their table. She followed her gaze and saw Kevin standing a few feet away. Her stomach fell.

He looked at both women, then their hands, then back to Willow. "Isn't that sweet," he muttered. He headed toward the bathrooms, which seemed to have been his destination when he spotted them.

"Shit," Christine whispered, pulling her hand away. "Damn it. I'm sorry, Willow."

Willow sat there for a long moment, her stomach in knots. She considered a lot of things in that moment. Sure, it was easy to be with Christine in the safety and privacy of her home, but that's not how life was. When you were with somebody, you went out, did things together, were affectionate together, used terms of endearment with each other.

Finally, she shook her head and met Christine's pensive gaze. "No. I hid who I was for so long," she said. "I know not everyone is going to be happy for us or like who we are, but I'm not going to hide this beautiful thing we've found together." She gave her a little smirk. "Fuck him."

The singer's eyes widened. "Alrighty, then." She grabbed her coffee mug. "Cheers!"

Willow clinked her cup to hers. Even though she

felt like she could vomit, she knew she was right and needed to keep her perspective in this new adventure. "So, puppies or kittens after this?"

"I'll definitely drink to that." Christine chuckled, sipping her coffee.

❧ ❧ ❧ ❧

"You said puppies *or* kittens," Christine said with a raised eyebrow as they sat on the floor of the living room. "Not dog *and* cat."

Willow grinned, accepting kisses from their new dog, a mix that looked like a Boxador, a mix of Boxer and Labrador, but the people at the pound weren't sure. He was a few years old and so sweet. His name was Buster at the moment, but the two hadn't decided if they wanted to change it or not.

Then there was Keaton. The gray tabby that had come into the pound with Buster, and the two were the best of friends. There was no way Willow was going to tear them apart. She watched as the cat made her way around the area, climbing onto furniture, eyeing the tree before, luckily, thinking better of it and moving on to sniff other things.

"We need to get her a really good cat tree," Willow said.

"Tell you what," Christine suggested, running her hand down Buster's dark brown back. "Why don't you go to the pet store, because we need to get her more litter too, and I'll hang here with the puss and pooch?" She met Willow's gaze. "Don't think it's a good idea to leave them alone quite yet."

"Okay. I'll get them their goodies and see what I can get her for the short term, but I think we should order her something online." Willow gave Buster some last loves before getting to her feet.

"Something grand?" Christine said dramatically.

Willow grinned. "Yup! In fact..." She reached over and grabbed Christine's phone from the table. "Be productive while I'm gone."

Christine quirked an eyebrow at her.

⁂

"Thanks so much," Willow said, giving the kind pet store clerk a smile of gratitude for loading the heavy bags of cat litter and dog and cat food into the back of her truck, as pretty much everything she'd bought exceeded the weight limit her doctor set for her to be lifting.

"You're welcome. Have a nice evening," the clerk said, pushing the emptied cart back to the store.

Willow closed the tailgate and walked around to the driver's side door when she heard a familiar voice behind her.

"So, the dyke come with a dog?"

She whirled around to see Kevin standing behind her, a plastic sack dangling from his fingers with the logo of a store in the shopping center. "What?"

He nodded toward the bed of the truck. "Dog food. Cat food, cat litter. A scratching post?"

"Yes," she said, crossing her arms over her chest, feeling mighty small in front of him in that moment. It was so hard for her to not fall back into the pattern of, "Yes, sir." But, she thought about what Christine would do in that moment, and it gave her strength. "We got a dog and a cat, not that it's an ounce of your business."

"Well, I'd say it is my business," he said. "I don't want my baby around those creatures."

"Which ones?" she asked, cocking her head slightly to the side. "Dogs and cats, or dykes?"

He smirked. "Yes."

Instinctively, Willow placed a hand on her baby bump. "You mean, the baby you don't want?" she challenged. "The baby you wanted me to get rid of? That baby?"

His gaze slid down her body to her hand on her belly. "Clearly you didn't, so yes, *my* baby."

She looked at him, disgusted. "What do you want, Kevin?" She held out both of her arms, wrists up. She shoved her coat up so her wrists were exposed. "Want some blood? Shall I cut? Want your pound of flesh?"

"Don't be ridiculous, Willow," he growled, looking around to see if anyone was paying attention to them.

"Come on, Kevin. We always said that if it wasn't working, we'd make changes. Well, it wasn't working for me." Hand on hip, she eyed him. "Or, was that just if it wasn't working for you?"

"Why do you always make me out to be the bad guy and you're the victim?" he yelled.

A burst of laughter escaped from her lips. "I think you're projecting a little there, Kevin," she said. She turned away and opened the door of the truck, only to be spun around as he grabbed her wrist. She whipped it away, whirling on him. "Don't you ever touch me again."

He had the decency to look contrite as he took a step back. "Is she living there?" he asked.

"I don't know, Kevin," she said, angry and over

it. "We're working out what exactly our relationship is. Would you like a front-row seat to that conversation?"

"I just don't want my kid living with a whoring drug addict."

She stared at him, stunned and disgusted. "Who are you?" she asked. "You've always been capable of being an asshole, but you've never been cruel." With that, she climbed into her truck and slammed the door shut.

Her hand was shaking as she tried to insert the key, she was so angry. Finally, she got it and the truck roared to life. She peeled out of the parking space a little more aggressively than she'd intended to, but she kept going.

⚜ ⚜ ⚜ ⚜

They sat quietly, Christine holding Willow's hand, Willow having just explained her encounter with Kevin, her words hanging heavy in the air like a dialogue bubble lined with lead. She smiled when, to her surprise, Keaton, who had very quickly bonded with Christine, climbed into Willow's lap, staring up at her with big, gray-green eyes.

"Hey, pretty girl," the nurse said softly, using her free hand to rub the soft gray-and-black fur. "They've been here a whopping two hours and I already can't imagine this place without them." She looked over at Christine, who nodded.

"Is he dangerous?" Christine asked softly.

Willow let out a heavy sigh and shook her head. "I don't think so," she responded. "I think his very fragile ego is struggling mightily with the fact that, first of all, *I'm* the one who walked away and ended the marriage. And, two, I'm with you." She sat back on the couch to give Keaton room to lie down on her lap, her hand absently stroking her fur. It was so calming. "He could handle another man, baby. But he has absolutely no defenses against someone like you."

Christine sat a bit sideways on the couch, planting an elbow into the back cushion to cradle her head. "What do you mean, 'someone like me'?"

"Well, a woman, for one. He always hated me spending any kind of time with Julie and Remmy, yet had no compunction at all for me to spend time with Rachel and Andrew. Deep down, I think he always knew and was threatened by Julie and Remmy and their relationship."

"Well, come on, now," Christine joked. "Remmy is more of a man than Kevin could ever be."

Willow chuckled. "So are you, and he knows it. I think it absolutely kills him that you're so successful in your field, what you've done with your life. And of course, money. It's all about the Benjamins for him."

Christine looked down at Keaton, even as her free hand stroked Buster's silky ears, whose chin rested on her leg. "I see," she murmured, almost as if to herself. "Willow, he threatened to try for custody, essentially, using the fact that I'm a drug addict as a reason."

"And a dyke. Don't forget that one."

The singer grinned. "Yeah, well, that's not gonna change anytime soon. But," she continued, growing serious again. "Yes, I'm almost a year clean and sober, and that's a wonderful thing, a huge milestone. But in the grand scheme of things, it's nothing. Especially when he tries to play that card over what's best for the baby." She swallowed, hard. "I'd rather walk away from your life forever than be the reason you lost custody of your child."

Panic set into Willow's heart, her stomach turning over at the very thought. "No," she said, placing a hand to Christine's face. "No," she said again, shaking her head. "I will *never* let that son of a bitch dictate what I do or who I have in my life again. Don't you see?" She caressed the soft skin. "That's what he's trying to do," she said, realizing it as the words came out of her mouth. "If you walked away, not only would it break my heart, but you'd give him exactly what he wants—continued control of me, over the situation, even if he's no longer here." She smiled. "I'm not losing you over his teeny tiny self-esteem. That's not my issue to fix."

Christine was quiet for a long time, though it was clear the wheels in her mind were spinning. She turned her focus to Buster for a moment, giving him loves as he looked at her adoringly. "What do you want for us, Willow?" she said at length, glancing over at the nurse. "Like, perfect situation."

Willow considered her response. "I want us to continue to build on what we've already begun a foundation for. I love you and I know I want to be with you. I want this to be your home too. I want you to have your dreams, have your career, but also have that safe harbor, your lighthouse." She smiled, loving that the singer saw her in those terms. "I want this place to be that for you." She shrugged and gave her a sheepish look. "I was even thinking about the fact that I so happen to have land where things can be built. Like, a real music room, whatever you may need, or even—"

"A recording studio," Christine finished.

"Yeah. A recording studio." Willow raised her hands in supplication. "I don't pretend to know what you need as a singer or recording artist, but I want to learn, and I want to offer you the space to build… whatever." She shrugged. "Our little family complex, here."

Christine's smile was slow but ultimately brilliant. It was the very smile that had won Willow's heart so early on. "I want that too. I want you, all of this," she said, indicating the house they sat in. "These two newbies," she said, nodding toward their new furry pals. "And," she added, "I want this." She placed her hand on Willow's growing baby. "I will protect her or him at any cost, Willow. Just like I'll protect you."

"Her," Willow murmured with a shy smile. "They called while you were in California. The results came back from the fetal DNA test. Everything is fine, she's healthy, and she is a girl."

Christine looked away, but not before Willow saw that those beautiful, deep blue eyes were glistening. She took a long, shaky breath before turning back to Willow, Swann fully in place. "Then I'm gonna do all I can to help her rock this world."

Willow smiled before cupping her face and pulling her into a kiss. "You certainly rock mine."

Chapter Twenty-seven

Willow was working the mid-shift for a bit, so it was the perfect time to take care of some business. It was the new year and school was back in session. Christine drove to the school and trolled the parking lot until she found Kevin's car. From what Willow had told her in passing conversation, he'd be leaving in just a few minutes, if he left on time.

She found a nearby parking space and waited, which wasn't long. Soon enough, she saw him walking toward the parking lot, loosening his tie and top button of his shirt as he went. Climbing out of her Explorer, Christine walked over to his car. His steps slowed when he noticed her.

"Afternoon, Kevin," she greeted casually. He said nothing but eyed her warily. "We haven't been formally introduced, and I think it's important that we are." She gave him a dazzling smile. "After all, I'm not going anywhere. So, that being said, are you a beer guy or a coffee guy?"

"Why?"

"Because you and I are gonna go talk. Coffee shop or bar? Your call."

"And if I won't go?" Kevin challenged, feet planted wide in an aggressive stance and arms crossed over his chest.

"Then we talk right here," Christine said simply, arms held out in an expansive gesture. "In front of all your colleagues as they leave work. Fine by me."

Kevin's jaw muscles were flexing, but finally he sighed. "Do you know where Scully's is on eight street?"

"Nope, but clearly you do, so I'll follow."

The two parted ways, Kevin climbing into his car, Christine into hers. The short parade drove the couple miles to the bar and grill. They walked to the door where Kevin nearly ran to get to the door first. If it wasn't so important to Willow's life and that of the baby, Christine would have laughed. Instead, she graciously nodded acknowledgment and walked into the place, which was slow at three thirty in the afternoon on a random Tuesday.

Without asking his thoughts, she headed to the booth near the back, away from the bathrooms and the bar itself. He followed, the two sliding into opposing seats. She studied him for a moment, thinking the two of them couldn't be any more diametrically opposed if they tried, despite their gender. She had to wonder what made Willow, who had chosen this guy, who looked like the all-American Boy Scout, choose her, definitely not the all-American Girl Scout.

"Hey, Kev, how goes it?" a man, who was suddenly at their table, asked. He looked at Christine. "Howdy. Welcome."

She smiled up at him. "Thanks."

"What can I get you two?"

"Coke for me," Christine said. "And whatever Kevin wants. My ticket."

The man nodded and looked to Kevin for his order.

"Old-fashioned, Todd," Kevin said.

"Be right back."

Left alone, Kevin looked to Christine. His expression was an interesting one, seeming to be a mixture of anger and curiosity. "So, what do you want?" he asked. "I signed the papers, and in ninety days it'll all be done, so…"

"The baby," Christine said simply.

The anger took over the curiosity. "What, are you here to try and get me to sign that away, too?"

Christine shook her head. "Nope. Quite the opposite."

Kevin opened his mouth to speak but closed it when the older man returned, setting the soda in front of Christine and the cocktail in front of Kevin. Left alone, he cleared his throat. "What?"

"Willow and I, but the mother is who really matters here, think it's very important for a father to be in a baby's life," Christine said casually, grabbing her drink and taking a sip from the straw.

"Oh, I will," he assured. "Because it'll live with me, its father." He placed his hand over his own chest to emphasize his point.

"It?" Christine asked. "If you're so very interested in taking full custody of your child, the one you never wanted, by the way, why don't you even know the gender?" She cocked her head to the side. "I was sitting right next to Willow when she texted you the results."

He blinked at her for a moment before grabbing his phone, tapping and swiping until he stopped, staring at the screen. Letting out an irritated sigh, he slammed his phone back down to the table, Willow's week-old text visible.

He took a long sip of his drink, not looking at her. She could tell he was now angry with himself, as he'd just made himself look like a real asshole and quite uninterested. Clearing his throat, he set the drink down.

"My daughter isn't going to be raised by two dykes," he said, his angry tone completely undercut by what had just happened.

Again, Christine wanted to laugh, but the situation was far too serious for that. "It's twenty-plus years into the twenty-first century, Kevin," she said. "What judge in their right mind is going to grant you sole custody on those grounds?" She sat back in her seat, staring him down. "Especially when the birth mother is an absolutely beloved nurse in the community. Well known, well loved. Responsible. Has a solid home for her daughter."

"And then there's you," he spat, glaring at her. "What the hell kind of influence you could have on her?"

"On the baby, or Willow?" She had the distinct feeling that the baby was only in his periphery.

He looked away. "The kid."

Sensing she wasn't going to get anywhere with the direction the conversation was taking, she decided to change tack. "I grew up in Queens, New York," she began. "Parents were messed up, caught up in drugs, using and selling, all that jazz."

He looked at her. "Why are you telling me this? I don't care about your childhood, Swann."

"Christine," she corrected, keeping her voice even. "When I was eleven years old, I lost both my parents. I grew up without a father, Kevin. My father chose drugs and addiction over his only child. I grew up without a mother, Kevin," she said. "She, too, chose drugs and addiction over her only child."

He looked at her, his features softening as he seemed to be absorbing what she'd told him. He sipped quietly from his drink.

"I know what it feels like to grow up without a parent. Don't doom your daughter to the same fate. You said you'll fight for custody of her. That means lawyers, and lawyers mean lots and lots of money." She caught and held his gaze. "Who, between us, do you think can continue such a financial fight?" she asked, not unkindly. "Don't let your ego ruin a life you've worked hard to build. You deserve a place in your daughter's life, and so does her mother."

He was quiet, seemed downright deflated. He looked out the window for a long moment, his expression unreadable. Finally, he let out a heavy sigh and turned toward the bar, raising a hand. "I'll need another one, Todd," he called out.

❧ ❧ ❧ ❧

Willow's soft sighs and little whimpers aroused Christine almost as much as the feeling of the dildo strapped to her hips pressing rhythmically against her clit as Willow's hips rolled gently with the dildo buried deep inside. Ever since they'd gotten a strap-on harness a couple months ago, it had become a fan favorite in the bedroom, especially as Willow's belly had grown larger.

She rested her hands on Willow's hips, mindful to keep them away from engorged breasts—not an easy task, as she loved those breasts. They'd grown far too sensitive to the touch to be pleasurable for the mom-to-be, but her need for pleasure in other ways had skyrocketed.

Willow's already healthy sex drive had increased considerably during her pregnancy. It had become their private joke that if Willow said, "hormone surge," Christine knew what their evening was going to be like.

Now, as Willow slowly and sensually rode her, Christine was lost in both the pleasure and the tremendous love she felt. Every day they were together, she loved her more. Now, looking up at her as they moved together, she was blown away all over again by how beautiful she was, how sexy she was, how absolutely amazing she was.

As Willow's breathing began to increase, as well as the rhythm of her hips, Christine knew she was getting close. She moved one of her hands and used her thumb to rub against Willow's clit, eliciting a loud cry from her as her hips jerked. Christine didn't stop as Willow moved faster.

Christine's eyes fell closed as her own pleasure built, her thighs falling open wider to allow her own clit to be rubbed and pressed against even more with each thrust of Willow's hips. With a loud gasp and sensuous groan, Willow came, her body shuddering as she straddled Christine's hips. It wasn't long before the singer followed, her orgasm taking her hard and quickly.

After several moments, Willow brought her hands up, pushing her hair out of her face as she rose to her knees, the dildo falling out of her, the toy glistening with her spent desire. Breasts still heaving, Willow lay down on her back next to Christine, their hands finding each other.

Though the house was much warmer after they'd replaced all the windows and had the house reinsulated, it was a cold March night and spring snow fell outside. Christine released Willow's hand so she could unbuckle and remove the harness and dildo before climbing back in bed and pulling the covers up around them both. Willow turned on her side and Christine spooned up behind her.

"Oh, somebody was wet!" Willow giggled, her behind pushing back into Christine's crotch, her saturated but neatly trimmed pubic hair indicative of just how much she'd enjoyed their activities.

Grinning, Christine thrust suggestively against her behind. "Damn straight."

"God, I hope not!"

Christine chuckled against her neck before leaving a kiss there. "I love you."

"I love you more," Willow said, taking Christine's hand and lacing their fingers together where they rested on her belly. "How's the studio coming?" she asked. "I meant to ask you earlier, but kind of got distracted."

Christine chuckled, snuggling in even closer. "Can't imagine with what." She kissed Willow's naked shoulder. "It's going amazingly well. Sid says we should finish up ahead of schedule."

"Oh, baby, I'm so glad to hear it. I think the barn idea was brilliant. You can't even tell what it is."

"Yeah, well, I'm talented like that." Christine moved when she felt Willow turning to her back. She remained on her side, elbow planted into her pillow as she rested her head in an upturned palm.

"I've been thinking about something," Willow said, looking up at her.

"Okay," the singer said. "What's on your mind, gorgeous?"

"I told myself that I'd only ever marry once," Willow began softly, reaching up and running a fingertip along Christine's jaw before letting her hand drop back to the bed. "I still stand by that, but unfortunately I married the wrong person."

Christine listened, resting her hand on Willow's swollen belly, as she did all the time, most of the time not even realizing she was. She loved the feeling of her soft skin, yet so firm in the bundle inside.

"I want to get it right this time," Willow continued.

Christine's heart was racing. She'd had the thought so many times in the last few months, yet thought Willow would think she was out of her mind. Hell, her divorce was just final a matter of weeks before. "What are you saying, baby?" she asked softly.

"This little girl is going to be born in three months," she explained. "I want her to know her two moms are settled, love each other. Yes," she conceded with a grin. "You can certainly love each other and not be married, but…" She shrugged a shoulder. "Call me old-fashioned, but I want her moms to be married. And," she said, almost shyly. "I really, really want to be your wife." She cupped Christine's cheek. "I love you more than I ever thought possible. You've changed me in ways I never could have imagined."

Christine smiled down at her. "Yes," she whispered. "I will marry you if you'll marry me."

"Yes," Willow murmured. "My little phoenix from the ashes."

Christine chuckled. "Isn't that the truth." She used her fingers to brush some hair out of Willow's face. "I think for both of us. Both of us were trapped in our own ways. You rescued us both, do you realize that?"

"I think we rescued each other."

The singer nodded. "I can dig that. You know they're gonna say it's too soon for us to get married. I've only been here four months, basically."

"Yeah, but I'm pretty sure I've loved you since that night," Willow said.

"I would say the same, but you creeped me out too bad. Clowns just don't do it for me."

Willow laughed. "Oh, come on, now. You were hot for Bozo, and you know it."

"Oh, yeah," Christine said against Willow's lips. "Definitely hot for Bozo."

Epilogue

"Does that work?" Christine asked after the recordings she'd made earlier finished playing.

"I think that first song may need to be tweaked a bit," Oscar said, scribbling a few notes on the pad he'd brought with him to the production meeting. "I'm not sure it quite captures the scene and storyline there."

Christine nodded, adding to her own notes. She glanced across the table. "Christian? You're our dance girl, so…" She shrugged. "Would the choreography be a bitch?"

The retired dancer, who was now one of the best choreographers in the business, leaned her chin on the heel of her hand as she tapped the fingers of her other hand on the table. "You know, I think we need Gray." Her wife, Gray Rickman, was a celebrated novelist but also the book writer of the show they were working on to develop into a stage production. Christine was writing all the songs for it, Christian handling choreography, and Oscar in charge of production design.

"Where'd she go?" Oscar asked, looking around the conference area. The studio housed, among other things, a room with a long table that could seat twelve and had access to any number of technologies, from sound to video to graphics and anything else the team might need.

"She went in to check on Aria," Christian said, referring to her four-year-old in the house with Willow, Buster, and Keaton.

"Oh, right." The older man shook his shiny bald head before reaching for his giant sketch pad. "Okay," he said, flipping open the hard cover and several pages to what he wanted them to see. "I'm thinking about this for the feather bed scene."

Used to the fact that Oscar was old school and used paper and pen rather than a computer program, Christine rolled her chair closer to peek at his work. The lovely blond choreographer did the same.

All three were startled when Gray came bursting into the room, a wide-eyed Aria on her hip. "You guys, she's in labor."

᙭᙭᙭᙭

Standing next to the bed, Christine looked down at the exhausted woman lying there. She was pale with dark circles under her eyes. It had been a very long sixteen hours, but according to the nurse, she was getting close.

"I know, baby," she whispered, brushing damp bangs away from Willow's face. It was so hard to see her in such pain, but she knew it was part of the process. She held her wife's hand, noting the gold band with inlaid diamonds, a perfect match for her own. She leaned down and left a kiss on a sweaty forehead. "It's almost over."

"Okay, let's see where things stand," a nurse said, entering the labor room. Christine watched as she sat on a rolling stool to examine Willow. "Well," the nurse said after several long moments. "Wonderful news!" She grinned at them both, her teeth white against beautiful dark skin. "It's time."

Butterflies were dive bombing Christine's innards at those precious words. She squeezed Willow's hand and met her gaze. "Ready, baby?" she asked, almost unable to breathe.

Willow nodded. "Yes. God, yes. Just want her out," she said with a groan.

Christine stepped aside as Willow's team swarmed in like bees, preparing Willow and the bed for transport to the delivery room. While they were doing that, the singer quickly sent a text to the group chat which included Julie, Adam, Kevin, Bug, and Christian.

Christine: Here we go!!!!

Moments later they were settled in, the doctor showing her face for the first time. She gave a great big smile to Willow and then to Christine, who once again stood next to the bed, holding Willow's hand.

"Good evening, ladies," she crowed, excitement in her voice and in her dark eyes. "Let's have us a baby!"

"Yes, please," Willow murmured.

"Okay, sweetie. We'll make it happen," the doctor promised, patting Willow's arm before taking her place at the foot of the bed where she checked things out, the nurses coming in to help. "Okay, Willow," she said. "Everything is looking really, really good. So, when your next contraction begins, I want you to push, okay?"

Willow nodded, her eyes closed. Christine could see the pain coming, as she'd seen variations of that look last evening, all night, and into this morning. It was now almost ten thirty in the morning and it was finally happening.

A long, slow groan began as the contraction started, Willow seeming to be transported to a place of intense pain. Her hand squeezed Christine's as her face scrunched up and she began to push.

"Good job, baby," Christine whispered. Her hand felt like it was about to break, but she was pretty sure all the bones were powder by now anyway.

Willow let out a long, keening cry, the veins in her neck standing out in relief with her effort.

"Good, good, Willow," the doctor encouraged. "Give me another really good push if you can."

Willow gasped, her chest heaving as she gulped in air. A moment later, that intense look of determination distorted her features as she pushed. Christine watched in absolute awe of the strength of her wife. She honestly wasn't sure if she could've done it.

"I love you so much," she whispered, the words just slipping out of her mouth.

Willow let out another long cry, but this one was guttural, sounding otherworldly. She held her position of absolute strain, her entire body rigid, her fingers like a steel vise around Christine's.

"I see baby! She's crowned."

Christine's heart was racing almost as fast as that of both mother and baby on the monitors.

"You're doing so well, Willow," the doctor said, looking up the length of Willow's body to her face before returning her focus back to her task between Willow's spread legs. "Almost there."

Though still scared from such a new experience

that could go sideways so terribly easily, Christine felt her excitement growing with each rapid heartbeat. "Come on, baby," she murmured, repeating the doctor's words. "Almost there."

Willow took a deep breath, as though preparing herself for battle. She visibly threw her entire being into what she was being asked to do, pushing with everything she had. Her silent focus turned into a loud scream that ripped from her throat as her head thrust backward against the pillow.

Christine watched in awe as something incredible and magical happened. A tiny little being shot out of Willow's body, her angry cries renting the cold, sterile air. Instantly, she was in tears, unable to control her emotions as she watched the tiny, goo-covered baby quickly passed off to a nurse waiting with warm towels to dry her off, then gently placed in Willow's arms on her abdomen.

"Here you go, Mommy," the nurse said softly.

Christine looked down at the tiniest human being she'd ever seen. She was a bundle of dark reddish-purple skin with folds and rolls. Her little face was all scrunched up with a look of utter confusion.

"Hey, sweet girl," Willow whispered, leaving a kiss on the baby's head. She looked up and met Christine's tear-filled eyes. "Our little Phoenix," she whispered.

"She's so beautiful," Christine responded. "So much hair."

Willow's smile was amazing, Christine thought. After what she'd just gone through for so many hours, her body ripped open to give birth to this little human they were being put in charge of raising, she lay there calm, smiling and radiating love.

Christine leaned down and kissed her lips. "I love you, Willow."

Willow returned the kiss. "I love you, too, baby."

"And," the singer added, leaning down and leaving the softest of kisses on Phoenix's head. "I love you, little one."

❧ ❧ ❧ ❧

It was absolutely wonderful to have those closest to them in their home to meet the newest member of the Paxton family. When they'd gotten married in the very simple, private ceremony performed on their property. Christine and Willow had decided to take Willow's maiden name as their family name. Christine would keep Swann professionally, of course, but when she was home with her wife and child, it was Paxton all the way.

Julie held the week-old Phoenix, gently rocking in the rocking chair that Adam and Camille had given them as a baby gift while Christine sat on the couch next to Willow, an arm resting along the back and fingers lightly caressing the shoulder bared by the sleeveless shirt the new mom wore.

"I think this show will be pretty amazing," Bug said, he and his wife having flown into town to see the baby and check out the new studio. "I'm proud of you, lady," he said, lightly punching Christine in the arm.

Buster hurried to the screen door, tail wagging as newcomers stepped up onto the porch. He was excited as he got pets from Christian and Gray as they entered the house after being called in by Remmy, who was standing close by.

"Hey, there," Gray said, setting Aria down on

her feet. "This little one wanted to see the baby." She gave them a sheepish grin. "Me too."

Aria ran over to where Julie was seated and peeked over at the sleeping bundle. She gasped as she looked at her face. Christine watched in amusement. "Hi, Phoenix. I'm Aria." She grinned up at the new moms, little straight white teeth showing on the beautiful little cherubic face. Her long, dark hair was pulled back into a ponytail. "She's so beautiful."

"Thank you, sweetheart," Willow said, resting her head on Christine's shoulder. "Maybe you two will become friends."

Aria looked back down at the baby. "Yeah," she said, wonder in her little voice. "Maybe we'll be friends."

Willow lifted her head and looked at Christine, who was already looking back at her. She smiled. "Uh-oh."

Christine returned the smile. "I see trouble in about fifteen years."

Willow chuckled as she left a kiss on Christine's lips before replacing her head on the singer's shoulder, Christine's head resting against hers.

Christine let out a long, happy sigh. She'd never been so contented in her entire life. Yes, they were tired, and yes, sleep was hard to get, but as she cuddled with her wife and watched Aria with her newborn daughter, she knew it was all worth it.

About the Author

Kim has spent her life in Colorado and can't imagine living anywhere else. She's been writing since she was 9 and stumbled into her first book being published in her mid-20s. She's worked in the film industry as a writer, director and producer, but now enjoys the quiet, happy life of a professional author. She can be reached on Facebook and on her website at, www.kimpritekel.com

IF YOU LIKED THIS BOOK...

Share a review with your friends or post a review on your favorite site like Amazon, Goodreads, Barnes and Noble, or anywhere you purchased the book. Or perhaps share a posting on your social media sites and help spread the word.

Join the Sapphire Newsletter and keep up with all your favorite authors.

Did we mention you get a free book for joining our team?

sign-up at - www.sapphirebooks.com

Check out Kim's other books.

Zero Ward - ISBN - 978-1-943353-19-4

Danny Felts grew up in the heart of the Midwest on a dairy farm, expected to follow in her mother's footsteps and marry a farmer and become a mother. Danny had other ideas. As World War II heats up, she makes a decision that will change her life forever as she becomes a lie, serving with the Seabees in the Navy as Daniel Felts.

Kate Adams is about to graduate high school in her prestigious and elite San Diego neighborhood when she's dragged to the USO for a dance with friends and servicemen. There, she meets the person that will catch her eye and her heart, only for jealousy and vengeance to tear her apart.

Are Danny and Kate strong enough to win the battle within and fight for their love?

Connection - ISBN - 978-1-939062-24-6

Julie Wilson lives a charmed life as a beloved teacher and aunt in the small town of Woodland. Close to her brother and guardian of two adorable Yorkies, she loves her life, the only negative being ex-boyfriend, Ray who can't seem to understand the phrase, "We're done." Believing that's her only problem, Julie has no idea what hell awaits her during a normal summer afternoon.

Remmy Foster is the quirky, friendly drifter who has

never found roots after a difficult childhood, as well as the difficulties her very special gift brings into her life. Though she may call it exploring, the truth is she's running from ghosts that haunt her every step.

After a chance meeting with Julie while hitchhiking, Remmy will be thrown head first into darkness she could never have foreseen, regardless of her abilities. As the clock ticks, life and death is on her shoulders to make the right connection.

Warning - Some scenes may be too intense for some readers.

1049 Club - ISBN - 978-1-939062-97-0

Almost two hundred souls, one plane, six survivors, endless heartbreak.

When flight 1049, headed from Buffalo, NY to Italy falls from the sky, a firestorm of drama, pain, angst and sorrow ensues. Can an author, a business owner, a teenager, good ol' boy, veterinarian and ruthless lawyer survive? Better yet, can those left behind?

1049 Club is a story of survival, love, deep regret and miracles. Can the living make peace with the presumed dead? Can the presumed dead make peace with the lives and loves they thought they had before?

Blinded – ISBN – 978-1-943353-53-8

After a horrible explosion sends local television news reporter, Burton Blinde reeling both physically and emotionally, she walks away from her life and the dream job she was about to start at a major news network.

For six long years she hides out in a small mountain town, working at the local library, though is haunted by the life she had, including mysterious messages and gifts she was receiving before her life was turned upside down, a veritable bread crumb trail leading to the unknown.

Unable to resist, Burton begins to follow the clues, which will lead her into the darkest places of human nature that she may not be able to return from.

Damaged - ISBN - 978-1-939062-45-1

Family. A group of people you are related to by blood or love.

Nora Schaeffer has come home to her family after twenty years working around the world as a photographer for National Geographic. She's welcomed into the open arms of her father and siblings.

Family. A group of people who support you, lift you up when you fall.

Shannon, the youngest of the four Schaeffer siblings, has vanished, leaving her five-year-old daughter, Bella, terrified and alone. To help find Shannon, Nora has no choice but to turn to the dark-haired specter who has haunted her for twenty years. Along the way, she finds her own long-dead heart and uncovers chilling family secrets beyond imagination.

Family. A group of people who will stick together to hide the rotten soul at its core at any cost.

Who will live? Who will die? Who will be the most damaged? And who will learn to love again?

The Gift - ISBN - 978-1-948232-47-0

The dead do speak. You just have to listen. Homicide Detective Catania "Nia" d'Giovanni is the only daughter in a large Italian family of six children. The backbone—a position not applied for nor wanted—she continues to create new glue to hold the dysfunctional group together. For Nia, family time feels more like herding cats than spending time with her brothers and feisty, aging parents.

Her heart has always been in her career with the Pueblo Police Department, especially since it will never be okay with her very Catholic mother to openly give her heart to any woman, until she meets a secretive waitress who has her at, Can I take your order?

And then it begins…

Three murders that are so gruesome, so horrible, they rock the small town to its core. Nia and her partner Oscar are left to piece together a deadly puzzle to find the key to unlock the monster they hunt.

Or, are they the hunted?

As they dissect the murder scenes where not one shred of evidence is left behind, more bodies begin to show up, each cleaner than the last, the shadowy specter that is the killer vanishing without a trace, making the woman Nia loves disappear right along with it.

When there is no evidence to follow, Nia must trust her instincts…or, is she being guided?

The Plan – ISBN – 978-1-948232-43-2

As the dark days of the Dust Bowl came to an end, the midsection of the United States tried to rebuild and revitalize. In the small, dusty farming town of, Brooke View, Colorado, teenager, Eleanor Landry and her mother were dealing with her father, a self-appointment fire and brimstone preacher to his congregation of two. A plan to survive.

As the dark era of the robber baron comes to an end, giants of industry and innovation emerged with fabulous fortunes manifested in the mansions that dotted the landscape across the country. Lysette Landon, the teen daughter of the wealthiest family in Brooke View, was everything a good, proper girl of privilege should be. Only problem was, she wasn't dreaming of finding a young man to raise a family with. A plan to be free.

One look, one touch, all plans are off.

Secrets deeper and darker than the grave would bring Eleanor and Lysette together, their families connected by a web of lies and broken promises. A plan to escape.

Be careful because, life has other plans…

The Traveler Book One: The Hunted - ISBN - 978-1-948232-91-3

A story so epic one book can't contain it.BOOK ONE:

1977: In the era between flower power and the yuppie, Sonia Lucas is a young wife and mother, just starting out in life. Without warning, a strange presence and dark force enters her life, clouds building…

1917: …and a storm brewing as the world reeled from the horrific events of World War I just before it was ravaged by a Spanish flu epidemic that would kill millions. Sephora Lloyd is a 16 year old girl lost in the responsibilities of an adult world helping to support herself and her mother. A beautiful young nun-in-training enters her life, bringing love and hope with her. That is, until a force bigger than either of them threatens everything Sephora holds dear.

Four women - three deaths - two words - one house
THE HUNTED

The Traveler Book Two: The Hunter - ISBN - 978-1-948232-93-7

A story so epic one book can't contain it. BOOK TWO:

1890: In the dying days of the Old West, Sally Little runs her booming brothel with the passion and tenacity the business of sex requires. Savvy and indulgent, there's one itch Sally can't let herself scratch. Afraid of hurting the woman she loves, she instead unleashes...

Present Day: ...her renovation crew and fixer upper TV show on a dilapidated mansion that has known nothing but death since a murder there in 1977. Samantha Leyton sees ratings gold in bringing the sagging old house to life, but instead she discovers only she has the power to unlock the mystery that hunted four women across time, leaving death and destruction in its wake. Can she release her sisters who came before her and finally be granted the gift of love that is stronger than any evil?

Four women - Three deaths - two words - one house
THE HUNTER

Finding Faith - ISBN - 978-1-952270-16-1

Faith Fitzgerald thought that if she got an education and became a high-powered attorney in Manhattan, maybe—just maybe—she'd gain the attention and respect of her absentee father. Considering he was the only parent she had left after her mother's suicide when Faith was just a child, she thought that's what it would take.

She was wrong.

What she dreamed would be glamorous and satisfying turned out to be grueling and thankless. Since she wasn't willing to play the game between the sheets, she was forced to stay in the cubicle jungle doing all the heavy lifting while the men got the credit and the rewards.

Deciding she is done, Faith packs up and, with the flip of the bird to the rearview mirror, leaves New York and heads home to Colorado. She has nothing there: no job, nowhere to live, no relationship with her father. Truth is, she barely has a relationship with herself.

On the drive home, she finds herself in Wynter, a tiny mountain town at the foot of the Rockies. Looking more like it belongs in a made-for-TV Christmas movie than on the map, Faith is utterly enchanted. When she tries her luck and buys a raffle ticket at Pop's, Wynter's charming café, her prize is far more than meets the eye—or the heart.

Enter Wyatt, a feisty, sexy southerner and waitress at Pop's, who just happens to be married to a local sheriff's deputy. All is not as it appears with the All-American boy and his Georgia peach.

A colorful cast of unforgettable and charming characters will teach the jaded attorney that sometimes to find yourself all you have to do is go back to the basics…and have a little Faith.

Taking Liberty - ISBN- 978-1-952270-24-6

A victim of a massive corporate downsize, Liberty Faulkner suddenly finds herself without a job, without a home, and without a plan. Though certainly not part of her vision, Libby decides that the familiar is the safest path back to her life goals. In this case, the devil she knows is home: the tiny mountain town of Wynter,

Colorado, a close-knit place where everybody knows everybody and everybody's business. Seems like the perfect place for the twenty-five-year-old to start over and figure out who she is without being noticed…not.

Sergeant Grace Montez escaped her dead-end job and toxic relationship in New Mexico and moved to Wynter to help build their police department from scratch. Now an established figurehead in the community, she's got her professional life dialed in and even mentors new recruits on the force. After a challenging childhood and lifetime of abandonment and disappointment, Grace hasn't been interested in another relationship—especially because no one has caught her eye since a certain quirky college student who used to make her caramel macchiato at the local coffee shop moved away three years ago.

Now that quirky college student has returned as the beautiful, mature woman Libby has become. Can Grace keep her distance, or will she finally take liberties with what is being offered?

Justice Won - ISBN - 978-1-952270-36-9

In 1890, seventeen-year-old Justice Kilkoyne and her mother, Ninny, are one bad decision away from living on the streets of Azrael, Pennsylvania. Ninny's propensity for the bottle has left Justice to play the adult, her androgynous good looks helping her pass as a young man to gain employment and keep them—if just barely—above water.

Determined to find a better life for them, Justice saves

every penny to get them on a train headed west to the sunshine of California. Before they can leave, the bigotry of one shopkeeper sends Justice on the run, chased by the police for a crime she didn't commit and straight into the unwitting arms of a stunning young prostitute, who, after an unexpected connection, becomes Justice's Angel.

The day arrives to leave Pennsylvania for good. As Justice and Ninny get settled, they're surprised by the appearance of Angel, also wanting to start anew. When the trip is violently interrupted in Colorado, Angel just may be lost to Justice forever.

Can Justice find a new life when she makes her way to the fledgling mining town of Wynter, Colorado? Can her heart ever be whole again?

Curtain Call - ISBN - 978-1-952270-42-0

What do you do when you come from a long line of dancers that spans the globe and generations, yet you can't tell your right foot from your left? You fall in love with a dancer, of course!

Gray Rickman is an awkward seventeen-year-old when she first sets eyes on Christian Scott at the dance studio/theater Gray's parents own and run in Denver, Colorado.

Though only a handful of years older than Gray, Christian carries herself with poise and wisdom far beyond her years. A woman of few words, she speaks volumes with her body.

Before Gray even really knows what her type is, Christian stars in endless daydreams and even fulfills a couple of her fantasies before vanishing out of thin air, leaving Gray in an empty bed with nothing but bittersweet memories and broken dreams.

With no choice but to move on, Gray attempts love, even moving with her college girlfriend to New York City to pursue a career in journalism. But her standard has been set, the bar way too high for any other woman to reach or clear. It's an unexpected encounter in an obvious place when Gray sets eyes on her dancer again. Will the bright lights of Broadway illuminate the way back to the woman of her dreams? Or will they blind her to any other possibility of happiness?

Break a leg, Gray. The Great White Way calls.

Encore Performance - ISBN - 978-1-952270-52-9

Grey Rickman, a journalist for The New York Times, is offered the opportunity of a lifetime and a huge boost to her career—ghostwriting a memoir for one of the world's most beloved actors. She is deeply in love with her girlfriend, dancer Christian Scott, and her world couldn't be better.

Christian, though proud of Grey and all that she's accomplished, is facing her own career dilemma. All she's ever wanted to do is perform and create, her body her kinetic canvas. But, in one of the few industries where youth matters above all else, her time is coming to make decisions that no woman in her mid-thirties should have to make: is it time to retire?

As the career of one begins to explode into the stratosphere and the other's implodes after a career-ending injury that makes any retirement discussion irrelevant, Grey and Christian begin to drift apart. Changing priorities and newly built walls lead to fears and accusations, further tearing at the fabric of the love they've worked years to create.

Will cooler heads prevail to warm up the hearts of the deeply passionate couple in time to create a new dream for their second act?

Other Sapphire books from Sapphire Authors

Talk to Me – ISBN – 978-1-952270-20-8

Claire takes a turn for the wild side when she chances into a job at San Diego's KZSD radio to work with Marly, the sharp-tongued lesbian shock jock of Gayline. Under Marly's close tutelage, Claire feels the sparks fly as she learns to screen calls and handle board operations. It's enough that her formerly quiet life has been upended after separating from her husband, and at first, she keeps her feelings hidden. Even as bomb threats force the radio station employees to clear out, Claire's attraction to Marly's charisma, wit, and atypical beauty keeps her coming back. Meanwhile, she struggles to maintain a relationship with her teen daughter while her soon-to-be ex makes it clear he wants to try again. Its two steps forward, one step back as Marly and Claire grow closer and admit their feelings.

Will Marly's outrageous "anything goes" attitude be too much? As their on-air shenanigans and romance heat up, Marly's crazed plan to boost ratings threatens their relationship, and ultimately, their lives.

Keeping Secrets – ISBN – 978-1-952270-04-8

What would you do if, after finally finding the woman of your dreams, she suddenly leaves to fight in the Civil War?

It's 1863, and Elizabeth Hepscott has resigned herself to a life of monotonous boredom far from the battlefields as the wife of a Missouri rancher. Her fate changes when she travels with her brother to Kentucky to help him join the Union Army. On a whim, she poses as his little brother and is bullied into enlisting, as well. Reluctantly pulled into a new destiny, a lark decision quickly cascades into mortal danger.

While Elizabeth's life has made a drastic U-turn, Charlie Schweicher, heiress to a glass-making fortune, is still searching for the only thing money can't buy.

A chance encounter drastically changes everything for both of them. Will Charlie find the love she's longed for, or will the war take it all away?

Broken, not Shattered – ISBN – 978-1-952270-22-2

Even when it seems hopeless, there can always be a better tomorrow.

Jill Bishop has one goal in life – to survive. Jill is trapped in an abusive marriage, while raising two young girls. Her husband has isolated her from the world and filled her days with fear. The last thing on her mind is love, but she sure could use a friend.

Alex McCoy is enjoying a comfortable life, with great friends and a prosperous business. She has given up on love, after picking the wrong woman one too many times. Little does she know, a simple act of kindness might change her life forever.

When Alex lends a helping hand to Jill at the local grocery store, they are surprised by their immediate connection and an unlikely friendship develops. As their friendship deepens, so too do their fears.

In order to protect herself and the girls, Jill can't let her husband know about her friendship with Alex, and Alex can't discover what goes on behind closed doors. What would Alex do if she finds out the truth? At the same time, Alex must fight her attraction and be the friend she suspects Jill needs. Besides, Alex knows what every lesbian knows – don't fall for a straight woman, especially one that's married…but will her heart listen?

Diva – ISBN – 978-1-952270-10-9

What if…you were offered a part-time job as the personal assistant to someone you have idolized for years? Meg Ellis has just completed the school year as a nurse in the Santa Fe school system. It isn't her first choice of profession, but a medical problem derailed her musical career years ago. The breakup of a bad relationship is still painful. The loving support from her close-knit family and good friends has buoyed her spirits, but longing still lurks below the surface. She can't forget the intoxicating allure of the beautiful diva who haunts her dreams.

Nicole Bernard is a rising star in the world of opera, adored by fans around the globe. When Meg learns that Nicole is headlining a new production at the renowned New Mexico outdoor pavilion—and then is asked to accept a job offer to be her personal assistant—she is beside herself. After a short time learning the routine and reining in her hormones, Meg discovers that Nicole's family will be visiting for the opening. Her responsibility to the charismatic singer immediately becomes more difficult when Nicole's young husband Mario shows up and threatens the comfortable rapport between Meg and the prima donna.

The two women brace for a roller-coaster interlude composed by fate. Will the warm days and cool nights, the breathtaking scenery, and the romance of the music create summer love? A heartbreaking game? Or something very special?

The Dragonfly House: An Erotic Romance - ISBN- 978-1-952270-14-7

On the outskirts of a small, picturesque Midwestern town, sits a large, lovely old Victorian house with many occupants. This residence, known simply as The Dragonfly House, is home to Ma'am, the proprietor, along with several young women in her employ. One such woman, Jame, is very popular among the female clientele. One such client, Sarah, fresh from a divorce and looking for a little adventure, as well as some gentle handling, becomes one of Jame's repeat clients. Once Sarah enters the picture, Jame and Ma'am, as well as the brothel, will be forever changed.

www.ingramcontent.com/pod-product-compliance
Lightning Source LLC
Chambersburg PA
CBHW061052190726
48286CB00006B/1718